KINGSBANE

The servant climbed stiffly and mechanically to his feet, as though some outside force was directing him. He uttered a croaking cry that brought the others to fearful attention, and then chanted:

> Three will find what may be found
> When the sun shines underground.
> Two will stand when all have fled,
> Amid the voices of the dead.
> One will bleed and one will burn,
> Before the rightful rule return.

His eyes glazed over and he crumpled to the ground. The travelers looked at one another in profound astonishment and confusion. *The servant had been mute.*

"It's magic," one said. "The magic is returning...."

IRONBRAND, GRAYMANTLE and **KINGSBANE** form the Iron Angel Trilogy

"**GRAYMANTLE** is many cuts above the usual Sword and Sorcery novel. I look forward to reading Morressy's other books."

Parke Godwin,
author of *Firelord*

Other books by
JOHN MORRESSY

Ironbrand
Graymantle

KINGSBANE

JOHN MORRESSY

PLAYBOY
PAPERBACKS

Once again,
as always,
for Barbara

KINGSBANE

Copyright © 1982 by John Morressy

Cover illustration copyright © 1982 by PEI Books, Inc.

Published simultaneously in the United States and Canada by Playboy Paperbacks, New York, New York. Printed in the United States
of America. Library of Congress Catalog Card Number: 81-85181.
First edition.

Books are available at quantity discounts for promotional and indus-
trial use. For further information, write to Premium Sales, Playboy
Paperbacks, 1633 Broadway, New York, New York 10019.

ISBN: 0-867-21098-2

First printing June 1982.

THE
HEADLAND

CAPE OF
MISTS

THE
CRYSTAL
HILLS

NORTHMARK

THE
FASTNESS

THE PLAIN

THE
STONE
HAND

LONG
WOOD

THE
FOOL'S
HEAD

THE
HIGH
CITY

THE
SISTERS

THE
BROTHERS

SOUTHMARK

MISTLANDS

THE SOUTHERN FOREST

THE
CITADEL

Then life was good—until the day when evil stirred
    once more,
And Ambescand was dead, and dead were those who on
    the shore
Had knelt with weary arms and given thanks for
    victory,
And gone was Staver Ironbrand, beneath the whelming
    sea.
Then bitter days returned, and fear lay heavy on the
    north,
And trembling people prayed for a new hero to come
    forth.

They looked aloft on moonless nights; they searched
    the deepest skies;
They sought the Iron Angel, and the place where Staver
    lies;
For all believed the prophecy that in an age of pain
Great Ironbrand would hear their cry and walk the world
    again;
But no one heard, and no one came; the stars were
    bright and cold;
The ancient cause was left to men unlike the men of
    old. . . .

From *The Last Deed of Ambescand*

CHAPTER ONE

TROUBLE AT BALTHID'S KEEP

In the chamber of state in Balthid's Keep stood a semicircular table. Here the lord of the keep sat in council, with his high-backed chair against the western wall, at the straight edge of the table, where he could look each speaker in the eye and see every man's face, and no glances could be exchanged without his knowledge.

His councilors sat side by side, equidistant from their lord a half mark across the oak table. In Balthid's day, when a man spoke in council, his eyes remained fixed on Balthid, regardless of whom he addressed or answered. Those who could not observe this decorum, or would not, did not serve on the council after the first breach.

Now Brondin, son of Balthid, ruled in Balthid's Keep, and he ruled with a lighter hand. He had found that he could learn more from men who felt free to speak with one another while he listened to the argument move back and forth between speakers and observed the interplay of personalities; and he wished to learn. Brondin ruled, but he did not dominate. It was not his way.

Brondin was known in the north as a man firm but fair in all his dealings. He was slow to enact a law, examining all sides and hearing all viewpoints before pronouncing. But once he had established it, he upheld a law without exception. He seldom pledged his word; once it had been given, he never broke it.

He took pride in the fact that life at Balthid's Keep was better now in many ways than it had been in his father's time. Even the poorest crofter on Brondin's lands wore a woolen cloak, went shod in the winter months, and had meat and fish to eat, good ale to drink, and wood for a fire. No one who worked the land had fear of the men who wore the three broad green bands of Brondin's service on their sleeves, but rather looked to them as friends and protectors. Justice was dispensed equally to all at Brondin's court, from his lips. Accused and accusers came face to face in Brondin's presence. Exoneration or punishment followed without delay.

Partly because he was a good ruler and partly because he was the son of a powerful warlord and, despite his youth, a shrewd statesman, Brondin's realm had grown steadily in the six years since the rule of Balthid's Keep had passed to him. He had expanded his territories to cover more than nine thousand square greatmarks. From the edge of the Southern Forest to Riverbend beyond Southmark, from the seacoast to the mountains—all this was his. Only one man in the north ruled a greater kingdom, and that was Halssa, self-proclaimed King of the High City, Brondin's rival and in recent years his bitter enemy.

The council had assembled early on this day and quickly disposed of routine business. Nothing out of the ordinary had arisen except for a domestic mystery: A servant had been found in the lower passage, stabbed to death. The matter was turned over to the Master-at-Arms, and the rest of the agenda was then considered.

When the last item of the day, a small petition, had been seen to, Brondin terminated the session; but instead of dismissing his councilors, he ordered that food and drink be brought to the chamber. "We will have visitors on matters of importance. Eat well. We may be here for some time," he announced.

When the last of the food was removed, two men entered the chamber. The dust of far travel was still on their cloaks and boots. They were both tall, with the solid, lithe build of men of war. Their hair was light brown, their eyes blue, and their complexions florid. They were westerners, from the lands beyond Mistlands, whence Brondin's own father had come to seek his fortune in the collapse of the northern kingdom.

Brondin raised his hand. "Welcome, Stallicho and Zathias. Join us in peaceful council and assist us in judging wisely," he said in formal greeting.

Stallicho, the elder of the two, replied for both. "Our

swords are blunted against Brondin, son of Balthid. We come as friends and offer him all we know and all we have seen."

Room was made for them at the table. They sat side by side, and no sooner were they settled than Brondin asked, "What news from the High City? Is there progress in the dredging of the harbor?"

"Very slow progress. The harbor's been long neglected, and the equipment is poor," said Stallicho.

"But they make progress," Brondin said.

"Yes. It's costing them lives, though. They're taking the muck far out to sea for dumping, out where the Stone Hand is supposed to have been. It's rough water out there. They've lost six barges that I know of."

"Halssa has no objection to losing other people's lives. We all know that. How long before the harbor is cleared for shipping, if things move at the present pace?" Brondin asked.

"It cannot be done before winter, that's certain. If all goes right, it might be ready this time next year, but I doubt it. Even Halssa can't drive men that hard without trouble."

Brondin turned to an aged man who sat listening attentively. "How does this tally with the historical accounts, Espar?"

The old man frowned in concentration and pursed his dry lips. Then, fixing his gaze on the bare tabletop before him, he said in a slow, measured recitation, "We know nothing certain before the time of Ordred. When he came to the High City, the harbor had long been neglected by the people of the Game. He began a regular schedule of harbor maintenance, and it was long followed. We must recall, though, that sea traffic was small in those times. It was only in the last days of the Vannensons, in the time of Madorian and Stiragos, that large vessels from the east entered the harbor. In those times, the dredging was carried on continuously."

"But it hasn't been kept up since the Long Winter. That's over fifty years of neglect. The harbor must have been choked," Brondin said.

Zathias nodded. "At the lowest tide, it was no more than a long mud flat. But all Halssa needs is a channel so he can bring in men and supplies. He can have that in a year."

"So a year is all we have. If we haven't overcome Halssa by then, he'll be too strong for the alliance."

"There are those who say he's too strong for us now," said Zathias.

"They might be right," Brondin admitted. "But in a year, with reinforcements for his army from the east and supplies for a long campaign, there'll be no doubt at all. So either we act soon and risk defeat, or wait and make it certain. I don't like the choice, but I see no other."

"And will you lead us against the High City?" Zathias asked.

"I will help plan the assault."

"But who's to lead us into battle? It must be you. No man has a better claim," Stallicho said.

Brondin gave a short, self-deprecating laugh. He looked away, and his glance rested for a moment on the sturdy oaken crutch that stood within easy reach at his side. Slowly shaking his head, he said, "My claim might seem less impressive once I set foot on a battlefield, Stallicho. I appreciate your loyalty, but there are better men to lead our forces into battle than I."

"My troops will follow you," Stallicho assured him. "I've met with Witigense and Trugurian, and they're both willing to accept you as war leader. They supported Balthid, and they support you."

"How many men do they have?"

"Witigense has sixty swordsmen and ninety archers. It's a small force, but they're tough and well disciplined. They've beaten back Halssa's men at three-to-one odds. Trugurian's men are archers, about three hundred of them."

"Trustworthy?"

"Absolutely," said Stallicho.

Brondin directed an inquiring glance at Henorik, the Master-at-Arms, who calculated for a moment and then said, "Added to our present strength, that brings us close to Halssa's numbers. We have about nine men to every ten of his."

"Not enough to take the High City."

"No, my lord. We need more. If we could enlist men from Long Wood, we'd be ready for an assault. There are many in Long Wood loyal to the Vannensons still, with no love for Halssa."

"They've a great love for themselves and their own safety. And for profit, too," Zathias said bitterly.

Brondin thought it best to avoid this subject. Distrust of possible allies was not to be encouraged. "At any rate, our strength is growing. By next spring we'll have the men we need," he said confidently.

"The only problem is the waiting. Spring is a long time off. Halssa might learn of our plans and take the offensive," Zathias pointed out.

"If he attacks any one of us in force, the rest of the alliance will move directly against the High City. We've all agreed to that," said Brondin.

"What about assassins?"

Henorik spoke up. "Assassins have already been sent after my lord. We sent the last one back with his hands hung around his neck on a string."

Brondin said evenly, "Since Balthid was struck down in his own chamber, I've learned to be watchful. The next assassin won't get me the way he got my father."

"I have no doubt of your courage or of Henorik's," said Zathias, "but I've heard disturbing things about Halssa's adviser. He seems to have come out of nowhere, and he's said to have powers unknown in the north since the fall of the Stone Hand."

"A wizard?"

"I've heard it said."

Brondin gave a little mirthless laugh and replied, "A mighty poor wizard he is, then, Zathias. If he were any good at his trade, we'd all be dead."

Dostilla, the treasurer, who had been silent since the arrival of the two visitors, said tartly, "Talk of wizardry is a waste of breath. All the magic in the north died with the crushing of the Cairnlord."

"So I believe. I only repeat what others have told me," said Zathias.

"What can you say of this, Espar?" Brondin asked.

"Dostilla says what all men have heard. Zandinell and Ordred both said on many occasions that all the magic in the world was consumed in the final battle against the Cairnlord and its creatures. Their words are recorded in nine separate accounts. However, some say that when Zandinell spoke of all the magic in the world, he referred only to such magic as he knew and could employ and that his words are not to be taken as absolute. As proof, they cite the spells and curses that still lie upon certain places and objects. Whatever one believes, there has been no evidence of major magic in the north since the day of the final battle, and Zandinell seems to have spoken plain truth."

"Let us hope so. And if it's true that there's still some magic in this world, let's hope that we can find a wizard of our own. In the meantime, we'll trust to secrecy and our strength of arms," said Brondin.

The conference went on until dark. Little of actual substance was discussed, but Brondin was aware by then that the real purpose of these meetings with his fellow warlords from near and far was not purely practical. In their eyes, he had come to be the symbol of resistance to Halssa and the power of the High City. Seeing his resolution, hearing his defiant words, and sharing his confidence knit them more closely together in alliance against the common enemy. Brondin knew that he could not hide away or remain aloof from their concerns and still retain their loyalty.

In his few quiet hours, Brondin often wondered at his situation. His was a hard and lonely calling. He could ask no woman to share the daily threat of death; there would be no secure place for a wife and children until his work was done. Still, he had no regrets. He was a young man, and if his efforts succeeded, a long life lay ahead, a time to live as others lived. Given the opportunity to withdraw from his present struggle, he would reject it in an instant. But he was bemused by the succession of chance events that had led him, a youth unfit for battle, to his present eminence.

Balthid, his father, would have been a more likely battle leader. He had come out of the western wilds at the head of a small band of adventurers and seized a prosperous settlement, whereupon he created an island of sanctuary in the turmoil of the north. After more than two hundred years, the dynasty of the Vannensons was ended, and the northern kingdom was dissolving into chaos. But the word soon spread that the gate of Balthid's Keep was never shut in fear. He attracted hard-working men and women to till his lands and the best fighting men in the north to protect them. Smaller, weaker neighbors assessed the situation and chose to become his liegemen. While the other warlords and adventurers—

some old friends among them—were preoccupied with the siege of the High City, Balthid remained at home, building a base for the future.

It seemed for a time that he had acted wisely. After the fall of the city, the victors busied themselves with clumsy intrigue and random murder. New rulers sprang up like weeds and were as quickly cut down. Then Halssa emerged and survived. In time, he became master of the High City.

Balthid himself had claims, through his marriage, to rule in the High City, but he was by that time preoccupied with enlarging and strengthening his own territories. Those councilors who expressed concern at his delay in pressing his claim were rebuked for their lack of confidence in his power. Halssa was an old follower and a friend, Balthid told them, and would serve as his deputy until Balthid was free to assume his rightful place in the High City.

Then, in the seventh year after Halssa came to power, Balthid was slain by an unknown hand for an unknown reason. His only son became lord of Balthid's Keep, and Halssa declared himself King of the High City and the northern lands.

Brondin did not rule as his father had; he learned ways of his own. When it was possible, he won men to his side by reason rather than force. When force was required, he used it swiftly and effectively, without cruelty. He was in no hurry to assert his family claim. The High City was far away, and he did not concern himself with it or with Halssa.

When he was not immersed in the affairs of his domain, Brondin delved deep into the history of the north. Though little remained of what had been written, the oral tradition was rich, and in old Espar he had a walking library of the annals of the land.

He was surprised to learn that the very site of his fortress was hallowed ground. Balthid's Keep stood where once had stood the great hall of Goldengrange, with its ties to Ambescand. This discovery stimulated Brondin's interest in the past and led him to further investigations. He particularly prized the fact that his mother, who had died at his birth, was distantly related to the last of the Vannensons to rule in the High City. Through her hands had come the amulet that attested to his rightful claims.

Brondin's love of the past grew as his knowledge increased, and he soon came to think of himself as a northerner—which, in truth, he was by birth and half by blood—and a preserver of the old ways. When his western ancestors were still living in squalor and brutality, the northern kingdom had been a place of high civilization. People had traveled freely from the Headland to the Lake Isle, from the border of Mistlands to the Crystal Hills. Precious goods had been traded safely over a thousand greatmarks' distance. Invaders had been driven off, and a powerful sorcerer had been defeated by the might and magic of the north.

All this was changed now. From a single mighty kingdom made up of three interdependent realms, the north was rapidly becoming an archipelago of petty states separated by burnt and bloody zones of conflict. Trade was all but extinct. What could not be grown or made within one's own walls was taken by raids or simply done without. Brondin mourned the lost greatness and the coming of the long night of ignorance and continual strife, but he knew that it was beyond his present power to remedy matters.

Then there came an attempt on his life. Thanks to Henorik's quickness, the would-be assassin had been slain in the act, and now Brondin was warned. The second assassin was taken alive, and he revealed that Halssa had marked Brondin for death, just as he had marked his father. They had done him no harm, and he bore them no malice; but they represented potential rivals, and he was removing them out of prudence.

From that moment, Brondin was Halssa's implacable enemy and his rival for dominion over the north. Beyond the simple hatred that grew between them, neither could have comprehended the other's motives. Halssa did not care what the north had been or what it might become after him. He wanted power and the enjoyment of power here and now. Brondin wanted to restore the north to greatness, not for his own ambition but for the sake of something even he did not fully understand.

And so Brondin planned and plotted and sought out word of Halssa's doings. He met with his growing band of supporters and waited for the day when the alliance would be strong enough to strike, hoping all the while that Halssa would not strike first with some unexpected blow that would undo all his work. There was no certainty, only unending effort and constant alertness.

When the conference ended, Stallicho and Zathias departed at once. Their way lay across land more safely crossed in darkness, and they were anxious to reach Brondin's border outposts by the next nightfall. The others at the table took their leave one by one until only Henorik and Dostilla remained.

Brondin stretched and leaned back, lacing his fingers behind his head. "You may leave whenever you wish, unless there's something more to discuss," he said to them.

"The matter of the dead servant, my lord," said Dostilla.

"I think we can safely leave that to Henorik."

The Master-at-Arms spread his big hands on the table and nodded. "I'll see to it," he growled.

Dostilla gently persisted. "It might be best, my lord, for you and Henorik to inspect the site personally before we remove the unfortunate lad's body and scrub the stones. It is a most unusual occurrence."

"Servants are always squabbling. This quarrel turned out to be more serious than most, but it's hardly unusual," said Henorik.

"He was found by the treasure room."

"But there was no sign of entry."

Brondin wearily raised his hands to silence them. "Perhaps it's worth a look. It will do the servants good to find out that I won't tolerate this kind of behavior."

Brondin pulled himself erect and slipped his crutch under his right armpit. The three men made their way below, with Henorik in the lead, until they reached the cellar. There, in a central vault whose walls were made of stone a full two marks thick, stood the treasure room of Balthid's Keep. The body of a young boy lay sprawled on his side by a door, his fingertips just touching the stone sill.

"That's the position in which I found him, my lord," Dostilla said.

Brondin studied the body. "Stabbed, you say?"

"Just under the breastbone."

"Turn him over," Brondin said. He leaned forward to look

closely. In the lantern light, the dark stains on the boy's jerkin were difficult to see. "There's very little blood. This looks like the work of an experienced hand."

"An assassin?" Henorik asked, suddenly much interested.

"In truth, yes. But it's absurd. Who'd send an assassin to kill a kitchen boy?"

"He was sent for you, my lord," Henorik said.

"That makes no sense, either. I seldom visit this level. I use another corridor to approach the treasure room, and my visits follow no regular pattern. I might go months without coming down here. Halssa wouldn't waste an assassin on such a random mission."

"Then perhaps it was as Henorik suggests, my lord: a quarrel among servants. The kitchen boys are quite handy with a knife. I'm sure several of them are capable of such a stroke," Dostilla said.

"Possibly," Brondin said, sounding unconvinced. "I think we'd best look at the treasure room."

He turned and went at a brisk rocking gait over the flagstones, his uneven step swift and sure. As Dostilla held the lantern close, he studied the locks on the massive door.

"The door was locked, and there was no sign of tampering. Surely, no thief would have dared to enter with a body lying so near," said the treasurer.

"He might have been coming out when the boy happened by. Keys, both of you," Brondin said, reaching inside his shirt.

Three separate keys were required to open or secure the door of the vault. Dostilla carried one and Henorik another; Brondin retained the third.

Once the locks clicked free, Brondin pushed the heavy door inward and hooked it in place. While the others stood watch outside, he inspected the room carefully. All seemed in order, yet the uneasiness in him grew. A fatal quarrel between servants; a kitchen lad in the cellar of the treasure vault, a murder by a practiced hand—none of these things were unheard of, but taken together they were cause for concern.

He made a second cautious circuit of the room and still found no sign of intrusion. He stopped before a massive chest that stood in an alcove, concealed from the view of anyone outside the door. The chest was a half mark from side to side and nearly a quarter mark deep. It reached almost to his waist. Its rounded lid was flung back to reveal close-packed bags filled with coins from all the known world: ancient golden oaks and half oaks, silver eagles, the thick square arkads and delicate waferlike nirexes of the east, crude western hawkheads—all jumbled together in close proximity.

Brondin laid his crutch carefully against the chest and hung his lantern from a hook in the low stone ceiling. Gripping the rim with both hands, he lowered himself to one knee, his bad leg extended awkwardly to one side. Reaching into his shirt, he drew forth a tiny key on a golden chain. He inserted the key into an all-but-invisible slot on the side of the chest's massive lock plate and turned it gently. With a soft click, the lock plate swung down, revealing a cache the size of a small child's fist.

Brondin looked in and caught his breath. He dug his fingers into the space, but to no avail. The cache was empty. The most precious object in the northern lands was gone.

He knelt for a moment with his forehead pressed against the cold iron of the lock plate; then he rose stiffly and drew his cloak more closely about him. The chill of evil lay on the air of the treasure room, and he had to fight back the despair that threatened to overcome him.

CHAPTER TWO

AN OFFER OF
HONEST EMPLOYMENT

The trail at this point was level and straight, packed hard by a summer's constant use. The solitary man in brown loped on at a steady pace for three greatmarks, until he came to the stone bridge. Pursuers would anticipate a trick, he knew. He would give them a few tricks they had not foreseen.

At the far side of the bridge, he stopped and drew two large squares of rough cloth from inside his shirt. He bound them firmly around his feet. Then he began to walk backward, bringing his heels down lightly to leave the marks of a man proceeding in haste toward the bridge. He went on this way, moving at almost normal walking speed for a little more than a greatmark, until he came to a crossing.

A large party with several wagons had passed on the transverse road a short time before, obliterating all earlier tracks. He pulled off his footgear and joined his barefoot tracks with those of the wayfarers, following the road westward for several greatmarks until he came to a place where a sturdy branch overhung the way.

The branch would have been out of the reach of an ordinary man, but the traveler knew that he could just reach it. He was a tall man, and though his long limbs were slender, they were very strong. He was also a skilled climber and something of an acrobat.

He sprang, and his fingers closed around the rough bark. Pulling himself up, he worked his way to the trunk, where he took a moment to check the contents of his shirt. The little packet was still there, doubly secured in a special pouch.

So far, all had gone well. There would be pursuit, certainly. Perhaps not at once, for the theft might long go undiscovered; but pursuit would come, and it would be relentless. Brondin would not accept the loss of such a treasure without making every effort to recover it and punish the thief who had dared to violate the treasure vault of Balthid's Keep. But capture would be no easy task. Brondin might be powerful, but he could not work miracles.

The only witness to the theft was dead; no danger, then, of being identified. He had escaped swiftly and left a devious, confusing trail. Even Brondin's most skilled trackers would be hard put to follow him this far. But he could spare no time for gloating; he could scarcely allow himself a moment of rest. He worked his way around the thick trunk and inspected the branches that pointed into the woods, away from the trail. The farther he could go without leaving tracks on the ground, the less hope there was for his pursuers.

He finally dropped to the ground about twenty marks into the woods and started north at the best pace he could make. He reckoned on five days' hard traveling to the foothills and another five days before he was deep enough in the mountains to lie up for a time and plan the best way to get word to Halssa that the cloak pin of the Vannensons was available to him if he was prepared to pay generously. It was a matter that called for delicate handling, and he had no intention of acting in haste.

All went as well as he could have hoped. On his second day in the forest a hard rain fell, effacing all tracks; if pursuers had not found his trail by this time, they never would, however tenacious they might be.

It seemed that they had not, and he was safe. Day followed day without a sign of pursuit. He did not slacken his pace or relax his caution; he ate and drank on the trail and forced himself to cover sixty greatmarks each day, walking from before dawn to after dark. But he began to feel safe.

On his fifth day in the mountains, he still had not reached the resting place he sought. He pressed on and two days later came to the spot, a small concealed valley with a grove of trees and a spring of fresh water. Rock goats were plentiful, and they were tame as pets. With one good daytime fire, he could prepare a supply of meat that would last for the rest of his journey.

There was one problem. A thin wisp of smoke was rising from the center of the grove.

Whoever was there could not be Brondin's men. That was

impossible. Nevertheless, he had no intention of sharing his
sanctuary with strangers. Nor did he wish to go on. The next
safe resting place was eight days' hard traveling over barren
trails, and he had scarcely food or water for one.

He studied the trail carefully and found signs of only two
travelers. One, much bigger than he, walked with an erratic,
dragging step that often wandered from the path. The other
was smaller, perhaps an old man. There was no trace of
guard or servant and no sign of other recent visitors.

The situation was better than he had first assumed. He
moved quietly through the low brush to the source of the
smoke for a closer look.

The travelers were what their tracks had led him to expect.
The larger man was tall and softly corpulent, with long white
hair hanging loose around an ageless face. The other was
slender and reached barely to his companion's shoulder. Over
his left eye he wore a dark patch. He was heating something
in a pot over the fire, while his companion looked on with
an expression of eager anticipation. The smaller man spoke,
and the other gave a gurgle of childlike laughter and clapped
his hands together clumsily but with great enthusiasm.

The watcher was reassured. A one-eyed old man and a
half-wit surely were not robbers. They could be dispatched
easily, and it was unlikely that anyone would raise inquiries
about a pair of wandering outcasts. He withdrew and made
ready.

From around his waist he uncoiled a silken cord and
tucked it, folded into eighths, under the strap of the dagger
on his forearm, where he could pull it loose with a quick
tug. His plan was to wait until the half-wit slept and then to
dispose of the old man with a dagger thrust from his blind
side and use the strangling cord on the half-wit, whose clumsy
weight would make the job easier.

With his preparations complete, he returned to the trail
and started for the campsite. His appearance changed with
every step: His sure, smooth motions became hesitant and
uncertain, his manner cowering. He seemed almost to shrink.
When he reached the clearing where the two men sat, and
threw himself groveling to the ground before them, he was
a pitiful sight.

"Please, masters, please let me sit by the fire, just for a

little while," he whined, not raising his eyes. "Please don't drive me off."

The old man turned to bring his good eye to bear, while his companion stared open-mouthed and silent at the wretched apparition.

"Kind masters, just a sip of water and a little warmth, please," the newcomer went on, venturing a quick, imploring glance at the one-eyed man. "I'm so cold . . . so very hungry."

The one-eyed man looked down on him, appraising what he saw. The stranger was covered with the dust of long traveling. He wore no lord's colors. His plain earth-colored tunic and trousers were of sturdy stuff, not rich but serviceable: the garb of a working man. His dark beard was scant and patchy, shot with white; his hair was cropped close to his sun-browned scalp. His boots, though dirty and much worn, were of good quality. He appeared from his abject manner to be a thoroughly broken-spirited man, perhaps a fugitive. Whatever he was, he was in need.

"The fire has warmth enough for three, stranger, and you're welcome to share our pottage. I only wish we had meat to offer you, but these goats are too quick for the likes of us," said the one-eyed man, gesturing to a place by the fire.

The newcomer crept forward and held his grimy hands to the warmth. Glancing nervously at his host, he said, "If it would please you, masters, I can kill a goat."

"That would please us very much, stranger. It's long since we've tasted fresh meat."

"I'll do it, masters," the newcomer said, and made as if to rise.

"No need to hurry. Warm yourself first. Have some soup if you like. Thin stuff, but it fills an empty belly. And there's no need to call me master. I'm Traissell, and my assistant's name is Janneret. What do you call yourself?"

At the mention of his name, the big white-haired man laughed aloud and, nodding his head wildly, pounded his open hands on his thighs. Traissell reached over and patted his forearm gently to quiet him.

The newcomer thought for a moment and recalled a name he had used once before, far from this place, among men who were now all dead. "I'm Stoggan," he said.

"Welcome to our campsite, Stoggan. May I ask where you're heading?"

Stoggan glanced about furtively, as if he feared that the bushes around the little clearing were filled with listeners. He lowered his voice and said, "To the Fastness. I've heard that a man can be safe there."

"So he can. We're going there ourselves eventually, but not to stay. Purely on business."

"Are you merchants?"

"No, not us. Merchants have to carry too much and travel in huge caravans for safety. Janny and I prefer to travel light, just the two of us." Traissell smiled a dry, humorless smile and added, "The caravans seem to prefer it that way, too. They don't make us feel welcome."

"Suspicious, those caravans are," Stoggan said.

"They are indeed. Though what they fear from the two of us is something I've never been able to figure out."

"I travel alone, mostly."

Traissell nodded in approval. "Not the safest way, but it's always fastest."

"That's what I want now, the fastest way," Stoggan said, rising. "I'll catch a goat for us," he said, turning and making his way up the trail.

When he returned with a small rock goat slung over his shoulder, Traissell had built up the fire and was peeling the bark from a long, slender green branch. Several peeled branches lay at his side.

Waving to Stoggan, he said, "You sounded so confident that I built up the fire and made us skewers."

Stoggan worked fast, and before long the three men were eating their fill of the strong dark meat. The soup pot was crammed with bones, and chunks and strips of meat hung over the fire, drying in the smoke. No one said a word until all were finished, sitting content around the fire in the gathering dusk with full bellies and warm bones.

"You're as good a cook as you are a hunter, Stoggan," Traissell said contentedly. "Janny and I haven't eaten like this since . . . oh, since we were in that fishing village on the Fool's Head. Even then, all we had was smout for ten days. Decent fish, but it needs a good spicy sauce. This goat meat has a real flavor all its own."

"Are you fishermen?"

"We haven't the patience for that, Janny and I. We're healers," Traissell said. Perceiving the look of surprise that passed over Stoggan's features at this announcement, he went on. "My partner's got the mind of a child, I know that, but he has a gift I've never known anyone else to possess. He can lay his hands on a sick person and then go out and find the cure—just walk into the woods and pick leaves or berries or bark, or dig up roots or special kinds of stone—and he doesn't fail. Of course, I have to mix it up properly, and I do all the bone setting and cutting and the stitching up. But we're partners, Janneret and I."

Janneret, hearing his name, was looking eagerly from one man to the other, making impatient wordless sounds. Traissell patted the back of his big, pale hand paternally and said in a reassuring voice. "It's all right. Everything's fine. I'm just telling our new friend about how special you are at helping sick people."

Stoggan, with some time to think, had altered his plan. These two might be useful to him, particularly if Brondin had sent word about the north and put men everywhere on the alert for a solitary traveler. No one would suspect the hangdog servant of an old healer and his half-wit assistant of being the boldest thief in the northern lands.

"You're a good man, Traissell. You've been very kind to me," he said awkwardly, looking down at his hands. "I want to tell you the truth."

"I'll be glad to hear it. Running from someone?"

Stoggan nodded and began to recite, in halting, hesitant phrases, a tale he had heard by a similar fireside long ago in a distant land. It was a tale of innocence violated by brute power, of long patient planning and bloody retribution and headlong flight from a tyrant's cruel sons. Traissell listened without saying a word or even nodding as Stoggan's long account unfolded.

"I thought that once I'd avenged my wife and daughter, I wouldn't care what happened to me. But I do care. I want to live, and so I have to keep running," he concluded.

"And do his sons still follow you?" Traissell asked.

"They'll follow me as long as they live."

"Do they know what you look like?"

"They only saw me once, that first day at my cottage, when their father set his men on me, and they weren't close enough for a good look. I expect they've bribed or tortured a description out of someone by now."

"But if they walked into this campsite, they might not recognize you."

"Maybe not."

Traissell made no response to that. He sat silent for a long time. Darkness had come while Stoggan spoke, falling swiftly over the upland valley, and Traissell's expression, visible only by the fading fire glow, was not easily deciphered. At last he said, "Maybe we can help each other."

"How?"

"You're a good hunter and a good cook, and you probably know how to set up a camp a lot better than I do. It's hard traveling, just the two of us. This fellow is strong, but he can't do much on his own. I get tired, and sometimes I'd like someone to talk to."

"Do you want me to be your servant?" Stoggan asked, his voice filled with excitement.

"You won't get to the Fastness as quickly as you would if you traveled alone," Traissell warned him, "but you'll be safer. I'll tell anyone we meet that you've been with us for a long time. I'll tell them any story you like."

"You're very kind."

"It's just plain sensible. We'll be helping each other. Besides, I don't like to think of a man having to run all his life just because he acted like a man."

"I'll get more wood for the fire, master," Stoggan said, springing to his feet. "And I'll bring leaves for us to sleep on."

He smiled to himself as he walked from the fireside. These two would bring him safely through any net Brondin could cast and never be the wiser. Once safe within the Fastness, he could make his plans and his contacts at leisure, free from fear. Things were working out far better than he had dared hope.

CHAPTER THREE

ORANNAN MEETS
A GRATEFUL LISTENER

And on the plain beside the sea, on the day the magic
died,
When the three sons of Vannen met, and two fought side
by side,
And one set out across the waves to face the demon
lord,
Each bore the blood of Ambescand in his enchanted
sword.
The web was woven tighter when that day's work was
through,
And men rejoiced, for men believed no more was left
to do....

From *The Last Deed of Ambescand*

The words drifted off on the soft night breeze, and a silence fell upon the little group around the fire. Orannan struck one final chord, laid his harp aside, rested his elbows on his knees, and stared into the flames. For a time, the only sounds in the clearing were the faint rustle of cloth and leaves as one of the travelers shifted position, or the comforting gurgle of wine as a flagon passed among them.

Finally one man rose, stretched, and went to Orannan's side, where he stopped and dug for his purse. He drew out a coin and dropped it in the harper's outstretched hand. Waving off any expression of gratitude, he said, "It's a good tale you tell but a sad one. Too sad for me."

"The sons of Vannen delivered the north from the Stone Hand and founded a dynasty that ruled in peace and plenty for two hundred years. What's sad about that?" Orannan asked.

27

"It's all over. That's the sad part," said a second man gruffly, tossing his offering at the storyteller's feet.

"The wizards are gone, and they'll never return. The Kernlord lies under the sea," a third man pointed out.

"That's as may be," retorted the second. "But the days of peace and plenty ended before you and I were born. Look around you, man," he said irritably, with a gesture that encompassed their camp. "You can't travel anywhere in the north unless you travel with an army. Robbers on all the trails, and every fifty greatmarks some petty warlord demanding tribute for the privilege of crossing his domain."

The third man was persistent. "Robbers and warlords can be dealt with. Would you rather have gray men coming after you or sorcerers shriveling your body and spirit and shaking the earth under your feet?"

"I'd rather have peace and prosperity, just as my father did when he was a boy, before outlanders and thieves took over everything. Why, when my father was less than ten summers old, he and his mother—just the two of them; no guards, no private army, just a woman and a boy—used to travel everywhere in the north without fear," said the second man, turning away. "And look at us—a hundred grown men, one of every four a guard, all of us armed. I tell you, the north has seen its greatness. Our day is over. You don't have merchants coming from the east and the south anymore. We're a dying land."

Voices were raised in rebuttal, but their arguments grew indistinct as the disputants moved off. The crowd around the fire dispersed. Most of them dropped a coin into Orannan's hand or at his feet, murmuring a polite phrase of gratitude before returning to tent or wagon. Orannan smiled and nodded and gave his thanks to all.

He was pleased, and not only because he had done unexpectedly well that evening. It was good to be able to tell his best stories freely once more, without having to slip away before the audience had a proper chance to show their appreciation. Soon, if all went well, he would be in a place of sanctuary, a land where tales of the old heroic times were cherished and rewarded, not forbidden and punished.

Orannan rose, wincing at the stiffness in his knees. He glanced to the far side of the fire, where one man remained:

a burly fellow, one of the guards, relaxing after his turn on duty. He sat cross-legged, and a stone flagon rested against his knee. Looking up from the fire, he met the storyteller's gaze and shook his head. He dangled an empty coin purse upside down, tossed it away, and shrugged.

Orannan smiled and saluted him. "Another time," he said.

The guard nodded and returned the salute. Orannan flexed his knees, stretched, and took up his harp. As he turned, he gave a start at the sight of the two men who had been standing silent behind him.

"Hello, Orannan," said the taller of the two, smiling.

"Good evening, gentlemen," Orannan replied, regaining his composure. "I trust you enjoyed my tale."

"It's our favorite," the short man said.

"I'm very gratified to hear that." Orannan clinked the coins in his hand suggestively, glancing from one to the other.

"We heard you tell it in the High City," the short man went on.

"In the High . . . City?" An unpleasant suspicion sprouted in Orannan's mind.

The two men stepped to either side of Orannan. The taller one, still smiling, said in a lowered voice, "You're a hard man to find. You kept moving around, and when we finally heard you, you slipped away before we could speak to you."

"I'm so glad we were able to meet. I hope you'll come to hear me tomorrow evening," Orannan said, backing away.

There was a soft metallic whisper, and Orannan saw the gleam of light on a dagger point. "We'll hear you, Orannan. Tomorrow you'll be with us, on the way to the High City. We have a friend who wants to hear your story," the taller man said.

"Friend?" Orannan asked in a barely audible voice.

"His name is Halssa," said the tall man, and Orannan emitted a low groan.

The shorter man said, "Don't give us any trouble, and we'll make it an easy journey. If you try anything, we'll truss you up and drag you all the way. Understand?"

Orannan's heart sank. He nodded, unable to speak. In the silence, he heard a loud yawn behind him and then the sound of slow, heavy footsteps approaching.

"Get rid of this drunk fast," said the tall man, turning Orannan around to face the guard.

The guard was walking with the careful step of a man who knows that he has drunk too much but believes that he can conceal his state from others by adopting a dignified gait. Closer, he was not so tall as he appeared from a distance. The massiveness of his body gave the impression of great size; actually, he was only a bit taller than Orannan and slightly shorter than the man who stood with his dagger point at Orannan's back.

The guard radiated curbed strength. Seeing the forearms, thicker than his own thighs, that hung from the short-sleeved tunic, Orannan dared to hope for rescue. When the guard stopped and stood unsteadily before them, looking blearily from one to the other, Orannan's hope vanished.

"That was a good story you told. You're a good storyteller," the guard said thickly, nodding his head.

"Thank you," Orannan replied almost inaudibly.

"Wasn't that a good story?" the intruder demanded of the shorter man.

"It's our favorite. We were just telling him that," the man said, moving a few steps to place the guard between himself and his companion, who remained at Orannan's back.

"Good story. Best story I ever heard," the guard said dogmatically, addressing no one in particular. "Are you going to tell it tomorrow night?" he asked Orannan.

The storyteller gave a little jump as the dagger point pricked his spine. He quickly replied, "Yes! Tomorrow night, definitely."

The guard looked at him with sudden concern. "Your voice sounds funny. You need some wine."

"I'm fine, perfectly fine. It's . . . night air . . . too much talking," Orannan said, clearing his throat.

"No wine?"

"No, thank you."

The guard extended the flagon to the others in turn. "It's good wine. Plenty left."

"None for us. We're working tonight," the shorter man said.

"Too bad. Good wine."

"We'll all meet tomorrow night. We'll hear a good story

and drink some wine. How about that?" the taller man said, smiling amicably.

"Tomorrow night," the guard said, grinning and raising the heavy flagon as if it were a cup. He drank, wiped his lips and his long thick moustache, and clumsily refitted the stopper, swaying as he worked. He half turned as if to go and then brought the flagon up and around in a level backhand swing. It struck the taller man's temple with the sound and effect of a club hitting a melon.

The shorter man was not fast enough to save himself. His dagger had just cleared the sheath when the flagon came around in a descending arc, with the guard's full strength behind it. The blow landed just in front of the man's ear with a loud crack and sent him rolling. He lay motionless where he stopped, and a dark pool spread around his head.

Dagger in hand, the guard inspected both men closely. He tossed their weapons to the fireside and searched their clothing. From each he extracted a fat purse.

"They've had good pickings. They were stupid to get so greedy, right here in camp," he said. The drunken slur was gone.

"You saved my life," Orannan said, awed by the speedy reversal of his lot.

"That's what I'm paid for. Besides, I really did like your story." The guard rose and went to the fire, where he took up the daggers and scrutinized them thoroughly. "They carried good equipment. Either of these would cost close to a quarter oak in the High City. That's good workmanship."

"Thank you," Orannan murmured, still dazed.

"I saw them skulking around when you were finishing your story. They were watching all the time you collected. I figured there'd be trouble."

He seemed about to say more, but at this point the guardmaster and another man, their swords drawn, marched into the ring of firelight. The guardmaster knelt to inspect the fallen men; then he rose and joined Orannan and his rescuer.

"Thieves?" he asked.

"They tried to rob the storyteller."

"Any more of them?"

"Just these two."

"You should have given the alarm."

"I think they would have killed him and made a run for it."

Orannan blurted out, "Yes, they would have. They would definitely have killed me. This man saved my life."

"That's his job," the guardmaster said curtly, and returned his attention to the big guard. "What did they carry?"

The guard dropped the two well-filled purses into his waiting hand and then stooped to pick up the daggers. "These are worth something, too," he said.

The guardmaster gave a little grunt of approval as he hefted the purses. He spilled the contents of one into his palm and whistled softly at the sight of gold. "You did well. Every man will thank you for this," he said.

It was the custom among the caravans for the guards to divide any property taken from a captured thief. With two quick blows, Orannan's rescuer had assured his comrades of as much as they could hope to earn in a year of hard, dangerous work.

The guardmaster dismissed him, and Orannan fell in beside him. They went on for a few steps in silence, and then Orannan said, "You saved me from a bad death. They weren't just thieves. They were going to take me back to the High City."

"Why?" the guard asked without turning to look at him.

"I tell stories and sing of the old days. Halssa's forbidden anyone to do that."

"Halssa's getting stupid. What does it matter to him if someone tells a good story about the old kings?"

"I think he wants people to forget the kind of men who once ruled in the north. Halssa's not very impressive when you compare him with Ordred or Geerdran or any of the Colberanes from the Lake Isle."

The guard gave a low laugh. "No, he's not."

"Even after all these years, he doesn't feel safe. He made a lot of enemies in those early years. I think he's just trying to make himself as safe as he can."

"Safe from storytellers?" The guard laughed again.

"From everyone. Anyone. And I don't even care what becomes of Halssa or the High City. All I want is to get to a place where I can do what I do best and not have to fear being killed for it."

"That's reasonable. Tell me, doesn't all this talking make you thirsty?"

Ahead of them was the wagon of Boshko, the wine merchant, brightly lit by lamps hung from the side, with a good fire going nearby and stools set around it. A low buzz of talk came from the men seated in twos and threes by the fire, and an occasional loud laugh stirred the night.

"It does indeed," Orannan told him. "And since you seem to have broken your flagon, allow me to buy something to replace it."

The guard's name was Cabanard. He did not say where he came from, and even though Orannan listened carefully, he could not trace his new friend's origin from his speech. Cabanard had traveled too widely. Words, phrases, and intonations from every region of the familiar world were mingled in his conversation with expressions completely unknown to Orannan.

His age was as difficult to determine as his origins. In the brighter light of Boshko's fire and lamps, Orannan could see the gray in the guard's hair and moustache. The man's arms were latticed with scars. Most were faint with the healing passage of time, but one looked fairly recent. His large hands were like upturned roots: two fingers of his left hand were crooked and could scarcely bend, and the knuckles of his right hand were enlarged and crisscrossed with scars. His face might have been scarred, too, but it was so deeply lined, so leathery from long exposure to sun, wind, and hard weather, that one could not tell. And yet, for all the marks of time and travail that he bore, Cabanard's eyes were bright, and he made no complaint.

He took a long draft from his tankard, sighed with satisfaction, and turned to Orannan. "You were all talking too low for me to make anything out, but I heard Halssa's name clear enough. That's when I figured you needed help."

"Then you knew that they weren't thieves."

"I had my suspicions."

"But you said nothing to the guardmaster."

"No point in complicating things."

"No, no point whatsoever," Orannan agreed wholeheartedly. He glanced at those seated nearby. Then he leaned closer to Cabanard and said, "I'd be just as happy if the word didn't get around."

"Halssa's got you worried, hasn't he?"

"Yes. I didn't think he'd pursue anyone this far. The caravan is twenty days' travel from the High City. Another six days, at most, and we'll be in the Fastness. I thought Halssa's influence was far behind us."

"He probably offered a bounty. That gets people like those two mighty interested."

Orannan's eyes widened, and the tankard in his hand shook a little, spilling wine on his boot. "Bounty?" he asked in a small voice.

"If he wants you bad enough, that's a good way to get you, and no trouble for him." Cabanard took a sip of wine and went on. "He just waits for someone to bring you in, then he pays them. Probably cheats them, too."

"Then there might be others. Even in the Fastness."

"It's possible."

Orannan groaned and stared at the ground, an image of desolation. Cabanard was silent for a time, and then he looked cautiously around, hitched his stool closer to the storyteller's, and said, "There are some good men walking guard on this caravan. I'll talk to them and see that someone's always got an eye on you. Next time somebody calls you by name, don't answer. You gave yourself away to those two."

"I'll be careful. I don't know how I can ever repay you for your help, Cabanard."

Draining the last of his wine, Cabanard, with an expectant grin, handed the empty tankard to the storyteller.

When Orannan returned, he said, "A few tankards of watery wine is small return for saving my neck. Even at Boshko's prices."

"I'm the one who repaid tonight, storyteller. I've heard you a dozen times, maybe more, and never did I have a coin to drop in your hand to show my appreciation. When all those others got up and gave you something, and I had to sit there without two copper bits to rub together, I felt as low as I've felt in a long time. I'm glad I had the chance to help you."

"So am I," Orannan said fervently. He raised his flagon, and they drank.

"I'm curious. Surely you did more than just tell of the old times," Cabanard said. When Orannan merely shrugged, he went on. "As I recall, you could create a song right on the spot. They were funny songs, too, the ones I heard. You could make a man look like an awful fool, but you'd do it in such a way that he'd be laughing along with the rest."

"Halssa didn't laugh," Orannan confessed.

"Halssa never was much for laughing."

"Actually, it was a very witty song. Everyone else liked it. But Halssa considered it offensive."

Cabanard nodded his head but said nothing. He sipped his wine and waited for Orannan to continue.

"I found all this out later, of course. At the time, I wasn't even warned. If I'd known, I would have been more careful where I sang it and taken a closer look at my audience. But I had no idea Halssa was angry."

"How did you find out?"

"I performed at Kalogan's tavern, in the big basement room. The crowd was good. A lot of Halssa's men were there, mostly around the entry, but I didn't suspect anything at the time. It was a good show—very responsive audience —and when I had finished with my main story, a few people called for the Halssa song. I was a bit reluctant to sing it with so many of his men there, but I couldn't disappoint my audience. So I sang it. And while I was singing, a fight broke out. I heard someone shouting, 'Get the storyteller!' so I looked for a place to hide. The trapdoor to Kalogan's cellars was right there. I went down and then got out by a chute."

"Very sensible," Cabanard said.

"But I still didn't know what trouble I was in. The next day I was on my way to Kalogan's to collect my money, when Zupassa—she's Kalogan's mistress—pulled me into an alleyway and told me that Halssa's men were looking for me all over the city because of that song. She hid me for two nights; then I got out and made my way to the inn at Plain's End and waited for a caravan heading north."

"You may be safe now. At least you can be sure of help if anyone else comes after you." Cabanard set down his wine and added, "Some day I want to hear that song."

"I'll sing it as often as you like once I'm in a safe place."

They sat in silence for a time. Cabanard pulled his stool closer to the fire and began kneading his shoulder and moving his right arm stiffly. He winced when he tried to raise his arm too high, but he said nothing. Three of Boshko's other customers departed, leaving only a solitary drover, two merchants deep in an intensely secretive conversation, and the two new-found friends.

"Do you know Halssa well?" Orannan asked.

"Not well. Long, but not well," Cabanard replied, still working his shoulder slowly and methodically, as if it were an old habit. After a time he went on. "We came east together under Balthid. He was a good captain, but he decided to settle down, and Halssa and I weren't ready for that. We were still a pair of wild boys, and there was plenty of work for us in those days. We fought together at the siege of the High City. I commanded a squad of swordsmen, and Halssa was under me."

"Were you friends?"

"Halssa didn't make friends. He was a good fighter and smarter than any of us realized. I think he knew back then what he wanted to do, and as soon as the city fell, he got to work."

"I've heard that it was bad in the city in those days."

"It wasn't bad if you were one of the conquerors," Cabanard said. "I suppose it was hard on the people. I lived pretty well for a few summers, but it started to get boring. I could feel myself getting soft. So I headed south and joined a warlord who was having trouble with his neighbors. Next time I heard of Halssa, he was King of the High City."

The remembrance seemed to breach the reticence that Cabanard had displayed earlier. He talked on, recounting his travels and adventures; and though he was vague in referring to times and places, and sparing of names, Orannan knew enough about the recent history of the north to know that the stories were true. There was scarcely a major battle in which he had not taken part and few warlords he had not known.

In the years that had passed since the last descendant of the Vannensons had been deposed and slain in the High City, misrule had spread across the north. The long hegemony of the High City was ended. The majestic bridges, proudly re-built in the peaceful early days of the Vannenson dynasty, were torn down, and the Headland and the Crystal Hills withdrew into vigilant isolation. The Fastness, long a great gathering place for travelers, became a fortress city-state.

The Southern Forest and Long Wood were now wary of strangers. Petty kingdoms, some of them no more than ten greatmarks from side to side, came into being, grew, merged, and sometimes disappeared. Every sizable house became a garrison as each ambitious man turned hungry, suspicious eyes on his neighbors. The farmers, crofters, and smallholders looked to their local warlords for security, and sometimes they found it; more often they found oppression and the demand for tribute and forced service.

Life in the northern lands became an ongoing war that now and then abated but never ceased entirely. Amid the turbulence and uncertainty, rumor flourished. There was constant talk of an alliance of the warlords of the plain against Halssa and the army of the High City, and though young Brondin was generally held to be their leader, every whisperer had his favorite candidate. Some people spoke of distant powers observing carefully, awaiting their moment to strike and conquer the northland in a single bold stroke. Others held that a full-blooded descendant of the last Vannenson still lived in hiding and would return at the head of a mighty army to punish the usurper and reclaim his throne. A few raised their eyes to the heavens, to the twelve stars that formed the Iron Angel, and repeated the old legend that Staver Ironbrand would return to deliver his people in their need.

In such times, there was no lack of work for a man like Cabanard and no lack of listeners for Orannan. One promised safety in the present; the other revived, for a while, the glory of the past.

Orannan found himself moved by the veteran warrior's artless, straightforward account of battles won and lost, assaults and escapes, and old friends fallen. Here was a man who had lived the life that Orannan could only recreate in well-wrought phrases. The sword at Cabanard's side was the tool of his profession; the dagger that hung from Orannan's belt, still unstained with blood, was no more to him than an article of dress. He felt a pang of envy for Cabanard even as he pitied him for his scars and his poverty.

Cabanard emptied his tankard and set it aside with a deep sigh. "And look where it's all ended. Halssa rules in the High City, and I hire out as a caravan guard. Halssa drinks out of a gold cup, and I cadge overpriced wine from the people I'm supposed to protect."

"More wine?" Orannan asked.

"No. I can't even drink the way I used to."

"Cheer up, Cabanard. Luck changes," Orannan said.

"Mine gets worse."

"Not tonight. Your share of those purses ought to keep you in comfort for a year."

"If I lived in comfort for a year, I'd probably die of boredom."

"What will you do with the money, then?"

Cabanard reflected for a moment and then said, "First thing, I'll get cleaned up. Get myself some new clothes and burn these rags. I don't even have a cloak for winter. I want to sleep indoors on a soft bed; eat a slow meal, sitting down at a table, with people waiting on me; hear a woman's voice and feel her softness. It's been a long time since I was civilized." He sighed and then went on. "And then I'll look around the Fastness. I'm sure to find people I know. I've often thought of starting a school to train caravan guards. Something like that is really needed. I wouldn't go out myself anymore, but I'd supply the best in the north."

"You could become a prosperous man."

"About time, too, storyteller. I've done a lot of fighting, and other people always got the rewards. What about you? Will you stay at the Fastness?"

"For a time. Then I'll go on to the Headland."

Cabanard nodded approvingly. "That's smart. Make it to the Headland, and you won't have to worry about Halssa any more."

"Yes. If I can get there. It's a long way, and I have no promise that I'll be admitted."

"Don't worry about problems until they come," said Cabanard, rising stiffly and rubbing the small of his back. "The first thing to do is to get to the Fastness, and I'll see to it that you make it safely."

CHAPTER FOUR

BUSINESS IN THE HIGH CITY

The master of the harbor works gave a long and detailed explanation of the causes for his slow progress, managing to avoid all personal responsibility. The keeper of the treasury, in his hushed, melancholy voice, announced that the harbor works were exceeding all anticipated costs and severely draining the resources of the High City. Mourut, the tax gatherer, then smugly described his latest schemes for wringing tolls, tribute, and passage fees from traders and travelers. No sooner had he finished than the master of the harbor works and the keeper of the treasury burst into an anxious duet of self-justification.

Halssa let them babble on without interruption. All three were thieves, he knew, but they served his present purposes. He glanced at his adviser, Karash-Kabey, who sat at his right hand. The old man was listening with apparent interest to the woes of the harbor master, nodding sympathetically as the beleaguered official tried to explain himself.

Halssa returned his attention to the speaker. The facts were all too familiar to him by now, and he still wondered whether the whole project had not been premature. He had reservations about an alliance with the forces of the east and small desire to place his trust in sea power either for war or for commerce. He was a landsman, with a landsman's inherent suspicion of the sea. But he respected the wisdom of Karash-Kabey and heeded his advice, even on those occasions when it went against his own instincts. The old man had counseled him well in the past. He seemed to know the ways of acquiring, keeping, and expanding power, and he had so far shown unswerving loyalty. There were things about him that Halssa found disquieting, but since the old man roused far more disquiet—even stark fear—in others, Halssa retained him and made use of his talents.

The keeper of the treasury fell silent. Halssa nodded to the next man, and the conference proceeded. Only when all had reported did Halssa speak.

"You've done well, Mourut, and now you must do better. I'm assessing all land holders one-twelfth of their worth and all tenants one twenty-fifth, to be paid on demand in coin or in labor. That should put a small amount in the treasury and provide all the men needed for the dredging of the harbor."

"As Lord Halssa commands," the tax gatherer said smoothly.

Turning to the master of the harbor works, Halssa said, "You'll have all the men you need, Crollo. I want the harbor clear by spring."

"It will be cleared, my lord."

"You're taking the silt mighty far out. Why can't you dump it closer to shore?"

Crollo glanced up and looked nervously at Karash-Kabey. The adviser, in his gentle slow voice, said to Halssa, "Crollo takes a wise precaution, my lord, and avoids the error of past generations. The current north of the islands sweeps the silt out to sea. Any closer in, tides and current would only return it and undo our work."

"It costs us boats, workers, and time."

"Doing the work properly will repay all costs, my lord. The harbor will be clear once and for all."

"But will it be done by spring?"

"It will be as you command," said the old man.

Halssa nodded, accepting his adviser's word, and turned to the commander of the outer guard. "What word of the storyteller Orannan?"

"None, my lord. I've spread word of the reward, but no one's claimed it."

"A man with a price of forty eagles on his head doesn't just disappear. I want the storyteller. If he mocks me unpunished, others may try."

"You'll have him, my lord," the commander announced confidently.

"I've learned of a theft from Balthid's Keep. Nothing definite yet, but it appears that something of great importance to Brondin may have been taken. Have you heard anything?"

"Nothing at all, my lord. Not even a rumor."

Fixing his eye on the commander of the city guard, Halssa demanded, "What about you? Have you heard of any strangers worth noting? Any valuable item offered for sale in the city?"

"Nothing unusual, my lord. Certainly nothing that could be traced to Brondin. I'll have my men look to it at once."

"Have them look to it more carefully than is their custom. If the story is true, we're looking for a master thief. Your men could not manage to capture a storyteller who didn't even know they were after him."

Commander Letanza lowered his eyes under Halssa's cool scorn. Halssa flicked his gaze about the table from face to face and then addressed his commanders with an admonition: "Keep alert, both of you, but be discreet about it. I want the thief and whatever he took. And I want that storyteller."

That ended the business of the day. Halssa dismissed the council, and all left but Karash-Kabey, who remained seated at Halssa's right.

"Another wasted morning," Halssa said sourly.

"Not so, my lord," Karash-Kabey corrected him gently. "Your council members are kept alert by your show of interest, and regular contact with them keeps you informed."

"It informs me that most of them are helpless idiots. I sometimes wish I were still a soldier." Halssa was silent for a time. Then he asked, "Can't you learn anything more about the theft at Balthid's Keep? Can you at least find out what was taken?"

"If anything was indeed stolen, I will learn of it. My informant told me only that Brondin entered his treasure vault and said upon emerging that nothing had been taken, but his manner and appearance suggested otherwise."

"I didn't know you had a spy that close to Brondin."

"Such a matter is best kept confidential, my lord," Karash-Kabey said softly.

"Confidential from me? I think not. What else are you keeping confidential?" Halssa demanded.

"I do not wish to clutter your mind with details, my lord."

"If it has to do with Brondin, I don't consider it cluttering

d. Let that be understood. Not that I fear him."
gave a short, hard laugh at the idea. "But I know
tha___e's the man in the north who can cause me the most
trouble. Anything that's bad for him is good for me."

"He may be a source of great danger."

"Brondin? He's a nuisance but no danger. Brondin is all
words and no action. His father was a man I wouldn't want
for my enemy, but Brondin . . . a clever boy with a twisted
leg, nothing more."

"Nevertheless, he must be watched."

"I leave that to you. In a way, Brondin makes it easy
for us. We need only watch Balthid's Keep, and we know
everything our enemies are doing," Halssa said.

"Perhaps not. I have had indications—faint indications, no
more than hints—that others in the north may eventually
pose a great danger to you."

"Who? And don't talk of cluttering my mind. I want to
know."

Unperturbed, the old man said, "When I learn, I will in-
form you. As yet, all is vague."

"But there is danger, and it's growing."

"Yes." Karash-Kabey looked up, and his pale blue eyes
were piercing, as bright and full of life as a young man's.
"This is why work on the harbor must continue. With the
strength of the east at your command, you can crush all resistance. With a fleet, you can extend your power as far as
your ambition urges you. The harbor is the key."

"You've told me so often enough."

"I say it because it is true."

"If a clear harbor and a strong fleet are so important, why
didn't anyone else think of them? Ambescand didn't, nor did
any of the Vannenson kings. Even Tallisan, when he fought
the sea raiders, fought on land. Now, all of a sudden, deepening the harbor becomes all-important."

"The others were welcomed to the throne. You are called
usurper. Your help must come from without," Karash-Kabey
said.

"Yes, and Brondin, with his half dozen drops of Vannenson blood, thinks to rally all my enemies to him." Halssa
strode angrily the length of the chamber and back, while
Karash-Kabey sat unmoving, loosely clutching his staff, his

eyes fixed on the distance. Returning to his side, Halssa said, "I could solve the whole problem of Brondin and his alliance with a small force of good men. I'd lead them myself. We could attack while they're gathered in one of their conspiracy sessions and butcher the lot of them. Level Balthid's Keep to the ground."

"The danger of such a course is too great."

"There's greater danger ahead if the alliance grows strong enough to attack us before the harbor work is finished."

"You think as a soldier thinks, my lord, but now you are a ruler and must learn to think as a ruler," said Karash-Kabey, sitting like a dark effigy, still as stone.

"A ruler acts. That's why he's a ruler."

"A wise ruler acts wisely and does not put his life in hazard without great cause. A raid on Balthid's Keep is a desperate measure. You would lose many men, and you yourself might fall."

"I've led scores of raids like this in my time," Halssa said impatiently.

"The risks are too great," his adviser persisted. "You would face danger in the approach, danger in the attack, danger on your return. If Brondin's followers rallied to avenge him, you might face a siege of the High City before you are prepared to withstand it. First the harbor must be cleared, and then you will have the strength to dispose of your enemies as you will."

Halssa grunted irritably. "I hate waiting and plotting. That's not how I came to power. Brondin is in my way, and I want to remove him."

"There are other ways, my lord. As soon as we learn the truth about the theft, I will see that Brondin is slain."

"This spy of yours—is he an assassin?"

"An assassin will be found."

Halssa paused for a moment, pacing the room thoughtfully. "I've wanted others removed, and they still live. Brondin's survived my assassins before."

"I did not choose the assassins," said Karash-Kabey.

"No," Halssa admitted. "Well, you have your chance. You can leave now and be about it. Don't act until I give the word, but put everything in readiness."

Karash-Kabey rose. He was a tall man, thin of frame, his slenderness accentuated by his simple dark robe. He walked at an unhurried pace from the room, the sound of his staff as rhythmic as his soft footsteps. Halssa looked with distaste at the crystal atop the staff, and as he looked, a beam of sunlight struck the crystal carving with a rainbow flash that dazzled his eyes. He looked away quickly, and a chill ran down his spine.

CHAPTER FIVE

RESOLUTION

Against a hardened warrior there rose a valiant youth:
His mind was quick, his heart was bold, his word was
full of truth,
And brave men rallied to him—but their faith was
damped with doubt,
For though they saw his eye was keen, and his sword
arm swift and stout,
He could not march in battle, nor lead the headlong
charge,
Nor meet a foeman blade to blade and targe to ringing
targe. . . .

From *The Last Deed of Ambescand*

Brondin held the secret within him until he was bursting to speak. Every new message from his followers made it more difficult to conceal the theft. And yet he told no one.

Messengers arrived at Balthid's Keep every few days, and the word they brought was seldom reassuring. The alliance was deeply divided, and the very men he needed most were quarreling among themselves. Some wished to move against the High City at once and let surprise do the work of great numbers. Others urged that they wait until spring, when their armies were certain to be as large as Halssa's. Some called for a direct assault on the High City, while others wanted a long siege or slow infiltration and a sudden eruption from within.

Each petty warlord sought the honor of leading the attack, and it was these messages which rankled in Brondin's heart. He well knew that whatever role he might play in Halssa's overthrow, it could never be on the field of battle.

Like every man of his time and position, Brondin remained in constant practice with the sword. He was as good a bowman as any of his followers. Lifelong use of crutches had given great strength to his chest and shoulders, and he was in robust health. But he was hampered by his crippled leg. He had the blood of Ambescand and Colberane and the Scarlet Ordred in his veins, but he could never hope to match their prowess in battle. He could not lead a charge, scale a wall, fight blade to blade against the enemy who could dance around him like a child taunting a chained dog. On the battlefield he would be not a leader but an obstacle to his own cause.

He could not help but wonder what this might signify for the future, once he was on the throne. How long, he wondered, would fighting men follow a leader who fought with words and not steel? Perhaps such a man would retain their loyalty only while his right to rule was uncontested. If that was so, the theft had cost him dearly.

He kept his secret locked inside him until one blustery night late in the month of Harvest, after a day filled with dispiriting reports. Stallicho and Witigense were at odds over some cause Brondin could not fathom; it seemed unclear even to the men who were prepared to do battle over it. Zathias lay ill of a fever, and there was little hope for his recovery. Parhender, one of the most powerful warlords of the plain, was threatening to gather all those with a taste for glory and plunder and lead them against the High City before winter if Brondin delayed any longer. Everything, it seemed, was falling apart.

He rose from his chair by the fire, stretched, and went to the door, where a servant waited with the guard. He sent the servant for his chief advisers.

Henorik arrived almost at once; Brondin wondered whether the faithful old warrior ever rested. Dostilla came soon after, yawning, and finally old Espar made his slow, silent way into the chamber. Brondin bade them sit in the warmth before the fire.

"You must know I've been troubled of late, and I've said nothing to explain it to you," he began. "All the warlords have been pressing me for a decision. They want to know when and how I plan to attack Halssa and who'll lead the men. I haven't given them an answer, so they're getting restless. I don't think the alliance will last much longer without a decision."

"It is no easy decision for you to make, my lord," Henorik said.

"No, but it's made. That's not why I summoned you. I want you to know why I've been delaying and what I've decided to do." He glanced at the door and then leaned forward, drawing his three advisers closer. "Something very important to me and to the alliance has been stolen from the treasure vault. We must get it back."

"What is it, my lord?" Dostilla asked.

"A cloak pin. A simple iron cloak pin, inlaid with gold and silver wire and set with garnets."

Dostilla looked about in confusion. "But surely, my lord . . . an iron cloak pin. What value can it have?"

In his soft, measured voice, as if from a distance, Espar said, "The cloak pin of Ciantha is beyond value. It is the emblem of the Vannensons."

"Say what you know of it," Brondin directed him.

"There are four separate accounts, and all agree that the cloak pin belonged to the first Ciantha, bride of Ambescand, who brought it from the Crystal Hills. No one knows who fashioned it or where or when it was made. It is said to be of no earthly metal but of iron fallen from the sky. There are some who believe it holds magic, but the accounts disagree on that. Ciantha passed the cloak pin on to her eldest daughter, and that daughter to her eldest, and thus it was passed down through all the generations of the Vannensons. It has not been seen since the death of Stiragos and the end of the Vannenson dynasty. His wife, Eudotia, wore it; but her children were all slain and she herself never seen after the fall of the palace," said Espar.

"My mother's mother was cousin to Eudotia."

"This is so," Espar said. "And the accounts mention no other women surviving."

"So the cloak pin passed to her and then to my mother. And when Dolsaina married Balthid, she brought it here and concealed it in the treasure vault, until she should have a daughter. But both my sisters died in infancy, so it remained hidden until the time I should marry and have a daughter of my own. And now it's gone," said Brondin.

"My lord, forgive my ignorance, but of what real importance is this cloak pin to you?" Dostilla asked.

"It verifies my claim to rule. I have Vannenson blood in me, the blood of Ambescand and his descendants, and should rule by right of that, I know," Brondin said, raising a hand to forestall their objections. "But these are troubled times. The north teems with ambitious men, and there are those who would respect the claims of force above the rights of blood. I would be challenged, and whatever came of it, the kingdom would remain fragmented. I need the cloak pin to prove my rightful claim until I'm firmly in power."

"But would it suffice? Such a thing could easily be duplicated, my lord. Those who wished to reject your claim would say you had falsified the cloak pin of Ciantha," Dostilla objected.

"I've heard that the cloak pin has a power about it. I've held it in my hands, and I felt nothing, but my father told me a story about the times of Theora." Brondin turned to his old chronicler and asked, "Do you know the story of Theora and Grendoorn? I can recall it only vaguely."

The old man nodded. "I know it, my lord. It is in a secret palace account. Theora was a descendant of Ordred, third to rule after him in the High City in the times of peace. She was much beloved. Theora wore the cloak pin, given her by her mother, Jemmesne, on all public occasions. Since she had four sons and no daughters, she intended to present the cloak pin to the eldest daughter of her cousin Geminlan, of the line of Colberane, so that it would, as always, be worn by a woman of Vannenson descent.

"But her eldest son was married to one Grendoorn, who desired the cloak pin for herself. Grendoorn was a great beauty, the accounts say. She came from the Crystal Hills and had been heard to say openly that she had equal right to Ciantha's legacy. She induced her husband, Dexal, to steal the cloak pin from his mother when Theora lay in her final illness.

"Dexal did as she wished. He was a weak man and a feeble ruler, and his reign was of blessed brevity. Theora died, and on the first state occasion after Dexal's coronation, Grendoorn appeared, wearing the cloak pin at her breast. On the steps of the palace she suddenly cried out and fell forward and lay writhing at the foot of the steps, shrieking in an inhuman voice, and then she died. When her garments were removed, a great wound was found on her breast, just where the cloak pin had rested. It was as if a flaming sword had been thrust into her heart. Dexal had the cloak pin conveyed to Geminlan's daughter the very next day," the old man concluded.

"I knew of the death of Grendoorn," Henorik said, looking about uneasily, "but I never heard of any magical wound."

"Nor did I, before this," Dostilla added.

"Perhaps it's a weary chronicler's embellishment, and perhaps it's true. Does it matter?" Brondin asked. "It shows that people believe in the power of the cloak pin to preserve the line of the Vannensons and punish usurpers. If I'm to rule effectively and have time to put things in order without having to worry about others claiming my throne, I need the cloak pin."

"True, my lord, true," Dostilla said. "But if this tale of Grendoorn is true, the cloak pin would be of no use to a usurper."

"The mere fact that I do not possess it would be help enough. You've heard what Parhender has been saying. Others share his feelings but do not yet dare to speak openly."

Henorik scowled and laid his hand on his sword hilt. "Parhender is a jealous man and a boaster, my lord, but he would not dare defy you. If he did, I'd see to him."

"He might move too subtly for us, Henorik. I dislike him and distrust him, but right now I need him."

"Then we must indeed get this cloak pin back. What are your orders?"

"I wish it were so easy, Henorik. I have no idea where to begin or whom to suspect. No one on earth but I knew where it was hidden. I fear that there may be more to this than mere thievery. There's a touch of something more than mortal power in it." As Dostilla began to speak, Brondin raised a hand to silence him. "I know your feelings on such things, Dostilla, but I cannot help myself. What power but magic could pry a secret from a man's mind and steal an object without leaving a trace?"

"The dead servant was not slain by magic, my lord."

"No, he was not. But I cannot say that his death and the theft are connected."

"You found the cloak pin missing the day he died. Is that not so?"

"True enough, Dostilla. But it might have been taken months before."

The three counselors looked helplessly at him and at one another and were silent. The fire crackled, and a log fell, sending up a spray of sparks, but no one moved or spoke until Brondin cleared his throat and said, "I told you I'd made a decision. I think the only course for me is to tell all my supporters that the alliance marches on the High City in the spring. The war leader will be chosen before we set out. Meanwhile, I'll send my best spies to hunt for the thief. I'll swear them to absolute secrecy, promise a huge reward, and hope for the best. But when spring comes and the roads are open, we march against Halssa, with or without the cloak pin."

The counselors accepted Brondin's decision without question. They saw no alternative.

In a short time they left Brondin. He sank deep into his chair, while the freshly fed fire grumbled and muttered in the windy chimney and the warmth soothed his aching leg. In a little while, he fell asleep.

High in a dark corner, a shadow stirred. Slowly, in total silence, a black shape swooped down, circled the sleeping figure thrice, and then flew like a bolt from the chamber window, heading north to the High City.

CHAPTER SIX

ONE EVENING
AT ENNET'S HOSTEL

Orannan found the variegated, ever-changing crowds of the Fastness a most receptive audience for his tales and songs. He twice extended his stay beyond the date he had set for departure, and the generosity of the crowd on this particular evening had made him consider doing so once more. In fact, had it not been for the inflexible regulation that anyone who remained within the walls of the Fastness for more than forty successive days would be drafted into the defense force, he might have thought seriously of settling there.

But Orannan was not a warrior and had no wish to be one. With fourteen days left until the critical date, he judged that he could spare another eight or ten, especially when the coins came his way so freely. The way ahead was long, and there might be unforeseen expenses.

He stepped up to the platform at the rear wall of Ennet's Hostel, where he had been performing since his arrival, and raised his hands in greeting. A rumble of leather tankards and pewter mugs pounded on tabletops greeted him, and cries of enthusiasm and encouragement echoed about the capacious low-ceiled room. He looked around to see whether Cabanard had shown up this evening, but his friend was nowhere in sight. On the first ten nights of Orannan's performance, Cabanard had been in regular attendance. He had come but once since then and stayed only a short time.

A loud voice nearby arrested the storyteller's attention. He turned to nod to a strapping young swordsman at a front table, with one of Ennet's girls seated at either side of him. Orannan had seen the youth here before but did not know his name, only that he liked tales of battle and rewarded them generously. He was a good-looking fellow, decently dressed but with a swaggering way about him. Had he been smaller

51

or less self-assured, he would certainly have been knocked about before this.

"Tell us of Ambescand at the tower!" he cried in a deep voice that carried above the uproar.

Other voices were raised to call for other stories, but the swordsman outshouted them. Finally he rose, and coins glinted in his upraised hand. "Two silver hawkheads for the tale of Ambescand at the sorcerers' tower!" he cried. The crowd, impressed by such largesse, grew still. He tossed the coins at Orannan's feet and with a lordly wave of the hand said, "You may begin, storyteller."

Orannan was not happy with the youth's manner, but the choice of story pleased him. This was an ancient legend from the days before the emergence of the Kernlord and the sons of Vannen. He had heard no less than six versions of it, and over the years he had developed a version of his own, a tale of subtle magics in confrontation and the clash of mighty wizards. He picked up his harp and began to strike a rhythmic sequence of deep, thrumming notes, setting the mood for his story. Louder and louder swelled the music, then softer and softer, until it faded in the attentive silence. Orannan clutched the little harp to his chest and began.

"In the days when the great king Ambescand ruled in the north, when the three realms were one, he was lured by deceitful magic to take arms against his friend Daun Sheem of the dry lands. And he rose and took up his sword and drew over his shoulders the gray mantle of power and went forth, leaving his throne and his realm and the safety of the beauteous Ciantha and their children to his brother Feron, whom he trusted."

Here Orannan paused and laid the harp aside. He waited unmoving, while his listeners became uneasy in the silence. Then he leaned forward confidingly and said, "Now, this Feron was not a man like other men, and most of all was he unlike Ambescand. For Ambescand was tall and straight and fair to behold, and Feron was a slinking little muddy-faced man with the eyes of a serpent and the teeth of a rat. It is said, in Long Wood, that the midwife who delivered Feron cried out in pain and swore that he had bitten her. And the next day she was found dead. Her arms were black and swollen from the fingertips to the shoulders, and her hands were covered with the marks of small teeth."

He paused and looked slowly around. This particular embellishment was his own creation, and he enjoyed observing its effect on an audience. He went on then to tell of the perils and enchantments that befell Ambescand on the way south, of his solitary battle with the gray men in the deserted village, and of his final reconciliation and oath of eternal friendship with Daun Sheem. At the end of this happy episode, he paused and signaled, and Falshreene, the youngest and by far the prettiest of Ennet's girls, stepped daintily up to the platform to hand him a small flagon of cold mild wine.

He sipped it slowly, keeping a watchful eye on his audience, gauging their attention. When they seemed ready, he handed the empty flagon to Falshreene, kissed her hand politely, and addressed the crowd.

"So Ambescand turned his footsteps home, to his beloved Ciantha. But as he walked one night in a moonlit clearing, a bolt of lightning blazed across the sky, and he looked up and saw a great bird overhead. It was the White Falcon of the North, and it circled him slowly before it landed as lightly as a butterfly on his waiting wrist and screeched out a single word: 'treason'!"

Orannan let the word die into silence. He took a step forward, folded his arms, and said in a firm voice, "It was so. Feron had betrayed his trust, and now the High City lay in the grip of a fellowship of sorcerers, and none but Ambescand could deliver it. But I warn you—the faint of heart must go from here at once. The things I tell of now will whiten the hairs of their heads and chill their blood with terror." He spread his hands wide and slowly shook his head. "I accept no responsibility for those who choose to stay, and die of fright."

He saw the wave of uneasy head turning, the sidelong glances, the forced smiles; heard the whispers and the gruff declarations of bravado; and knew that he had this audience in his grip, to do with as he pleased.

He plunged into the story of the battle at the dark tower, and not a sound came from his audience—aside from subdued murmurs of awe—from start to finish. When he ended, with the tower in ruins and Ambescand, restored to his human form, in the arms of Ciantha, the silence was profound.

The young swordsman rose and stepped to the platform. Picking up the two hawkheads, he placed them in Orannan's hand. In a voice husky with emotion he said, "Well done, storyteller. A noble tale well told."

The shouting and drumming of tankards rose then, and the crowd pressed forward to place their coins in Orannan's hands. Aside from the swordsman's, the contributions were modest—lunes and half lunes, brass daibas, copper bits—and Orannan was beginning to feel unappreciated, until a slender, aging man with a patch over one eye dropped two arkads into his open palm.

"You're most generous, sir," Orannan said.

"My friend and I enjoyed your tale. Fond of the old tales, we are."

Orannan glanced down at the arkads and smiled appreciatively. "So I see. I wish everyone were as fond as you."

"Will you take a drink with us before we leave? I'd like to speak with you about a point in your tale: when Ambescand healed the injured archer. I'm curious about such things."

"It will be my pleasure to join you, sir."

Orannan watched the stranger move off, walking with unhurried, shuffling old man's steps, and seat himself at a table apart from the rest. A huge white-haired man was seated there, awaiting his return. They had no other company. Even Ennet's girls seemed more inclined to avoid them than to offer their companionship.

But when Orannan joined them, it was Falshreene herself who bore his flagon to the table. His host fumbled through a scattering of coins as varied as those in Orannan's purse and pushed a generous portion into Falshreene's soft hand. She favored him with her most fetching smile and walked slowly, smoothly off, glancing back twice with that same smile.

"Falshreene makes me wish I were twenty years younger," Orannan confessed, looking wistfully at the rhythmic sway of her hips.

"She does more than that for me. Makes me wish I were fifty years younger and could look at her with two good eyes.

Fine woman. But at least I can still enjoy my wine," the stranger said, raising his tankard to Orannan.

He and Orannan sipped the chilled wine, but the giant white-haired man took up the tankard in both his hands and gulped it down noisily, swallowing a bit but spilling most of it over himself, the table, and the floor. He placed the empty tankard down cautiously, looked at the others, and gave a happy, childlike laugh.

"This big fellow is my partner. I hope you'll excuse his manners," the older man said.

"Certainly. To judge from the variety of coinage on the table, you've been doing business here. Are you a storyteller, too?"

"Oh, no. I haven't your gift. I'm a healer. Traissell is my name, and this is Janneret."

Orannan frowned and scratched his chin, trying to recall a time and place. Then he brightened and said, "Yes, I know your name. I stayed at Darath's Hall for a time, when you had just left. Darath said you were the greatest healer in the north."

"I cured his boils and his wife's cough. The ones I can't cure seldom speak as well of me," Traissell said with a faint, dry smile.

"I've heard of you from others, too."

"There's plenty of work for a healer these days, what with everyone ready to pounce on his neighbor, and the High City just waiting for the right time to pounce on them all. Bad times we've come to, storyteller," said Traissell, shaking his head slowly. "Bad times."

"Bad enough. Though I sometimes wonder if they're not better than the old days."

"That's a refreshing observation. Everywhere I go, I hear people whining for the good old days." Traissell laughed self-consciously. "I just came close to doing it myself, didn't I? You'd think that if we could push the sands back a few hundred years, we'd all be fat and happy."

"And that just isn't true. Nowadays, bad as things may be, we don't have the Kernlord and its servants to contend with."

"Is that what they call the old enemy here?"

"Most of the time. Some say 'Cairnlord' or 'Lord of Stones,' but most of the time they call it 'Kernlord.' Doesn't much matter what they call it, I say, as long as we're rid of it. There's plenty of evil in the world still, but it's human evil."

"That can be bad enough."

"Well, yes," Orannan conceded. "But there was no place to hide in the Kernlord's time. No refuge anywhere. Now we've got the Fastness and the Headland. Some people are even traveling to the west."

"That's where we're going one of these days, Janny and I. I wouldn't want to go to the Headland, even if they were letting strangers across."

"They pass strangers quite frequently, I've heard."

"Maybe. Don't see why anyone would want to go there, myself. Crazy lot, those Headlanders," said Traissell, "them and their silly bridge. Twice now, they've gone to all the risk and expense of putting a bridge across the Fissure, and both times they've decided to tear it down again. Now they have that giant drawbridge, and from what I hear, they're mighty reluctant to lower it. Terrified that someone will slip over and murder them all in their beds and steal their gold."

"I suppose that is a bit odd," said Orannan. He did not like the thought of the drawbridge being raised to shut him out. His heart was set on refuge on the Headland, and he wished to hear no discouraging news. "Still, there's no point in being murdered in your bed if you can avoid it."

"No point in building a bridge if you don't want people crossing."

They were both silent for a time, and then Traissell said, "I wanted to ask you about something in your story. Remember the part where Ambescand restored the man's arm after the gray man had lopped it off?"

"Yes."

"Do you know any versions of the story that give details of how he did it?"

"No. They all just say that he did it. Enchantment, I suppose. Ambescand was a powerful wizard."

Traissell grunted. "Too bad. Sometimes you can learn a trick or two from the old tales. If I could learn how to put back an arm, I could do a lot of good."

"I'm sorry I can't help. It's a pleasure to find someone who respects the old stories."

"Oh, I do, storyteller, that I do. You won't find a man in the north who has more faith in the old tales than Traissell the healer. Now, finish your wine, and we'll have another."

"No, thank you," Orannan said, rising to leave. "I never have more than one. Bad for my throat."

"It's the best thing in the world for your throat, storyteller, and don't you listen to anyone who says otherwise. But I never force a man to drink against his will. Good evening to you, and my thanks for a fine tale, even if you couldn't tell me what I wanted to know."

"My thanks to you, healer. And to your partner."

Orannan turned and made his way from the table. Janneret stared at him, gave a low, wordless moan of anxiety, and reached out a groping hand. Traissell took his wrist gently and drew it down.

"Never fear, Janny," he said. "We'll see him again."

CHAPTER SEVEN

THE PROTECTOR

On a brisk, cloudy morning near the end of the month of Harvest, Traissell and Janneret, with Stoggan close behind them, threaded their way through the crowds toward the main gate of the Fastness. The healer and his partner each carried a pack, while Stoggan trudged along, bearing everything else the three of them possessed.

As they passed the doorway of an inn, a tall young man in a plain worn traveling cloak fell into step with Traissell. "May I speak with you, healer?" he asked politely.

"Speak away, as long as you don't mind walking. Walk on this side so I can see you without turning my head."

The man moved to Traissell's right. The healer looked him over and said, "I know you. I've seen you at Ennet's, haven't I?"

"Yes. I . . . I spent some evenings there."

It was obvious to Traissell that the young man had spent more than time at Ennet's. There was a broad pale ring around each wrist; Traissell recalled the heavy gold-trimmed wristbands the youth had worn the last time he saw him and the fine green cloak with gold clasps he had had on then. He steeled himself for a tale of penitence and a request for the price of breakfast. He sighed.

"And now you have nothing left but the clothes on your back," he said.

"Those and my strength and my skill with the blade and the bow," said the young man with no vestige of humility.

"Fine things, but you can't eat them."

"I can earn my living with them. I've heard that you're going west. You'll need a guard," the swordsman said flatly.

"Will I, now?"

"Yes. You'll be safe with me."

"Well, listen, son. What's your name, anyway?"

"Call me Daike."

I've been making my way around the north since before you were born, Daike—since long before you were born—and my only companion has been this big fellow, who, as you can plainly see, is no swordsman. And never once, in all that time, have I needed anyone to protect me."

"You've never gone west of Long Wood."

"Have you?"

Daike paused for a moment before replying. "No. But I've spoken with men who have. It's dangerous out there. Even Long Wood is unsafe for travelers these days."

"Anyone who wants my purse is welcome to it, Daike."

"They won't stop at theft. They're men without kin, without names. They have no ties to the world, these robbers. They'd kill you for sheer sport. And the women are worse than the men."

Traissell walked on a few steps before responding. "Mighty poor sport that would be. Tell me, Daike, why are you so concerned about my welfare? Are you so eager to come up against a gang of cutthroats to save an old man's skin?"

"I'm a swordsman and an expert bowman. I can follow a trail and provide food. I want work, healer, and these are the things I do best, so I want to work as a guard."

"Sign on with a caravan, then."

Daike's response was quick and contemptuous. "I don't want to be part of that pack. They're all scum."

"Some good men serve as caravan guards."

"Maybe," Daike conceded reluctantly. "I've heard of too many who cut a merchant's throat and then call him a thief so they can claim his purse."

"I suppose you find that kind, too," Traissell said.

The gate was in sight before them now, and Daike, in an open, man-to-man manner, said, "I may as well tell you, healer. I plan to go west myself. There's no one leaving for five days, and I'm not a man used to waiting around for strangers. I'll guide you to the western edge of Long Wood and a hundred greatmarks further, and all I ask is my food and drink along the way and twelve hawkheads when I leave you."

Traissell scratched his jaw and said, "I'll give you seven arkads."

"Eight."

"Seven. But I'll give you two right now so you can get yourself fitted out for the trip."

"Done!" said Daike, extending his hand.

Without breaking his step, Traissell dug into his purse and drew out two coins. "We'll wait at Voyagers' Well," he said, and dropped the coins into the young man's palm. Daike grinned, saluted him, and dashed off into the crowd.

"If he comes back, we've got ourselves a guard cheap," Traissell said to his servant. "If not, well, maybe he's learned something from his misfortunes and will now go back to his father's hall and behave himself. What do you think, Stoggan? Will the bold swordsman return and bring us safely to our destination?"

"I think he will, master. He looks to be a man of good blood. Dependable."

"What about yourself? Haven't had any second thoughts?"

"Oh, no, master. I want to go west with you and Janneret."

"And so you shall. I'm glad you changed your mind about staying here, Stoggan. A few more days and you'd be dragged into the defense force, and after that it might be difficult to leave."

"That was my thinking, master."

Voyagers' Well stood before them. Traissell pointed out an unoccupied spot on the broad stone terrace that ringed the well, and here Stoggan gratefully set down his burden and seated himself. Janneret was content to lean on the rim and gaze down into the dark well, listen to the echoing slosh and splash from within, and wonder at the glitter of sunlight on the surface of the updrawn buckets. Traissell settled with a long, old man's sigh of relief at Stoggan's side. They sat in silence for a time, enjoying this respite that had come so unexpectedly before the start of their long trek.

Stoggan was grateful for the chance to reflect. He had concerns of his own, and they had grown more serious than he liked in recent days.

Once arrived at the Fastness, Traissell had had little need of a servant, and so Stoggan had been at liberty to pursue his own affairs; yet in the eyes of the officials he was merely the servant of a transient healer and scarcely worth their notice. He found this status ideal for his purposes.

If there was news in the north, it could be heard at the Fastness, where information was as much an article of trade as comfort, precious stones, or pleasure. Stoggan set out to learn all that was known of the theft at Balthid's Keep.

The first day he heard nothing, and this puzzled him. Nine days later he had still heard nothing, and he was much disturbed. By the time Traissell announced his intention of moving on and asked whether he wished to come along, Stoggan was ready to go to any lengths to get safely out of the north. His expectations had collapsed into utter confusion. In all his seeking, he had heard not a single mention of his theft. He did not doubt that by this time it had been discovered, yet no word of it had reached the Fastness.

In the face of such total silence, Stoggan was helpless. To probe any more deeply would be to risk revealing himself. He was wondering even now whether he had been sufficiently cautious and indirect in his conversations with strangers. The very silence might have been a stratagem of Brondin's to trap the thief.

To Stoggan, it was otherwise incomprehensible. The cloak pin concealed inside his shirt was Brondin's most valuable possession: ages old, unique, beyond all price. Any other man would have had his forces scouring the north, his spies in every tavern, brothel, and inn. Rewards would be posted in every public place. But Brondin seemed to have accepted the loss calmly and done absolutely nothing to recover the cloak pin. Stoggan was an experienced thief; had there been pursuit, he would have been aware. There was none.

Yet the theft was real, and the cloak pin was genuine. And Brondin was, with the possible exception of Halssa, the most determined, powerful man in the north. And he had done nothing.

Confronted with an enigma, Stoggan chose to flee. Having made his choice and acted on it, he still could not put his mind at ease. Everything about this affair of the cloak pin was odd. In a long life of thieving, he had never experienced anything like it before. Even the very beginning, when he first learned of Brondin's treasure, had been unlike any other undertaking, a matter of sheer chance that defied all probability.

Stoggan had been curled up in the chimney corner of Longfoot's Inn, dozy and comfortable. His purse was bulging, his hide was warm, and his belly was filled with meat, bread, and Longfoot's best beer. He was at peace with the world.

He became aware of low voices nearby. At first he ignored them, but the mention of a priceless treasure arrested his attention and held it. Two men were speaking. One, with a hard, hoarse voice, did most of the talking, while the other, gentler-voiced, contributed only phrases and monosyllables. They seemed unaware of his presence; from their seat before the fire, Stoggan would be difficult to see. Stealthily, he cupped his hand to his ear and inclined his head toward the voices.

"And not just Halssa, either. A dozen men in the north would give their weight in gold for that cloak pin," said the hard voice.

"Why?" asked the other.

"Because it could make the holder king of all the north. The time is right. A strong man could make himself ruler over the three realms."

"But what about Halssa?"

"He's a usurper. No one will support him once all the north rises. Brondin has the blood claim and the cloak pin, but he's no warrior. If a real fighting man, a war leader, had the symbol of rightful rule, you'd see some changes mighty fast. As it is. . . ."

The voices dropped too low for Stoggan to hear. He dared not try to move closer. When they were once more distinguishable, the mood of the hard-voiced man seemed to have sunk to despair.

"Get us to the door of Brondin's treasure vault, that's all. There's a triple lock, and no man but Balthid and Brondin has ever seen all three keys. Even when you get inside—if you ever do—the cloak pin is concealed. It could take days to find. No, the map is useless."

"We could seek help."

"If anyone learns how we got this map. . . . No, no one else must know."

"Then we killed him for nothing."

The other man muttered angrily. The hard-voiced man cursed. Suddenly a scrap of soft leather was flung onto the fire. It slid off a log and lay on the dead cinders within Stoggan's grasp. He could distinguish lines and markings.

When he heard no more voices for a time, Stoggan ventured a glance. The bench by the fire was vacant. He snatched up the map and studied it carefully; then he folded it and placed it inside his shirt.

He made up his mind on the spot. From that night, he gave all his efforts to planning the theft that would make him the greatest thief in the north, a kingmaker, and a wealthy man. The preparations took nearly a year, but he succeeded. He had the cloak pin, but now he could not work out his next step.

He no longer felt the confidence he had enjoyed when his fingers closed on the treasure. Lately, he had even begun to wonder whether he had somehow been manipulated into the theft. Why, or by whom, he could not begin to imagine; but he sometimes felt that he had been subtly maneuvered.

He found himself, for the first time in his life, unable to decide between alternatives. Would it be best to await further developments in the security of distance or to stay on at the Fastness in obscurity as a worker-guard? Might it be wiser to seek out Halssa and tell him all? In the face of utter silence, he could not judge, and so he remained with Traissell and Janneret and left events to work themselves out.

"Daydreaming, Stoggan?" Traissell asked, causing him to start.

"No, master. Only resting."

"Sensible man. Look, here comes our swordsman in his patched cloak, with his wrists flashing like the sun. I hope his courage is as great as his vanity."

Daike stepped before them, flung back his shabby cloak, and struck a bold stance. "Whenever you care to leave, healer, we'll be on our way," he said.

"No pack? You travel light."

"I carry all I need," Daike said coolly, slapping the pommel of his sword. With the other hand he flourished a short bow.

"Good." Traissell glanced upward at the bright sky. "It's

getting on to midmorning. We'll take a little food and drink and then be off. Stop to rest just after midday."

"That's slow traveling," Daike observed.

"We're in no hurry. Are you?"

"None at all. Just an observation, healer."

"Make any observations you like, Daike. Just don't try to rush me along. I'm an old man. I hate to rush."

As Daike had observed, their pace was unhurried. For about fifty marks around the Fastness, the region was patrolled and relatively safe. Nevertheless, Daike seemed determined to make up for his slow progress by excessive attention to duty. He deliberated long before selecting a stopping place for the night, investigated every potential ambush, and every night carefully laid his bow and quiver within close reach. When he insisted on setting up a regular guard rotation for their sleeping hours, Traissell voiced no objection; but once on guard he went directly to sleep, trusting Stoggan to awaken him before Daike arose.

At Riverroad Camp, the last secure stopping place before the ford that led to Long Wood, Traissell declared a long halt. They would be spending many nights to come under the trees, in the gloom of thick forest, he said, and he wanted to have another glimpse of starlight under the open sky while the moon was dark. The others welcomed his decision. They had been on the road only a few days and had moved at an unhurried pace, but a rest was something one took when one could.

They spent four lazy days relaxing at Riverroad Camp. On the fourth day, early in the afternoon, two travelers arrived at their encampment. And at that point, the journey became very different.

CHAPTER EIGHT

THE HUNT BEGINS

Shivering in the night chill, the servant poked the fire in Halssa's chamber. When it began to blaze, he laid on some dry pine, and when that caught, he carefully placed three slabs of fine maple on the firedogs and watched until the flames curled up the flesh-colored face of the wood. Warmth touched his cheeks and hands, and he surrendered to a long, jaw-cracking yawn. The air of the little room began to grow almost comfortable.

Still half asleep, he huddled close to the feeding flames and thought of how it must have been before the Long Cold. He remembered the old men's stories, their boasts that they had never had to light a fire before the dark of Gleaner's Moon and sometimes not until well into the month of Yellowleaf. Nowadays, the fires began to burn in the chill nights at the end of Harvest, and frost could strike as late as Flowerdown. Life, he thought, must have been good in those times. Whatever evil stalked the north, at least a man's bones were not chilled from one end of the year to the other.

As soon as the fire was burning brightly, the servant quietly left the chamber to take up his post outside the door. Halssa was not the gentlest of masters, even under the best circumstances. Roused at this hour, he might vent his annoyance at the handiest target, and the servant had no desire to feel his master's fist or foot.

Halssa soon entered, drawing his fur cloak about him, and stood before the fire, rubbing his eyes. He took a mouthful of the cold weak beer that stood on the table, swished it around in his mouth, and spat it into the fire. He had just settled in a high-backed chair when Karash-Kabey entered and stood in the firelight, leaning on his staff.

The hideous little face carved in the crystal flashed and

glittered in the flickering light. Halssa turned aside and rubbed his eyes once more. He disliked the sight of the Doomstaff. There was a wrongness about the grotesque face that bothered him.

"Move that thing out of the light. It flashes in my eyes," he said.

Karash-Kabey stepped back and drew the crystal face into the shadows. "As my lord wishes," he said softly.

"What news is so important that it can't wait for daylight? Have you learned something of the theft from Brondin?"

"I have, my lord."

"Speak it, then."

"A single object was stolen from the vault of Balthid's Keep: a cloak pin said to have been worn by the first woman of Vannenson blood in each generation since the time of the first Ciantha, wife of Ambescand."

"Valuable?"

"In the material sense, a trifle. But as an emblem of rightful rule, it is beyond price. If you were to acquire it, much of the support Brondin now enjoys would vanish."

"Have his followers no more loyalty than that?"

"Men are loyal to what they perceive to be their own interests. They follow Brondin because he claims legitimate succession, even though you rule. They think that a legitimate ruler increases the chance of a return to prosperity and peace. The cloak pin, in your possession, would lend force to your claim and weaken his."

Halssa grunted and nodded his head thoughtfully. "Perhaps. Yes, it might." He was silent for a time; then he turned to Karash-Kabey and said, "Wait, now. If this cloak pin is to be worn by a Vannenson woman, what good is it to me? Or to Brondin for that matter? The Vannensons of the High City were wiped out, man, woman, and child, when the nobles rose against them. Dolsaina was the last woman of her branch, and she had no surviving daughters, only that accursed cripple Brondin. There's no one to wear the cloak pin, so why is it valuable?"

"It may be all the more valuable under such circumstances, my lord," Karash-Kabey explained in a calm and patient voice. "Since no woman can wear it, it belongs to the ruling man, to hold in his custody."

Halssa pondered that for a moment. "I suppose it does. It won't hurt to have it, anyway. Have you any idea who the thief is and where I can find him? Or her?"

"I have learned of a man, the servant of travelers passing through the Fastness. He asked certain questions which suggested that he might have an object of great value to sell to the King of the High City."

"Where is this man? Do you have him?"

"No, my lord."

"Then I'll have patrols out after him at once. What do you know of him?"

"Very little, my lord. He was exceedingly cautious. He serves a wandering healer. Late in the month of Harvest, they stopped at the Fastness on their way west."

"They can only stay forty days. When did you learn of this?"

"This very evening, my lord."

"You did well to have me roused," Halssa said. "Is there any more news?"

"Brondin plans to march on the High City with all his followers in the spring. The word has been sent, and all are making ready for the assault."

Halssa gave an angry growl. "You save your bad news for last. Why do you waste time talking of cloak pins and thieves when there's an assault afoot?"

"The assault need never occur. My assassin is in readiness. Brondin need trouble you no more."

Halssa raised a hand. "Not yet. Not quite yet. Let him live for a time."

"As my lord wishes."

"I'm not getting tenderhearted. Far from it. If you're right about this cloak pin, I want Brondin to live to see his plans collapse and his followers come running to pledge their loyalty to me. Plenty of time for your assassin to do his work after that."

"Not so much time, my lord. The first snow is near, and the thief is yet to be taken."

"I'll have messengers on the way to all patrols before dawn, and I'll send out extra patrols until we have him. I'll get that cloak pin," Halssa said. He looked into the bright blaze and added, "If Brondin thinks his destiny is to overthrow me, so much the worse for him. He won't fulfill it. I'll see to that." Turning to his adviser, he said, "If there's nothing more, you may leave. I'll attend to the necessary business."

"As my lord wishes," said Karash-Kabey with a slight nod. As he turned to go, Halssa called his name, and the old man looked back. "My lord?"

"What's to come of all this? Do you know?"

"Does my lord believe that I can see the future?"

Halssa looked at him for a time before saying firmly, "I know no man can see the shape of things to come. I respect your wisdom and judgment and your skill at learning things that men wish to keep hidden."

With another slight nod, the adviser took his leave. Halssa returned his gaze to the fire, and after a time he settled in his chair, leaning forward into the warmth, deep in thought.

Karash-Kabey was a disturbing but necessary presence. Halssa knew the tales that circulated about the man but stubbornly refused to credit them. He told himself that the last wizard had died generations ago, and all the magic was gone from the world, consumed in the war of wizardry that had ended the reign of the Kernlord. If Karash-Kabey had ways of seeking and knowing that went beyond those of any other man, it was a mark of his intelligence and long learning, nothing more. To give in and accept the old tales of sorcery and magic would be for Halssa to confess his own helplessness in the face of destiny, and that he would not do. He had come far in the world, carving out his fortune with a keen blade and a strong will. No adviser had brought him to power, and no adviser could keep him in power or depose him. He was a man of his own making, and Karash-Kabey was nothing more than a useful aide.

Still, there was something about that soft-spoken, unhurried old man that made Halssa long for open air and bright sunlight and the reassurance of a sword hilt in his grip. The calm silence of Karash-Kabey was appraisal, and his deference held something close to contempt.

And yet he was useful. He frightened others far more than he unnerved Halssa, and he acquired knowledge that no one else seemed able to unearth. Halssa had no doubt that Karash-Kabey's assassin would succeed where his own had failed. He had no choice but to keep the man, use him, and never cease to watch him closely.

Halssa sighed and then shook his head angrily as if to clear it. These were not things to think about in the small silent hours before the dawn, when the bravest man can find fears growing in his soul. There was work to be done, and it was time he was about it. Patrols had to be alerted, orders given, the hunt for the thief set under way. He wanted the cloak pin in his hand before winter set in. He rose, pulled his cloak around him, and shouted for his servant.

Near the end of the month of Gleaning, word reached Balthid's Keep that Halssa's outer guard had been ordered to track down a group of travelers and bring them to the High City. The spy could learn no more, but his information was enough to alert Brondin.

Two months had passed since the theft from his treasure vault, and in that time his spies had been able to learn nothing. Brondin's mind was a jumble of desperate questions, all of them unanswered. Who had committed the theft, and how, and why; how the thief had learned of his possession of the cloak pin and of its hiding place; how he had entered the vault and left without a trace—all these things were mysteries still. Indeed, if the unfortunate kitchen boy had not been slain—probably a matter of sheer chance—the theft might have gone undiscovered for months.

Like most northerners, Brondin walked a narrow line between scepticism and superstition. In public, among his followers, he scoffed at the idea of magic, but in his heart he wondered whether such things might not be. Mysterious events left him troubled. He wanted explanations, answers, facts; and none could be found where the theft was concerned. Above everything, he wanted the cloak pin. He would have foregone all answers merely to have it safe in his vault once more.

The worst part of Brondin's problem had been the need for absolute secrecy, and that, at least, was no longer necessary. Whatever had passed before, now there were facts to be faced and dealt with. Halssa's outer guards were in dogged pursuit of a small band of travelers. It might have no connection with the theft, but it was a new fact. Brondin could act on it, and he meant to do so. He summoned his advisers, and before they had settled in their places, he was telling them the news.

"So now we'll move openly," he concluded. "We'll have a patrol watching every patrol of Halssa's. Whomever they follow, we'll be following after them. Any prisoners they take will be taken from them and brought directly here."

"The best course, my lord," Henorik said, looking pleased. "No more waiting and sneaking about. We'll take them head on."

Espar nodded in agreement, but Dostilla was hesitant. "Is it not possible, my lord, that this great hunt is motivated by some other reason? If so, our open action might reveal the theft and do us much harm."

"I've considered that possibility, Dostilla, but I don't think it justifies any further delay. Perhaps I've waited too long already. I'm sure Halssa knows of the cloak pin and seeks it."

"Do you suspect betrayal, my lord?"

"Only the four of us and nine spies—men I would trust with my life—know of the theft. No, I fear no betrayal. But however cautious a man is, however closely he guards his tongue, words slip out. And even if our agents were models of circumspection, Dostilla, what of the thief himself? He could have given himself away in fear or in his greed, perhaps in a drunken boast."

"True, my lord. It appears we have no choice but open pursuit."

"Not too open, I hope. I want Halssa kept in the dark as long as possible. I'll speak to the men about that myself, Henorik. Assemble the leaders at midday in the courtyard. The first patrols will leave tomorrow morning."

"As you say, my lord."

"One thing more," Brondin said, leaning forward, lowering his voice and smiling eagerly, "and no one else is to know it. After the patrols leave, I'm leaving, alone, to learn what I can. I think—"

"My lord, not alone! You must take me with you!" Henorik cried, interrupting.

"I'd like to do that, but you're too important here. Besides, if you once slipped and called me 'my lord' or 'Lord Brondin,' the game would be up. I'm quite safe alone, believe me." He rose as he spoke, tucked his crutch under his shoulder, and walked to the fireplace. His limp was like the vestige of some long-ago injury now become a habit rather than a forced motion. Turning to face them, he said, "You mustn't think of me as a helpless cripple. In a close space, with my back to a wall, I'm a match for any swordsman I'm likely to meet. I can't move fast, it's true, but my eye is good, and my arms are strong. You know that, Henorik."

"But if you're taken by one of Halssa's patrols. . . ."

"Halssa doesn't know what I look like. He thinks I'm a puny, crippled boy, afraid to set foot outside my own walls. I'll pose as a student of the annals, making my way to the Headland from a settlement in the Southern Forest."

"But the weather, my lord. It's nearly winter."

"We have plenty of friends in the Fastness. I can reach it before the heavy snows and spend the winter there. No fear of their dragging me into their defense force," he said, laughing.

"I think this is unwise," Espar said softly. "The north is in chaos. A lone traveler is never safe. Marauders would kill a student of the annals as readily as they'd butcher a caravan. The past means nothing to them."

"He's right, my lord. It's too dangerous. We'll need you to lead us in the spring," Henorik added.

"You don't understand at all," said Brondin. "How can I expect men to trust me, maybe to give their lives in my cause, when they see me take no risks myself? Men follow me because I'm Balthid's son, not for my own qualities or for anything I've accomplished. I've sat in Balthid's Keep for years, while other men did brave deeds in my cause. I can't do that any longer. I have a feeling. I can't explain it—a sense that there's something out there that I must do. No one can do it for me. I must go."

The others were silent for a time, and then Espar said, "It is what Balthid would have done."

"It is, I think," Brondin said earnestly. "I'll be back in the spring to take part in the assault. If I'm not, it must go on, anyway. You understand that."

"We do," Henorik said grimly.

"You can say that I name Parhender as the war leader. He's capable. Follow him as you would follow me."

"We want to follow you, my lord. No other."

"Cheer up, my friends. We've been reassured in a way. If Halssa's seeking the cloak pin, that means he doesn't have it yet. I'll be back when the snow melts, with the cloak pin in my hand. You'll see."

That night Brondin slept soundly. There was little in this whole matter to afford him comfort. Somehow his closest secret had been uncovered, his sanctuary had been violated, and his greatest treasure had been stolen without a trace. He was walking out, alone, into a turbulent, dangerous world, and he had a growing suspicion that the worst danger would not come from the hands of violent men. There was more to this than thievery and political intrigue. Perhaps the wild tales were true, and Halssa's mysterious adviser really did possess powers beyond any known in the north for generations; perhaps the old magic was astir again.

Brondin could only do his mortal best and await the outcome. It felt good to be acting in his own cause, whatever the danger.

CHAPTER NINE

ENCOUNTER ON
THE WESTERN ROAD

*A wordsmith and a warrior, and a man still half a
child;
And one whose deeds were dark and grim, but whose
way was meek and mild;
A boaster with an eager blade, and a healer bowed
with care
Foregathered one by one upon the road to none knew
where.
They journeyed into darkness, and they found at
journey's end
That dark was light, and wrong was right, and enemy
was friend. . . .*

From *The Last Deed of Ambescand*

On a fine crisp morning early in the month of Gleaning,
when a bright sun burnished the reds and golds and coppers
of the turning leaves and warmed the chilly air to the point
where cloaks were unfastened and flung back for comfort,
Orannan and Cabanard were walking at an easy pace along
the westward trail. They were in territory said to be safe for
travelers; but Orannan, with two fat purses tucked in his
shirt, was uncomfortable. He walked softly, and his eyes
darted everywhere.

Cabanard, a step behind him, burst into song in a deep,
loud, and not very tuneful voice. Orannan winced.

*"Halssa married a sweet young bride
On a lovely summer's day—
A month he tarried by her side,
And then he marched away, away,
And then he marched away,*

Cabanard bellowed, and Orannan looked wildly about, waving his arms frantically for silence.

"What's the matter? Don't you like your own song?" Cabanard asked.

"Wait until we're on the Headland, I beg you, Cabanard!"

"We're safe here. It's patrolled all the way to the river."

"So they tell you. I haven't seen any patrols."

"I've seen traces of two so far this morning. You have to know what to look for."

That reassured Orannan slightly. "Well . . . all the same, Halssa has no regard for borders or boundaries. He'd send a patrol up here if he knew I was on this trail."

Cabanard laid a hand on his companion's shoulder and said, "Stop worrying so much. Halssa's only a man. You talk as though he could see in the dark and fly and read our minds. He can't."

Orannan nodded halfheartedly. They went on a way in silence. Then, to forestall another outburst of song, Orannan asked, "How long will it take us to reach the Headland?"

"If we're not delayed, it shouldn't take us more than fifteen days."

"That's good. You'll be glad you decided to come along. They respect swordsmen on the Headland. And storytellers."

Cabanard grunted but said nothing.

"It's a nicer place than the Fastness. Everyone says so. Friendly people, and the women are beautiful. Really beautiful, not like that painted-up merchandise at the Fastness."

Cabanard gave another grunt and then blurted out, "May I rot if I ever set foot in the Fastness again! I never saw so many thieves in one place. When I found out how many people I'd have to bribe just to open a little school for caravan guards . . . and then I'd be expected to hire the sons and nephews and cousins of half the officials in the Fastness!" He growled in disgust and shook his head.

"We're well out of the place," said Orannan righteously.

They went on at an unhurried gait until midmorning. By Cabanard's reckoning, they were only a greatmark or two from Riverroad Camp, where they might reasonably expect to find other travelers and perhaps a patrol. It seemed to Orannan more prudent to take refreshment there, and so they continued without stopping.

As they passed between the two boulders that marked the entrance and onto the level greensward, Orannan looked around. Riverroad Camp was empty this day, save for a group of four travelers settled in by the rocks near the well.

"I know those people," Orannan said happily. "It's Traissell the healer and his partner. I met them at Ennet's. The big fellow, too. I don't know his name, but he's free with his money. Let's join them."

Orannan introduced Cabanard to the three he knew, and Cabanard laid aside his staff and exchanged greetings with them all. In his brand-new cloak of deep maroon, fastened with a golden clasp, splendid soft boots, and well-fitted dark clothes, he looked more like a merchant than a battered old adventurer. During his stay at the Fastness, his face and hands had been steamed and scrubbed until they glowed, his moustache clipped and oiled. His hair had been trimmed; he now wore it bound with a gold-embroidered headband. Only when he perched his foot on a rock and bent forward to brush the dust from his new boots did a sudden bulge reveal the sword beneath his cloak.

"What's your profession, Cabanard, if I may ask?" said Traissell.

"I'm a traveler. Just a traveler."

"Nobody's just a traveler these days. What's your real profession?" Daike said, stepping to Cabanard's side.

Cabanard gave his boot a last flick of the cloth, inspected it, and then straightened and turned to face the younger man. Daike, half a head taller, looked coolly down on him.

"Well? What are you, Cabanard?"

"Just a traveler."

The exchange was cordial. Both men were smiling. But the tension between them was almost tangible. In the silence, Orannan said loudly, "So he is, Daike, and quite a traveler, too. Cabanard's been everywhere you can name, and a few places you've never heard of."

Daike retreated a step. "As long as the storyteller vouches for you, you're welcome to stay. Nothing personal, Cabanard. I just have to be careful. I'm responsible for our safety."

"Nothing personal," Cabanard said, and turned to dust his other boot.

"We were about to take a light meal. Would you care to join us?" Traissell asked.

"It would be a pleasure," Orannan replied. Turning to Cabanard, he added privately, "You don't mind, do you? This may be our last chance to relax and talk with people we know."

Cabanard did not look up. "It doesn't make much difference to me who I eat with."

"Good. Traissell is an interesting fellow. He's spent a long life as a healer, been all over the north. You'll like him." When Cabanard merely nodded, Orannan went on. "We might even stay here tonight and go on to the ford with them."

"No."

"Wouldn't that be safer?"

"That friend of yours who's so free with his money is a lot freer with his mouth. People like that are always trouble."

"He was only doing his job, Cabanard."

"I know his job better than he does, and that's a poor way to go about it. We'll eat with your friends, but then we move on."

Orannan was disappointed, for he dearly loved an audience, however small; but he accepted the decision. Cabanard's judgment in such matters was to be heeded.

The meal was plain but substantial. By the time they finished eating, the sun was high and hot, and the cool shade of an oak was welcome. After the meal, Orannan offered to tell a tale, and Daike spoke up at once to request a story of the olden times. No one objected to this, and so the storyteller told of the great combat between Tapran, son of Staver, the youngest son of Ambescand, and the giant Izmann of the Balukki guardsmen. It was a brisk and lively tale, full of high boasts and bold deeds. When it was over, Daike applauded wildly.

"Those were the days of glory," he said warmly. "There were brave men in those days and great deeds to be done. Not like these times."

"There are still a few good men around," Cabanard said.

"I don't deny that, but it's not the same today. All the fighting these days is just scrabbling for petty pride and a

few greatmarks of land. I'll never have the chanc
wizard or a giant or a gray man."

"You're the first one I've ever heard complain ĉ
said Cabanard.

Daike, frowning, turned to respond to the remark. Before
he could speak, Janneret climbed to his feet. He moved
stiffly and mechanically, as if some force outside himself
were directing his movements. Flinging his hands wide, he
uttered a croaking cry that brought the others to fearful attention and fixed all eyes on him. Lowering his hands and
extending them to his sides, he began to move them as if in
time to unheard music and to chant in a deep melodious
voice.

> "Fate the Shaper, men the tools,
> Wandering in a misty maze—
> Bane of king who wrongly rules,
> Hear what waits in coming days!
> One will steal what one will save;
> Two go early to the grave;
> Three will find what may be found
> When the sun shines underground;
> Two will stand when all have fled,
> Amid the voices of the dead;
> One will speak and then be still;
> One will fight what none can kill;
> One will bleed, and one will burn
> Before the rightful rule return."

Janneret stopped. His eyes glazed over, and he stood motionless for a moment before he crumpled to the ground, limp
as an empty sleeve, and lay unmoving. Traissell hurried to
his side and called for water. While Stoggan fetched it, the
others looked at one another in profound astonishment and
confusion.

"His voice was as clear as any I've ever heard. But he
never spoke before. Traissell said he couldn't," said Daike.

"But the words . . . what did they mean?" Orannan asked.

"Nothing," said Cabanard.

"They sounded like a vision. A premonition," Orannan
insisted.

Daike said firmly, "It's magic. This is the working of magic."

"There's been no magic in the north since the Stone Hand," Cabanard said with equal firmness.

"How else can you explain it? Maybe the magic is returning." Daike turned to Traissell. "What about it, Traissell? Can he tell us any more?"

Without looking up from his fallen companion, Traissell said, "Janneret is dead."

"Dead? Like that?" Daike glanced about, awed. "Are you sure, Traissell?"

The old man knelt beside his friend, cradling the pale unlined head in his hands. He nodded but did not attempt to speak.

"He knows, Daike. He's a healer," said Cabanard.

"Then it's magic. That was a prophecy. Janneret was the vessel of some powerful magic."

"But why here, among us? It can't be," Orannan said.

Daike turned on him angrily. "You're afraid, aren't you? Janneret has told us of a great adventure to befall us, and you're afraid. You're willing to tell tales of courage and battle, but you want no part of them yourself."

Cabanard had restrained himself with increasing effort, but Daike had finally gotten to be too much for him to endure in silence. He took a step toward him, but then he stopped at the sight of a group of armed men approaching them. He counted seven, all of them wearing the sign of Halssa on their left sleeve: three black stripes on a red field, running from shoulder to wrist. They were formed in two lines, with four ahead and three in support.

"We have company," Cabanard said, pulling his cloak around him to conceal his sword. "Halssa's men. Cover that harp."

The storyteller did as he was told without hesitation, dropping his cloak in a seemingly casual motion over the little harp. Cabanard stepped out of the shadow of the oak to greet the guardsmen, and Daike stood his ground about two marks to his right.

"Greetings, Captain," Cabanard said to the leader of the seven. "Will you and your men take some refreshment with us?"

Ignoring the salutation, the captain demanded, "Who are you, and where bound?"

"A pair of healers and a pair of merchants, headed west. One guide and one servant to aid us, no more."

"Where from?"

"From the Fastness, Captain, every one of us."

"What's wrong with that one?" the captain asked, pointing to Janneret.

"He's sick. We're looking after him. There's no trouble here, Captain," said Cabanard.

The guardsman studied him. Even when he was respectably dressed, scrubbed clean, and doing his best to behave like a gracious host, Cabanard was a formidable man. "And before the Fastness?" he asked.

"Everywhere you can name, Captain. A healer and a merchant must make their living on the road, and we've traveled every road in the north."

"Why all the questions? This isn't Halssa's territory, and we're none of Halssa's business," Daike burst in angrily.

"Tell your guide to keep his mouth shut," the guardsman said, keeping his eyes on Cabanard and not giving Daike so much as a glance.

"Nobody tells me to shut up. We don't have to answer your questions. You have no power here."

The guard captain turned and looked Daike coldly in the eye. "There are six in your party, and you're the only one with a sword. There are seven of us, all armed, and more within call. The nearest patrol from the Fastness is ten great-marks from here. That gives us all the power we need. Now shut up, boy, or you'll regret it."

"No need for harsh words, Captain," Cabanard said soothingly. "Come, let us offer you some good chilled wine."

"We're here to work, merchant."

"No man talks to Daike Vundalson that way," Daike growled, drawing his sword.

Cabanard had hoped to avoid a clash, but he was ready for it. At Daike's first move, Cabanard's sword was out, flashing from the scabbard in a deadly upward arc to cut down the guard captain with a single slash. He was upon the man nearest him before the rest knew what was happening, and a second man went down before the others had drawn their swords and rallied to meet this unexpected attack.

Daike dropped the nearest man and closed at once with another. He beat down the second guardsman's blade, but the man caught him with a hard cut across the ribs as Daike's blade sank into his midsection. Daike staggered, recovering in time to block an overhand slash from a new adversary that sent him reeling back. A blow to the skull knocked him sprawling.

Cabanard cut down his third opponent and turned to face the last. The guardsman who had felled Daike ran to attack Cabanard from behind, but as he moved, Stoggan came from out of nowhere, slipped smoothly under his guard, and plunged a long dagger into his chest with a single expert jab.

With the seventh guardsman sprawled face down in a spreading pool of blood, Cabanard lowered his blade and looked around, rubbing his shoulder. His friends stood gaping.

"Thanks, Stoggan," he said.

"Glad to help, master."

"How's Daike?"

Traissell knelt beside the fallen guide. "He's dying. The blow cut him to the brain."

"Can you do anything?"

"He's beyond my help."

Cabanard wiped his blade clean on a fallen guardsman's cloak, sheathed it, and stepped to Daike's side. He dropped stiffly to one knee, still rubbing his shoulder, and looked closely at the deep wound in Daike's skull.

"Win? Did we . . . win?" Daike's voice was barely audible.

"We took them, Daike. If it hadn't been for you, they would have killed us all." Cabanard pointed to Daike's sword, lying where it had fallen from his grasp, just out of reach. Orannan picked it up and handed it to him, and he laid it gently on Daike's body, placing the dying man's hands on the hilt. "Here's your sword, Daike. You'll want your sword," he said.

"My head hurts. Dark. All dark. Gray stone . . . didn't work."

"Take it easy, Daike. Lie still."

"Gray stone," Daike said, and then he said no more.

Cabanard opened the dead man's shirt. Around his neck, on

a cord, Daike wore a chip of gray stone wrapped in silver wire. "Grimmenstone," Cabanard said, closing up the shirt and pulling Daike's cloak close around his body. He rose slowly, wincing. "It's found on the plain. Supposed to be the petrified carcass of a gray man. If you wear a bit of it on your body, it will protect you from the sword's edge. So people say. It looks as though they're wrong."

"Poor Daike," said Orannan.

"Stupid Daike is more like it."

The storyteller and the others looked incredulously at Cabanard, who explained, "If he hadn't gotten killed, I would have beaten him from here to the river. He did a stupid thing."

"But you won, Cabanard!"

"We were lucky, and they were careless. By rights, we ought to be dead." Cabanard moved his right shoulder cautiously, as if testing it. He winced at the motion and began to knead the muscle slowly. "One thing I learned a long time ago: When the odds are against you, run. If you can't run, hide. If you can't hide, offer a bribe or try to talk your way out of it. And if you can't do any of those things, then you fight. Only then, when all else fails."

Traissell smiled and shook his head. "That's sensible talk, but you'd never get a young hothead like Daike to follow it."

"I plan to die of old age, healer, and I don't want some glory-hungry kid spoiling all my plans."

"Do you really think you could have avoided a clash?"

"Why not? We don't look rich, and we don't look dangerous. That captain would have blustered a while, probably taken some food and money—just to show that he could do it—and then gone."

"And would you have swallowed that? A man who can fight like you?" Traissell asked, clearly unbelieving.

Cabanard stopped working his shoulder. "Nobody ever promised me I'd win every time. I've had my share of fighting. If I can avoid it, I avoid it."

"You couldn't have avoided this one. That captain said they were here to work. They're looking for someone or something."

"Just talk," Cabanard said, shaking his head.

"What about these bodies?" Orannan asked.

"Leave them where they are. There's no time to bury them." Turning to the healer, Cabanard said, "I'm sorry we can't do something for your friend, but we can't take the time. We have to move out fast. Halssa's men will be back in force."

"How will they know?"

"They work nine-man patrols. That means two have gone off for help."

"Just to leave them lying here seems wrong," Orannan said uneasily. "So many men, dead in less time than it takes to tell of it."

"You've told tales of such things often enough. It shouldn't bother you."

"It's leaving them that bothers me, Cabanard. Can't we stay here? There's sure to be a friendly patrol coming through before long."

"We can't trust anyone but ourselves now. Even if a patrol showed up, they might prefer to turn us over to Halssa's men rather than fight. Why should they risk their lives for us?"

Orannan looked about desolately and clutched his harp. Traissell and Stoggan glanced at each other but did not speak. At last Traissell said, "Is there nothing but flight for us, then?"

"Nothing, healer." Cabanard looked up at the bright sky, dappled with sweeps of high, thin clouds, and added, "Even the weather is against us. A good hard rain at our backs would slow up Halssa's men and help cover our tracks, but there'll be no rain soon. We'd best be leaving."

They set out at a brisk pace for the ford. They had gone little more than a greatmark when Cabanard, glancing back, saw the sky darkening behind them. Halfway to their goal, the eastern sky was black; a torrential rain was falling on Riverroad Camp, while above them and ahead all was fair.

"It seems the weather has changed sides," Traissell said.

"It does, healer. Though how a storm can brew so quickly . . . and in the east, when the western sky has been fair for days. . . ." Cabanard shrugged and shook his head.

They reached the ford at sunset, with the rain still a few greatmarks behind them, and here Cabanard called their first halt. His three companions dropped like stones, groaning and rubbing their feet.

"We'll take a rest here and eat something," Cabanard said.

"How long?" Traissell asked weakly.

"Not long. We don't want to stiffen up. I want to get well into Long Wood before we stop for the night."

Cabanard hunkered down on a stone by the water and wet his neck cloth to wipe his face and neck. When he returned to the others, he said, "I didn't think to ask before, Traissell, but where were you headed?"

"West."

"Anywhere in particular?"

"No."

"How about coming with us? We're going to the Headland. Once we're over the bridge, we'll have no more worries about Halssa."

"Thank you for the offer," Traissell said, sighing, "but no."

"You'd be safe."

"I can't keep the same pace as you three. Sooner or later, you'd have to leave me behind, and by then it might be too late for any of us to escape. It's better if you leave me here." Before Cabanard could object, the old healer raised his hand and added, "I have some friends near the Fool's Head, and on the Eye. If I can get to them, I'll be safe."

"I'd like to come with you," Stoggan said to Cabanard.

Cabanard looked to Traissell, and the healer shrugged. "Stoggan's free to go wherever he chooses," he said.

"Can you manage alone?"

"I got along without a servant before Stoggan. I can do it again. Don't worry about me, Cabanard. I'm a survivor."

"Stoggan goes with us, then. Is that agreeable to you, storyteller?"

"I don't object," said Orannan.

They ate in silence and then rested for a time. At last Cabanard climbed to his feet, stretched, and said, "Time to be moving. You'd probably be safest on Col's Way, healer. It's a busy road. Halssa's men may not follow you that far, and if they do, they won't track you so easily."

"That's what I planned to do."

"Then you ought to make it. Good speed to you and good luck."

Traissell watched until the last of the three companions had disappeared into the wood, and then he rose. On his face was an expression of great satisfaction. He slung his pack and then, with a light step, began to retrace his path, turning back toward the mountains, alert, wary, and purposeful.

CHAPTER TEN

THE BRIDGE OF
THE THREE BROTHERS

Cabanard set a relentless pace and allowed no rest until they had gone ten greatmarks. He stopped at a place where the road divided, one branch continuing north along the river-bank, the other bending westward into Long Wood. Either road would take them to the Headland; the western road was the way to the Fool's Head and Mistlands as well.

The others flung themselves down on the grass at the road-side. Cabanard sat on a flat rock, looking at the sooty sky to the east and rubbing his shoulder.

Orannan propped himself on an elbow, studied the old warrior, and asked, "Were you injured, Cabanard?"

"Just a sore shoulder. I've had it for years."

"Why didn't you let the healer look at it? He could have done something to ease it."

"It's nothing a healer can fix."

"Don't underestimate Traissell. He's the best." Orannan turned to Stoggan and asked, "Isn't that so?"

"Oh, yes. Traissell is the master healer in all the north," Stoggan said warmly.

"Even a master healer can't undo the years," Cabanard said, kneading his fingertips hard into his bulging shoulder. "I've spent too many cold nights sleeping on the ground or not sleeping at all . . . marching and fighting in the rain and snow until I was ready to drop and then marching and fight-ing some more." He sighed and shook his head. "I've been hit too hard, too many times. It catches up to a man."

"You looked pretty good against Halssa's men."

Cabanard grunted sourly and moved his shoulder in a cautious circle. Orannan knew that the conversation was over. He lay back, hands pillowing his head, shut his eyes, and tried to relax his aching muscles.

A disturbing thought occurred to him. He sat up and asked Cabanard, "How did Halssa know where to find us?"

"I don't know. I just want to make sure he doesn't find us again."

"But if he has a sorcerer helping him. . . ."

"Forget all that. We can't be sure that the patrol was looking for us. I might have found out if Daike had kept his mouth shut."

"Who else would they be after?" Orannan demanded, as if the possibility had never entered his mind.

"How would I know? You're not the only enemy Halssa has. That patrol could have been after anyone." Cabanard rose and stretched. "Time to move on," he said. "The deeper we get into Long Wood, the safer we are."

"Can we get to an inn by nightfall?" Orannan asked.

"No inns for us. They're the first place Halssa's men will look. We want to stay out of sight of everyone until we reach the Headland."

"We're almost out of food."

"We'll forage. Let's go."

They set off to the west, walking at a steady pace that covered nearly five greatmarks an hour and soon had Orannan panting and footsore. His legs felt as though knotted ropes had been inserted under the skin and were being tightened mercilessly with every step. He gasped out a few complaints to Stoggan, but he received nothing in return but a monosyllable and a nod, and he soon fell silent.

Toward evening, Cabanard dropped back and fell into step at Orannan's side. The storyteller turned tortured, pleading eyes on him. Cabanard smiled to encourage him but did not slacken his pace.

"Cheer up," he said. "We'll be stopping before dark."

"I'll never be able to keep this up," Orannan said in a taut, pained voice.

"Of course you will. When it's all over and we're safe, you can weave all this into a grand tale and recite it before Halssa's enemies. You'll make your fortune."

Orannan responded with a weak groan. Cabanard laughed and turned to Stoggan, who was plodding along silently a few steps behind them.

"How are you feeling, Stoggan?"

"I'm all right."

"You're doing well. I bet the healer and his friend never moved this fast."

"No."

"Must we, Cabanard? Can't we slow down?" Orannan asked.

"Halssa has couriers who can cover eighty greatmarks between sunrise and dark, day after day. They'll bring word of our fight to every one of Halssa's patrols, and they'll all be looking for us. We have to reach the bridge before one of the patrols cuts us off."

Orannan looked at Cabanard in wide-eyed terror. "Is it possible? Could they really get there ahead of us?"

"If we don't make our best speed, they might."

Orannan hurried on without another word, and Cabanard moved ahead to take the lead. Left to himself, Stoggan matched his pace to the storyteller's and set his mind to making sense of the day's puzzling events.

Stoggan had no doubt that the patrol had been searching for the thief who had stolen the cloak pin from Brondin's treasure vault. Somehow, news of the theft had reached Halssa, and he wanted the cloak pin for himself.

He walked on in the deepening gloom of the forest twilight, his eyes and ears alert, his mind turning over the problem, considering every facet. Perhaps his original plan was best after all. With guards alerted everywhere, it would be no more dangerous to try to leave the north than to make his way to the High City. It might even be wise to return the cloak pin to Brondin with some story that would assure protection and a good reward. But that, too, would require travel through guarded territory, and it was now certain that Brondin's men, as well as Halssa's, would be on the alert for the thief, as would every warlord in the north.

Placing himself in the hands of a patrol was too risky. They would be more likely to cut his throat and take the treasure for themselves than to conduct him safely to their master. He could not allow himself to fall into anyone's hands.

Cabanard seemed a useful fellow. The storyteller—Stoggan had not yet heard his name mentioned—was good for little but complaints and prattle, but Cabanard had fighting skill and seemed to know his way among the tangled pathways of Long Wood. He might well bring them safely to the Headland. And the Headland was a perfect place to lie up for a few months and work out his plans.

All in all, thought Stoggan, his luck was holding up. A little bit longer and he would be safe.

They slept that night by the roadside and were on the trail before sunrise, at the same unflagging pace. Orannan could not spare the breath even to groan, and the others maintained a stoic silence as they placed greatmark after greatmark between themselves and Halssa's lands. Day followed identical day in painful wordless progress until one chilly gray morning. As they chewed listlessly on shriveled stingberries and strips of raw fish in the predawn dimness, Cabanard announced that they would reach the Fissure that day.

By midmorning they emerged from Long Wood. Before them, the stony plain sloped downward to the brink of the Fissure, at this point some two hundred marks away. Beyond loomed the sheer cliffs of the Headland.

They turned due west, keeping to the edge of the forest. The dull thunder of the tide racing through the Fissure rose to a peak as the waters met and then began to subside as the tidal bore receded. A few greatmarks farther on, the plain widened. They stayed at the margin of the wood. Soon no sound reached them from the Fissure.

"How far to the bridge?" Orannan asked.

"Not far. If they let us across, we can be sleeping on the Headland tonight."

"We must, Cabanard. They have to let us across."

Cabanard grunted noncommittally, not even turning to look at the storyteller. Orannan persisted. "They can't refuse us. To have come all this way . . . escaped Halssa's patrols . . . only to be turned back. They can't do that, Cabanard."

"It's their bridge. They can do what they like. Sometimes they let people cross, and sometimes they don't. That's all I know."

"Surely they'll let us across." When Cabanard made no response, the storyteller turned to Stoggan. "You believe they'll let us cross, don't you?"

"They might," said Stoggan.

For the rest of the way, Orannan was silent. He had driven

the thought of refusal from his mind and did not want it recalled. Surely a storyteller would be welcome on the Headland. The others might be barred, but not he. That was un-
thinkable.

In the early afternoon, they saw the bridge tower in the
distance, jutting like a thumb from the sheer rock face of
the Headland. The sight gave them new strength. They hurried on and soon stood on the platform opposite the tower.

Directly across the gaping Fissure, the wooden bridge rose
thirty marks to its topmost beam. The tower turrets flanked
it, bulging like hipbones about a third of its height above
them. The great stone counterweight hung below. The bridge
was an awesome sight, one of the wonders of the north, and
the three gazed at it in silence.

Legends said that a bridge had spanned the Fissure in
the times of Ambescand and had been pulled down for
safety when the terror began to spread throughout the north.
Headlanders denied this, claiming that the first bridge over
the Fissure was the Three Brothers' Bridge, built in memory
of the sons of Vannen and Ciantha, who crossed the abyss
by magical means and went forth with all their powers to free
the north from the grip of evil. That bridge had been smashed
within living memory, during the chaos of the Long Winter,
and replaced by this mighty drawbridge, which yet retained
the name.

From the far side, a voice called out, "Identify yourselves!"

Cabanard stepped to within a single pace of the jagged
stone edge, cupped his hands around his mouth, and shouted,
"Three honest travelers seeking sanctuary. Lower the bridge!"

"Give your names and trades," cried the voice from the
tower.

Cabanard complied and waited for the response. Orannan
paced anxiously back and forth at the landward end of the
platform, while Stoggan sprawled out on the sparse grass
beyond.

"Is it the same Cabanard who fought for Derran of Seven-
oaks against the Red Brothers?" the far voice demanded.

"It is the same. Who asks?"

"Vessler the bowman."

"I remember you, Vessler. Can you still split a straw at
two hundred paces?"

"Most of the time."

"Will you lower the bridge for us?" Cabanard called. "We've come a long way in a great hurry."

"The decision is not mine. I'm only a guard. I must send for the Bridgemaster."

"Then send for him quickly. We're being pursued, Vessler, and we ask for sanctuary. Help us."

"I'll do my best," the voice from the tower assured him. "The Bridgemaster will be here before dark. Be patient until then."

Orannan glanced fearfully at the distant line of the woods' edge. "Halssa's men might be here any time. Can't you make him hurry? He's your friend," he said to Cabanard.

"I can't make him do anything. Nor the Bridgemaster, either. But Vessler was always a decent man. He'll help us if he can."

Since Orannan showed no inclination to rest, Cabanard set him to watch the forest, while he pillowed his head on his cloak and slept in the comfort of the afternoon sun. When Cabanard awoke, the sun was a hand's length above the horizon. He dug a few hard dried berries out of his pack and popped them in his mouth, chewing slowly and moistening them from time to time with a sip of water. Below, in the Fissure, the first faint rumblings of the tidal bore were stirring the air.

"If the Bridgemaster doesn't come soon, we won't be able to talk over the noise of the water," Orannan said.

"Vessler said he'd be here before dark."

"It's almost dark."

Cabanard yawned, sipped from his water bottle, and said, "Then he's almost here."

Even as he spoke, a different voice came to them from the tower, straining to be heard over the rising roar of the waters below. "We cannot grant you entry, travelers. You must seek sanctuary elsewhere. We can allow no more to come to the Headland."

"If you don't let us cross, Halssa's men will kill us!" Orannan cried.

The Bridgemaster did not respond at once. The deep thunder of the Fissure grew louder, and when his voice came to them again, some of his words were lost. "We sorrow for

you, but . . . cannot cross. . . . Council of Nine . . . ruled
that . . . safety of the people. . . ."

Stunned, Orannan turned to Cabanard. "Speak to your
friend. He must help us. Tell them we'll pay, we'll travel on
after a few days. Anything they ask, but get us to safety."

Cupping his hands, Cabanard shouted, "Vessler, tell the
Bridgemaster how Halssa's patrols treat their prisoners. You
can shelter us for a few days, can't you? We ask no more.
We need rest and food, and we'll move on when you tell us,
but give us a chance."

For a time, no response came from the tower. The sun
was touching the horizon now, and Cabanard was just preparing to shout to Vessler once more, when Vessler's voice
cried, "Men coming . . . woods! Ten . . . twelve . . . two full
patrols!"

"Lower the bridge!" Cabanard bellowed.

No sound came. The bridge remained erect against the
far wall, without a stir of motion. Cabanard cried out again
and yet again, and all was silence from the tower. If his
words had reached them, their reply had been lost in the roar
of the converging tides below. Then, out of the darkening
sky, an arrow with a blunted head landed on the broad stones
at Cabanard's feet. He snatched it up and tore free the scrap
of soft hide wound around the shaft.

"It's a map, a way to escape," Cabanard said. He waved
a salute to the tower, and a vague figure returned it.

Cabanard studied the rough sketch quickly and then set
off at a run, crouching low along the edge of the Fissure,
heading east. Fifty marks from the bridge, at a spot marked
by a great cleft rock, he halted.

"Down here," he told the others. "There's a ledge about
six marks below."

"We have no rope!" Orannan cried.

"You'll have no head if you don't hurry. Move!" Cabanard shouted in a voice that pierced the din arising from
below.

Stoggan was already out of sight. Orannan swallowed,
raised his eyes to the heavens, and lowered one foot gingerly,
then the other, clutching for dear life at the gray rock. When
his head disappeared over the edge, Cabanard followed him.

He clung to jutting rocks and exposed roots, and at last,

about two marks down, his groping toe fit snugly into a notch. He found the next and soon was moving smoothly down a series of handholds and footholds the size of a man's fist cut into the rock at quarter-mark intervals. At the sixteenth step, his foot landed on a broad solid surface. He looked around and in the deep shadow at the rear of the ledge saw his two companions collapsed against the rock wall.

The ledge was nearly a half mark deep. It began at that point and extended as far to the east as the eye could follow. A sharp overhang gave it perfect concealment from above.

Crouching beside the others, Cabanard said in a hushed voice, "We may as well spend the night here. You two sleep, and I'll take the first watch."

"Shouldn't we get as far away as we can?" Orannan whispered.

"We won't get far before it's too dark to see our way. I don't want to be walking this ledge in the dark. What do you think, Stoggan?"

"Right here is a good place to sleep."

"That's another thing," Cabanard said. "I'd hate to be stuck for the night in a place where the ledge is a hand's breadth wide. We'll stay here."

"What if Halssa's men follow?" Orannan asked.

"They'll never find this ledge by chance in the dark. We're safe. And even if they found us, they could only come at us one at a time. This is a good position."

"The Headland is a better one," Orannan whispered gloomily.

"We can't get to the Headland, so this will have to do. Vessler gave us what help he could. Be grateful for that."

They arranged themselves on the ledge, rolling themselves in their traveling cloaks against the night chill. Stoggan went to sleep at once. Orannan, tied in knots with anxiety and disappointment and fear of Halssa's wrath, took more time getting to sleep, but exhaustion finally overcame his unease. The last thing he heard was Cabanard's rough, unmusical voice singing softly under his breath:

> *"Halssa married a sweet young bride,*
> *On a lovely summer's day. . . ."*

CHAPTER ELEVEN

HOSPITALITY

Brondin crossed his western border just after a cloudy sunset late in the month of Gleaning. He traveled on through the night and for the nights that followed, resting by day and avoiding every chance of contact. He deemed it wisest not to be seen by anyone until he was well away from his own lands.

Recognition was not a serious danger, since he was known by sight to few outside Balthid's Keep. He simply thought it best to avoid placing himself in questionable circumstances.

For a disguise he had chosen the simple dark garments of a student of the annals as best befitting his person and his mission. Such students threatened no one, possessed nothing worth stealing, and provided welcome diversion for all with their lore and legends and curious tales of time past. They boasted neither the valued skill of healers nor the manifold talents of storytellers, nor were they as pitiable as beggars; but like these classes, they enjoyed something akin to immunity. They moved about the north freely, in relative safety. All others, most particularly merchants and money-lenders, moved cautiously in those restless times, fearful of brigands and liegeless men and equally fearful of those who posed as protectors.

Brondin felt safe. His interest in the past was genuine and his knowledge extensive; he could carry off his role under the closest scrutiny. His purse was lean, most of its contents daibas and copper bits, with a few half lunes among them. It was sufficient to get him to the Fastness without starving. In his pack was a fist-sized chunk of hard yellow cheese and some dry scraps of bread, and a flat water bottle hung at his belt. His clothing was new, but he had subjected it to several days' hard wear, and it hung on him with the look of comfortable service in its creases. He carried no weapon but a dagger; students of the annals were expected to know of the great swordsmen of the past but not to emulate them. In case of need, his crutch, fashioned from a single piece of seasoned oak, would serve as a club.

He headed westward. His plan was to cross the southern foothills of the central mountain range and then ford the river into Long Wood. In the absence of information, he had to guess, and his best guess was that the hunted men would go where it was most dangerous for Halssa's men to follow. Long Wood, with its traditional loyalty to the Vannensons, was just such a place, and it was also the best and safest avenue to the other areas where fugitives from Halssa might seek refuge.

Brondin entertained hopes but no illusions. He knew how small his chances were of coming upon the men he sought. But he told himself that the simple fact of his active seeking would, however slightly, increase those chances.

He made good progress in his travels. His bad leg was weak but not useless. It was not, as rumor had said, twisted or shriveled. It had healed poorly from a childhood injury and had lost the flexibility of a healthy limb. He lacked agility and quickness of movement, but with the aid of a crutch, he could walk a considerable way before the pain of use slowed him.

Toward evening of his sixth day of travel, when he was more than halfway to Long Wood, his disguise had a crucial test. He was walking a narrow trail, when an armed man stepped out from the cover of a boulder and ordered him to halt. Brondin obeyed, and only when the man flung back his cloak and came closer, his sword raised, did he see the red and black of Halssa on the man's sleeve.

"What's a solitary traveler doing on this trail, with nightfall close and no shelter near?" the guard demanded.

"I'm a student of the annals, sir, bound for the Headland in search of ancient lore," Brondin replied in a low, respectful voice.

"You have small chance of getting there alive, boy, alone and limping on a crutch, and only a dagger for protection."

"What have I to fear, sir? I've offended no man. I have nothing worth stealing—"

"You have boots and a cloak and garments that aren't rotted to rags," the guardsman broke in. "Probably a few coins in your purse and some food in your pack."

"True, sir, I have."

"There are men in these mountains—women, too, and children—who'd kill for such things."

"I would resist. I'm not helpless, sir," Brondin said firmly.

"They'd take what they wanted, anyway, and kill you with a bit more enthusiasm," said the guard. "Where did you think to sleep?"

"I've traveled by night, for safety. When morning comes, I seek out a hidden spot to sleep through the day."

The guard studied him for a time, shaking his head, and then put up his sword. Pointing to his left, he said, "That way, boy. You're in luck. Tonight you'll sleep safely."

A student of the annals was not expected to argue with armed men. Brondin did as he was ordered, slumping and letting his shoulders sag as he moved. Only when he turned did he see the bowman who had been behind him.

The swordsman guided him along a winding path until they came in sight of a fire. Six men sat around it, and as Brondin drew near, two of them rose.

"Who's this?" one said gruffly, while the other stood apart.

"The luckiest lad in the north, maybe," Brondin's guide replied. "He's been traveling to the Headland by night, alone."

"Are you crazy, boy?" the new speaker demanded.

"No, sir."

"He says he's injured no one and has nothing worth taking. He thinks that makes him safe," the swordsman explained with a touch of irony in his voice.

The new speaker looked Brondin over carefully, let out a great puff of suppressed breath, and shook his head just as the guard had done. "Where are you from, lad?" he asked.

"The Lake Isle, sir."

"And how long on the way?"

Brondin paused, frowned, and said, "This is the twenty-fourth day, sir, or the twenty-fifth. I've lost exact count."

"Had an accident, did you?" the other asked, pointing to Brondin's crutch.

"A long time ago. I'm used to this now, sir," Brondin said, slapping his palm against the crutch.

"You must be. That's fair traveling for a man with two good legs. Come into the light more, lad." Brondin did so, and the other man inspected him closely before commenting, "You've got western blood in you."

"I'm told my father was a westerner. I never knew him."

"How old are you?" the guard asked. When Brondin told him, he spoke quietly to another, nodded, and said, "That's about the age of Brondin of Balthid's Keep, isn't it?"

"That may be so, sir."

"It is. And Brondin has an injured leg. It may be a coincidence, lad, but I can't help thinking—"

"Brondin's injury affects his left leg, sir, not his right. And it's much more severe," Brondin interrupted.

"It is, now? And are you such a close friend of his to know such things?"

"My mother once brought me to a healer who had tried to cure Brondin. He told us that my injury was nothing compared to his. Brondin's left leg is yellow and twisted, he said, skinny as a staff and covered with bleeding sores. He can never hope to walk as I do," Brondin said confidently.

The guard who had brought him in said, "He speaks the truth, Captain. I've heard the same thing myself more than once."

"So have I," said a man who had been silent previously, stepping forward to inspect Brondin for himself. He laughed once and then gestured for Brondin to seat himself by the fire. He settled beside him. "I didn't think we'd be lucky enough to have Brondin walk into our camp, lad. But it doesn't hurt to ask," he said.

"I doubt Brondin can walk anywhere, sir," Brondin said mildly. The captain laughed again, and the others joined him.

"Tell me, have you seen anyone in your travels?" the captain asked, serious now.

"I've avoided all contact, sir. I was advised that it's the safest way."

"The safest way is to stay at home or travel in a caravan. How did you buy food?"

"I brought enough to get me to Long Wood. I was told that travelers are safer there."

"Anywhere is safer than these mountains. You're lucky to be alive, lad, I tell you truly. I'd advise you to travel with us. We're going as far as the river. We won't slow our pace for you, but if you can keep up, you're welcome to come."

"Thank you, sir."

"You'll earn your way. When we've eaten, you can tell us something from the annals."

Brondin ate his fill of roast mountain goat and then settled into a comfortable spot by the fire, his back against a log, cushioned by his folded cloak, and offered to begin a recitation. Six guardsmen gathered around him, and he went without preamble into an involved account of the battle on the bridge to the Crystal Hills, beyond Northmark.

He was no teller of tales. His narration was straightforward: no song, no gesture, no subtle effects of rhythm or rhyme or assonance, no striking imagery—only the plain facts told in a studiously flat voice, as one would expect from a student of the annals. In truth, only the intrinsic interest of the material saved it from being a dull performance.

The guardsmen were mildly appreciative, and one called for another tale of battle. Brondin told them a longer story of Ambescand's first foray against the brigands of the north, in his youthful days when he was known as Genlon of the Gray Mantle. This was more to their liking, regardless of the manner of telling.

"He would take no reward for himself, in keeping with his oath to Cathwar, his spirit-teacher," Brondin concluded. "But he decreed that a stone should be raised to his fallen comrades, and in it should be cut the legend 'To the memory of four who died so that you who read might walk this way in peace.' It is not known how many such stones were raised, though men once knew, but it is said that three still stand and may be seen."

"I've seen one," said a voice out of the shadows. "In the mountains north of the Fastness it was. Had words cut right into it, and you could still make them out."

"You can't read, Gradden," another voice called, and the men laughed.

"Captain could. He read it to us. Read it three times so we'd remember," the first speaker said.

His story done, Brondin rolled himself in his cloak and settled down to sleep. His excitement, his sheer exhilaration at sitting in the midst of Halssa's guardsmen and telling tales of his own ancestors, made him certain that he would not sleep that night. He had been awake only a short time and had traveled no distance at all that evening. But he had overlooked the toll of long days and nights alone, of fitful sleep taken in snatches, of constant alertness. Here he was surrounded by armed and watchful men. They were servants of his enemy, true, but for the moment they were his protectors. He went off to sleep almost at once and did not wake until the sky was light.

In the two days he traveled with Halssa's guards, Brondin developed a grudging admiration for them. They were tough, hard men, and he did not doubt that they were capable of the brutal deeds he had often heard ascribed to them. But they were well disciplined and loyal to their lord. With a better leader, they might prove to be better men.

The thought that these men he now walked among as a friend might one day face his own followers in deadly battle troubled Brondin. He did not fear their victory, for he knew that his followers were the match of any warriors in the north, but he abhorred the prospect of brave men dying when their deaths might be avoided. The warlords and even the common soldiers themselves did not seem to think this way. To them, war was the only solution to differences between armed men. Brondin knew that war could sometimes not be avoided; but he saw victory as meaningless to the dead and wondered whether victory might be possible without slaughter. He knew of no one who shared his hope.

When they separated, about two greatmarks from the riverbank, the captain took Brondin aside. "We'll be back here in twelve days, lad, and we'll camp here for two nights. If you should see or hear of a storyteller, a swordsman, an old healer, and his servant, you get word back here, and there'll be a reward for you from Halssa's own hands. Do you hear?"

"What do they look like, sir?" Brondin asked.

"I can't tell you much. The swordsman's a big, strong fellow. Getting on in years but tough. The storyteller is one of the best. Orannan is his name. Skinny little fellow, jumpy as a hare. We don't know anything about the others."

"What have they done?"

"They killed one of our patrols at Riverroad Camp, up

north. We want them, lad. If you see them or hear word of them, you tell us."

"I'll do my best to find them, sir."

Once out of sight of the guardsmen, Brondin stretched and arched his back luxuriously. Since his first encounter with the guard on the trail, he had been slumping and stooping, letting his shoulders droop, doing his best to appear a smaller, weaker man. He grinned and then laughed aloud. He felt triumphant, bold as a figure out of the old legends—like Tallisan when he posed as a renegade and spied on the sea raiders, or the Scarlet Ordred among the gamesmasters. He had met his enemies and outwitted them.

As he walked on and reflected on the captain's words, his mood grew sober. He knew slightly more about the fugitives than he had known before, but the important information was still missing, and the little he had learned had only confused him. An old healer and a puny storyteller did not sound like formidable opponents; yet they, along with a single swordsman and one servant, had defeated a full patrol. That was reason enough to hunt them, certainly; but had they already been fleeing for some other reason when the patrol reached them? If that was so, it was more than likely that one of them was the thief or at least the possessor of the cloak pin.

And if not, at least they were enemies to Halssa and might join his cause. He had only to find them: four wary men, fleeing for their lives, with all the north to hide in. They had evaded Halssa's patrols so far, and the captain did not sound confident. Brondin sighed and trudged on.

He crossed the river where it was nearly two greatmarks broad and no more than knee deep. A series of stepping stones took him across dry-shod, not without some awkward moments on the slippery surfaces. Once across, he continued due west for a day and then bore northwest to join Col's Way at the lowest point of the Fool's Head.

Safely in Long Wood, he determined to stop for one night at an inn as soon as he should come upon one, and on his fourth night he did so. The inn was an ordinary-looking building, but the food was hot and plentiful, and the ale was surprisingly good. No other travelers were stopping, and so he was assured of a bed all to himself.

Three men, woodwards by their dress, were by the fire when he sat down to eat. They ignored him for a time, but when he pushed his empty bowl aside and took up his tankard, one of them invited him to join their company. Brondin did so gladly. The woodwards were slow of speech and friendly in manner, but their questions were shrewd. Brondin stayed as close to the truth as he thought prudent, to lessen his chance of being caught in a lie, and so he told them of his coming to Long Wood.

"They stayed other side of river, guardsmen did, you say?" the oldest of the woodwards asked.

"Yes, they did. I crossed alone."

"Not wanted over here, they're not, and they well know it," another woodward muttered into his tankard.

"And they turned north, did you say, lad?" the old woodward asked.

"I don't know which way they went. I was over the rise, and I couldn't see the trail."

"Ah, yes, I know the place," the oldster said, nodding.

"Haven't caught those fellows yet, for all their threats and all their bribes," the third said, sounding pleased. "Won't get them, either, if we can help it."

"Ah, now, Tuvey, it's not wise to mix in the affairs of the powerful. I wouldn't turn those four over to Halssa's guards for a bootful of oaks, but I wouldn't go out of my way to help them, either," the old woodward said softly. "They have their troubles, and they're welcome to keep them. I have enough of my own."

"You talk like Domitane," the second man said without turning.

"Master Domitane is a sensible man. He's prospered by minding his own affairs and no one else's."

"I'll mind no one else's affairs as long as they stay other side of river. You've known me long enough to know that, Ritt," the second man said.

"I have, indeed."

"Well, then. Halssa's guards have come over here nine times since early Gleaning. Wasn't us who invited them, Ritt. They came looking for those four, and they came with drawn swords and loud voices."

"Just doing their job, Wayder," the old woodward said placidly.

"The ones I saw said nothing about crossing into Long Wood." Brondin volunteered.

Wayder responded, "They don't give warning, lad. Burst in on people and threaten them is what they do. And them who could stop it sit back and do nothing."

"Master Domitane is wise. He'll act when time comes to act and not before," Ritt, the old woodward, said.

Wayder muttered angrily, but the matter was dropped. Ritt and Tuvey began to discuss some local problem, and Wayder soon gave in and joined them. Brondin, left to himself, turned his thoughts to Master Domitane.

He was aware of the name, although he had never met the man. Few had, and little was known about him. Domitane did not travel, and he had no dealings with the alliance. He was said to be a man who took no interest in others' quarrels, and Brondin had never come across any evidence to the contrary. But now, with Halssa's patrols venturing into Long Wood, and with some of the woodwards aroused, there might be a chance of winning Domitane over to the alliance.

Brondin yawned widely and finished his ale. The woodwards rose to depart, and he wished them farewell. He went directly to his hard, narrow bed and slept soundly through the night.

He learned the next morning that Domitane's manor was only seven greatmarks west of the inn, and this set him to thinking once more of the man. Domitane could prove a valuable friend. He was said to have at his command anywhere from two hundred to five hundred men. His lands were placed so that he could bar easy passage north and south. He was respected in Long Wood, and if he could be won over, others would surely follow.

Brondin was tempted to visit Domitane and see what he could learn of the man. There would be no danger. A student of the annals was a welcome guest in any house, and Brondin felt secure in his disguise, having put it to the test against watchful enemies. Visiting Domitane was not part of his original plan, but it might prove helpful even if he did no more than listen to the gossip of the household. Servants were always a good source of information.

Before Brondin could decide, the decision was taken out of his hands. The landlord of the inn entered in the company of a compact, weather-browned man in dark green, with a sword at his side.

"Are you the student of the annals who travels to the Headland?" the swordsman asked politely.

"I am."

"Then I bring you the greetings of Domitane, Master of Green Hall. He bids you dine this day and rest this night beneath his roof."

"I am most honored," Brondin said, half rising.

The swordsman, smiling genially, urged him to keep his seat. "Finish your breakfast at your leisure, young sir. No need for haste."

Brondin settled back on his bench. He broke off a piece of warm dark bread and spread it thickly with butter and honey. There was enough on the table for a group of hungry men, and he asked the swordsman to join him. The man hesitated and then took a piece of bread and began to butter it.

"Am I on Master Domitane's lands now?" Brondin asked.

"You've been on his land since you took the northwest fork in the trail. Four days ago, was it not?"

"How did you know? I saw no one until yesterday, when I came to the inn."

"We're watchful. Master Domitane is much concerned for the safety of travelers."

Brondin nodded and said nothing. He had already learned something valuable about Domitane.

It was still early morning when they left the inn, and they made their way at an unhurried pace along a narrow, well-tended trail. The swordsman was congenial and talkative, but he kept to generalities and said nothing of any consequence. Brondin saw no point in pressing him. When they arrived at Green Hall at midmorning, he knew little more about Domitane than he had when they had left the inn.

Green Hall was a bold, imposing structure. It stood atop a low rise in a clearing, a cube about eight or nine marks on a side, made all of stone, with a steep-pitched roof of slate. No outbuildings stood within bowshot. The main entrance was a mark high and slightly more than a mark wide, with thick iron-banded oak doors. The windows were narrow slits high in the walls. It looked far more like a fortress than a dwelling, but that was only to be expected from a man who hoped to survive without allies in dangerous times.

Domitane himself was a surprise. He was short and round, with a jovial ruddy face framed in white hair and a snowy white beard. His nose was snubbed and his merry eyes a bright blue. He welcomed Brondin with a broad smile and an embrace, as if he were greeting a long-absent friend.

"Welcome to Green Hall, my boy, welcome!" he boomed in a deep, warm bass. "From what I hear, you've come a long way and still have a long way to go."

"I hope to reach the Headland before the first snows, Master Domitane," Brondin replied.

"You're a brave lad, traveling all that distance alone and with a leg that must be troubling to you. Have you injured it on the journey, lad?"

"It's an old injury. I'm used to it now, and it slows me not at all."

"Ah, you're a brave lad, brave indeed. Well, now, you must tell me all you've seen in your travels and all you hope to see," said Domitane, taking Brondin's arm and drawing him to a pair of large high-backed chairs by the fireside of his chamber. "I'm much concerned over all that's going on in the north these days, but since I never leave my own territories, I must depend on travelers for all my news. I warn you, my boy, you must make yourself comfortable, for I intend to tire you out with my curiosity," said his host cheerfully, waving Brondin to one of the cushioned seats.

"I fear I have little news worth hearing, Master Domitane. Traveling alone, I was wary of strangers and did my best to avoid meeting anyone."

"One can't be too careful these days. We live in troubled times, my boy. A man who wishes only to live out his days at peace with his neighbors or in quiet study of the past," he said with a spacious wave of his pudgy hand to Brondin, "is as likely to fall prey to violence as the veriest brigand. Troubled times, these," he repeated, shaking his head sadly.

"They are, indeed, Master Domitane. Yet I managed to come this far in safety."

"So you did. Protected by a squad of Halssa's own guards, too!" Domitane said, smiling broadly.

Brondin returned the smile but said nothing for a moment. He marveled at how quickly the information had reached Domitane. "I came upon them quite by chance," he said at last.

"I'm sure you did, lad!" said Domitane, laughing and clapping his hands on his knees. "No one throws himself in the way of Halssa's guards."

"They treated me quite decently."

"Ah, so. But then, they had something else on their minds, didn't they?"

Brondin frowned and said haltingly, "The captain spoke of being after some men—a healer and his servant, I think, and others."

"Ah, yes. Now, there's a story for you, lad! You students of the annals know all the curious events of the past, but here's a marvelous tale unfolding under your very nose, and I'll bet you don't know a thing about it." Brondin made a vague gesture to suggest his ignorance, and Domitane continued. "You'd hardly expect me to know what's going on, never leaving my own lands, seldom straying out of this house, but there you'd be wrong. I'm a curious man. I like to know things. I'm always talking to travelers, all sorts of people, about anything and everything, but especially about events in the north, just as we're doing now. And I've learned some amazing things. You must let me tell you."

Brondin nodded, and Domitane hitched his chair closer to Brondin's and leaned forward. He glanced about like some taproom informer and lowered his voice.

"Now, you know of the great battle at Riverroad Camp. Seven of Halssa's men killed by the old healer and his servant and another fellow."

"The captain did speak of that."

"Here's something the captain didn't speak of. In the battle, the servant slew one of the guards with his dagger. Now, that's the work of no ordinary servant, is it? That sounds to me like the deed of a professional thief."

Brondin tried to show no reaction to this news. He paused for a moment, as if in thought, and then shook his head. "Just because a man's a servant . . . the servant of a traveling healer would be bound to use a weapon skillfully. He'd be as much guard as servant."

"Ah, but you see, the healer had hired a guard, a young swordsman named Daike. He was killed in the clash."

That was news to Brondin, and it put the healer and his servant in a new light. He pondered the information and then said, "All the same, it's not that unusual for a servant to use a dagger well."

"No," said Domitane reluctantly. "But think of this: Why would a healer and his servant and a swordsman and a story-teller risk a clash with a patrol? And why would Halssa's patrol risk a daylight raid in Fastness territory?" He paused and looked expectantly at Brondin. "It makes one think that something or someone very important is mixed up in this, doesn't it?"

"That's possible," Brondin admitted. "Were Halssa's men pursuing them?"

"Ah, now, there's the question that needs an answer. But nobody seems to have one. We're forced to guess and piece together an answer out of scattered bits of information. And here is a morsel that will set you thinking, lad. Some days before the healer's party departed for the west, there was a man going about the more dubious establishments of the Fastness, making very circumspect and nervous inquiries about a recent theft. He was so very, very cautious that he would not identify himself or the object he believed stolen or the one from whom it was taken. But one who saw him recognized him as looking very like the servant of an old healer then staying in the Fastness. What do you think of that, now, my lad?" Domitane concluded triumphantly.

Brondin felt his heart beat faster. He took a deep breath and held it to calm himself before responding. "It's very complicated . . . but fascinating."

"Ah, now, you see, it's not quite so complicated to me. I'm accustomed to sifting and sorting and fitting facts into place, like an old woman trying to piece together a shattered pot. It's habit with me, lad. I can almost see the shape of the missing pieces in my mind's eye." Domitane squeezed his eyes shut and tapped his forehead with his fingertips. "It's in there, lad. Find the man who's lost something precious, some-thing held in secret, something so powerful that even a master thief is stricken with fear to find it in his possession. Find that man and you have the answer."

Brondin was impressed by his host's reasoning and accepted his conclusions. With a few minutes' talk, this man had answered some of his most troubling questions. He rejoiced at his luck in coming upon Domitane but said merely, "I fear you're too wise for me, Master Domitane. I grow dizzy trying to follow your line of thought."

"Well, we know the cure for dizziness here, my lad!" said Domitane with bluff cheerfulness, clapping his hands loudly. "The finest wine in the north, chilled to perfection. But in order to do it justice, you must work up a thirst equal to my own. Do you have a choice tale from the annals of Long Wood? Something curious and complicated and full of puzzles for me to ponder in the long dark nights to come?"

Brondin searched his memory. His knowledge of the annals of Long Wood was not extensive, but he recalled a story of Ambescand's youthful encounter with the three Misty Maidens who foretold his great deeds and his coming to power. It was a moral tale and rather dry—so Brondin thought—but full of cryptic sayings sure to please a mind like Domitane's.

He had gone only a short way into the narrative when a servant entered, bearing a tray on which stood a silver carafe and two drinking vessels. Domitane poured a small measure into each vessel and handed one to Brondin. They drank together, and Brondin marveled at the clean dry tang of the wine, lighter and more refreshing than any northern wine he had ever tasted before.

He resumed his account. Domitane sat attentive throughout, and when Brondin was finished, he beamed appreciatively and poured them a full measure of wine. Brondin drank his off at a draft, and his host, laughing boisterously, filled the vessel to the brim.

At this point, the swordsman who had been Brondin's guide entered the chamber. He strode directly to his master and spoke to him in low, urgent tones. Domitane listened, frowning. He nodded once and then raised his great bulk out of the chair. His expression and manner were somber.

"An emergency has arisen. My presence is required at once. Ivermay will keep you company in my absence." To

the swordsman he said, "See that our guest drinks his fill."
Then he left the chamber without another word.

Ivermay perched on the arm of Domitane's chair, folded
his arms, and grinned conspiratorially at Brondin. "You
heard the master, lad. Drink up. There's plenty more."

Brondin smiled and drank. At once, Ivermay refilled his
vessel to the brim. "Drink it," he said.

"Give me some time," Brondin protested, smiling. "I'll be
sound asleep in a little while at this rate."

"That's the idea, lad. It's the easiest way. Now drink."

Brondin blinked, shook his head, and looked hard at Ivermay. He felt the first sting of suspicion. "What do you
mean?" he asked.

"Master Domitane's a kindly man. He doesn't want to be
rough with you if he can avoid it. Just finish this carafe, and
you'll sleep soundly for a day. When you wake up, you'll
feel fine, and we'll know what we want to know."

Brondin suddenly felt his body grow heavy and sluggish.
He tried to rise, but Ivermay pushed him gently, and he fell
back in the chair. "What do you want to know?" he asked,
thick-tongued.

"Very simple, lad. We want to know whether you're a
student of the annals or Brondin of Balthid's Keep. We could
take you down below and question you, but by the time we
were satisfied, you might not be much good to anyone. So
we've sent for a man who knows Brondin. He'll look you
over while you're dreaming away, and if you're no more
than you say you are, you'll be on your way with a silver
eagle for your troubles and the protection of Master Domitane to bring you safely to your destination."

"What if this . . . this man . . . says I'm Brondin?"

"Then we'll have an auction. Now drink up, lad. Make it
easy for yourself," Ivermay said in a kindly voice.

Brondin raised the vessel and sipped from it, spilling a bit
of the drugged wine. He could feel the lethargy creeping
slowly through his body and knew that he must act promptly
or be lost. He held the vessel out to Ivermay, who laughed
softly, picked up the carafe, and leaned forward to pour.

Brondin brought the tip of his crutch into Ivermay's groin
with all his might, doubling the man over. Carafe and vessel
clattered to the floor. He pulled himself to his feet and laid

the head of the crutch hard across Ivermay's temple. The swordsman fell and lay still.

At once Brondin thrust his fingers down his throat. He gagged, retched, and spewed up the wine. By the fireplace stood two buckets of water, dust-filmed and stale. He drank deeply and forced himself to vomit again; then he doused his face and hair in the cold water. It made him feel slightly better, but he was still dizzy and weak, and the craving for sleep was strong.

He made his way cautiously through Green Hall, dagger drawn, but he saw no one. There seemed to be no servants, no signs of life, only the afternoon silence urging him to close his eyes and sleep. At last he found a postern, slipped out, and made his way to the woods.

All day and all night he forced himself on. His arms and legs felt like blocks of wood; he fell asleep while walking and had to drag himself to his feet a score of times, each time with more difficulty. His head throbbed, and his eyes burned, but he went on.

By late in the night, the influence of the sleeping drug had worn off. Brondin was exhausted and aching, but he knew that he was feeling the natural toll of his exertions and nothing more. He bathed his face and neck in the chill waters of a stream and sat for a time on the bank, thinking of his escape.

He had acted like a fool, and he knew it. Domitane had a keen mind—far keener than Brondin's—and it had been the height of childish vanity to believe that he could deceive such a man. His success with Halssa's guards had made him arrogant, and his arrogance had nearly lost him everything.

His escape from Green Hall had been sheer undeserved luck; he could not count on such luck's continuing. He sighed and looked up at the cold stars, brilliant in the moonless sky. Despite his escape, he felt close to despair. In a world so full of treachery and ambition, with greedy men taking up arms on all sides to plunder or to protect what they had plundered from others, there seemed little point to his search.

If Domitane had told the truth, and if his surmises were correct, the old healer or his servant had stolen the cloak pin. But by this time, the swordsman or the storyteller—or almost anyone—might have taken the cloak pin from the original thief. It might have been lost or sold or discarded as a cheap trinket. The men he sought might be scattered throughout the world or dead. It was all folly and madness, he thought bitterly.

The uncaring stars shone down, and he looked up at them, and after a time he laughed. The stars watched all and knew all but said nothing to any man. They had hung there, remote and cold and bright, for as long as men could remember, and they would be there, unchanged and unmoved, when the last man lay down to die. The stars felt nothing, feared nothing, believed in nothing.

But Brondin was not one of them. He was a man, he believed in something, and he had work to do. He pulled himself wearily to his feet, groaning at his deep fatigue and the ache in his leg, and started north.

CHAPTER TWELVE

FLIGHT

When the first gray light filtered down into the Fissure, the three fugitives began to make their way along the ledge. Cabanard led them.

The nature of the trail became clear as they progressed. For most of the way the ledge was a natural outcropping, but for some long stretches it bore the unmistakable signs of human workmanship. None of the work was recent. Someone, in some distant time, had hewn a path into the sheer face of the cliff, continuing by human effort the work of nature. Not one of the three had ever heard of this hidden trail or suspected its existence.

The way varied from nearly a full mark to little more than a toehold in depth. The overhang in some places was a broad roof too high to touch even with an extended sword's point, and in others it was so low that the three were forced to their hands and knees. But the trail went on unbroken, greatmark after greatmark, until they had passed the Fissure. For another score of greatmarks, they made their way along the sheer cliffs facing the sea that lay between the Headland and the Cape of Mists. There the air was moist and bright, and the waves crashed below them with a rhythmic booming, like a great drum setting their pace. At last, near nightfall on their second day of flight, the ledge ended abruptly, in a dizzying straight drop of at least sixty marks to the foam-washed rocks below.

Cabarnard studied the notches cut into the stone, rising to the limit of his view and vanishing in the curve of the cliffside. The brittle remnants of a seabird's nest lay in the notch at his eye level, and moss was thick in the notch below it. No one had passed this way for a long time.

"It's nearly dark, and I'm not sure where we are. We'll sleep here tonight and go up in the morning," he announced.

"We might find food if we go up," Orannan suggested.

"We might find a patrol, too. You've got some water left. Fill up on that. We'll have plenty to eat tomorrow."

Orannan sighed, seated himself against the rear wall, and dug into his pack for whatever tiny crumbs might have escaped his earlier excavations. Cabanard settled beside him, while Stoggan sprawled belly down at the forward edge and studied the rocky islets that lay below them, a few marks out to sea. After a time, Stoggan joined the other two.

"Can you make a guess as to where we are?" he asked Cabanard.

"A rough guess. I'd say we're just about due north of the northernmost point of the Fool's Head. About six or seven days' normal travel. We're about the same distance west of the river."

"Where do you think we should go?"

Cabanard did not reply at once. When he addressed Stoggan, it was with a question. "Did Traissell tell anyone at the Fastness that he was heading west?"

"I don't know."

"He told me," Orannan said. "I don't know if he told anyone else, but he didn't seem to be keeping it a secret."

Cabanard nodded. He seemed satisfied with this information and asked Orannan, "What about you? Did you tell anyone you were going to the Headland?"

"I . . . yes, I did. I told Traissell and Ennet. And I may have mentioned it to Falshreene and a few of the other girls."

Cabanard looked at him curiously for a moment and then asked, "Why didn't you just make a public proclamation at the gate? That way you wouldn't have missed anybody."

"I only told a few people, Cabanard. I didn't tell it to everyone I met," Orannan said indignantly.

Cabanard laughed and said, "I wouldn't mind if you had. I think you may have helped us, you and the healer."

Later, as darkness gathered, Cabanard outlined his plan of escape. "If Halssa's men found our trail, they probably found Traissell's as well. The ones following him are over to the west of the Fool's Head, along Col's Way. We don't have to worry about them. The ones who followed us are probably going to stay close to the bridge, waiting for us to arrive. They'll be there for a few days before they begin to wonder if we're coming."

"Unless the Bridgemaster tells them about us," Stoggan pointed out.

"Vessler said he'd tell them nothing. He'll see to it that the Bridgemaster doesn't, either. We can trust him."

"But then it will never be safe to try for the Headland," said Orannan.

"That's right. So we'll forget the Headland and go south, all the way to the Southern Forest, and then head for the west. Halssa's men don't expect that, and they won't be looking for us. We'll stay near the river. Better get some new clothes just to be safe." To Orannan he said, "You'll have to get rid of that harp. If you're caught with that, there's no chance at all for us. And I can't keep my sword, either."

"Couldn't we just go to one of Halssa's enemies? He has dozens in the north. Surely one of them would give us sanctuary."

Cabanard shook his head. "They're all too weak to stand up to him—all except Brondin, and he's a long way off. If Halssa found out and demanded that they turn us over, they'd do it."

"Would they really betray us to Halssa?"

"They wouldn't call it betrayal. They're more concerned for their own skins than they are for ours. In fact, Halssa might not even have to ask. Someone might make his own deal, trade us for a friend or a promise of safety. No, I think the best chance we have is to go south as quickly as we can."

"It's a long way," Stoggan said.

"And dangerous," Orannan added.

"We'll decide in the morning. If anyone can come up with a better idea, I'll go along. I just want to get out of all this and rest for a good long time," said Cabanard, drawing his cloak about him and getting ready for sleep.

When morning came, no one had thought of a better way. In the early mist, the three ascended the cliff and made their wary way across the open ground to Long Wood. Once safely among the trees, they followed Cabanard through the trackless wood until they came upon a narrow pathway, a foresters' trail that showed no evidence of recent use.

"We'll make good time along here," Cabanard announced. "The chance of a patrol is pretty small. I'll keep well ahead and let you know if I see anyone."

"What about food? We have to eat, Cabanard, or we'll all collapse," Orannan said desperately.

"We'll have food. And new outfits, too. Come along."

With those words of assurance, Cabanard left them and headed down the narrow trail. They had no choice but to follow. They walked on through the morning, until Orannan lost all track of time and all sense of movement. His belly ached and groaned in protest at its emptiness; his temples throbbed, and he grew light-headed. Stoggan plodded grimly before him, silent, his head turning from side to side with his wary glances. At last, when the sun was high, they came upon Cabanard seated on a fallen tree at the side of the path. He rose when they came into view.

"Rest here, off the trail. There's a clearing about six marks into the woods. I'll be back before dark," he said.

"Where are you going?" Stoggan asked.

"To look for an old friend. Wait for me in the clearing," Cabanard replied, and then turned and entered the woods.

For one panicky moment, in terror of being abandoned, Orannan wanted to run after him. But he held his ground, partly because he was too weak and weary to run or protest or even question Cabanard's action. Sighing, he sat down heavily, hopelessly, on the fallen tree.

"If you want to rest, let's get to the clearing," Stoggan said.

Once in the clearing, they collapsed on the sun-warmed grass and fell in a stupor, drugged by hunger and exhaustion and lulled by the overhead sun. Orannan did not wake until the first chill of evening shadow crept over him, but then he roused himself swiftly and looked around the clearing with fearful eyes, aghast at his long unguarded slumber. Seeing no sign of danger, he relaxed and sank down with his back against a tree. His pounding heart slowly resumed its normal rhythm, and he closed his eyes, squeezing them tight against the pain that was like an iron band around his forehead. He had been hungry before, and more than once he had run for his life, but never had he felt such utter despair as now overcame him. If Halssa could be so relentless in pursuit, what hope was there of escaping him? And once captured, what awful death must they suffer? Thinking of the future, he wondered whether it might not be better simply to give in to hunger and weariness and die quietly in the peaceful clearing.

Then Cabanard appeared, stepping forth from the woods like a glorious apparition. His face was split by a wide grin, and in his upraised hands were a beautiful dark brown dome of bread and a stone flagon. Tossing the bread to Orannan, he reached into his tunic and drew forth a fist-sized chunk of pale yellow cheese. Stoggan, starting into wakefulness, gaped at the sight.

"Eat up, and then we'll travel. Tonight we sleep under a roof," Cabanard said.

He set the flagon, which contained cold beer, between his two companions, and settled down to watch them eat, smiling like a proud parent at their ravenous appetites. Only when every morsel of bread and cheese was gone and the flagon drained of its last drop did the others even notice Cabanard's changed appearance.

"That's a woodward's outfit. Where did you get it? And the food—" Orannan began, but he was silenced by a belch.

"The outfit was my friend's. He died last winter, but his widow knew my name. She'll help us. We can eat and rest up at her place and then head south."

"Could we stay there a while?" Stoggan asked.

Cabanard shook his head. "Halssa's patrol stopped there six days ago. They were looking for four men."

"Us?" Orannan asked.

"'A skinny little storyteller and a healer,' they said, 'and an old-timer with a sword,'" Cabanard repeated, smiling. "They don't seem to know what you look like, Stoggan."

"Nobody pays attention to a servant," said Stoggan.

"Lucky for you. For all of us. We may have to buy food later on, and you can deal with people and not be recognized."

"Did they say anything more?" Orannan asked.

"Not to her. She heard them talking among themselves about the Headland. She couldn't remember exactly, but she thinks they're going to set up an ambush at the bridge."

Orannan swallowed audibly and closed his eyes for a

moment at the realization of their narrow escape. Stoggan said, "We're putting our lives in her hands."

"We can trust her. She's from an old Long Wood family, and the people here have no love for Halssa. They had a special loyalty to the Vannenson kings, and they don't much care for the ones who took their throne. They don't like to see Halssa's men here at all, and when they come in force and ask a lot of questions, no one helps them." Cabanard picked up the empty flagon and rose. "Her place is about three greatmarks west of here. We can make it before dark."

The sun had just set when they reached the edge of the cleared land where the widow's house stood. It was small but well made, with a patterned roof of thatch, and glass in the windows. Behind the house stood a barn of modest size and two or three outbuildings, indistinct in the twilight.

The deep echoing bark of a dog came to their ears, and a lantern flared to bright life in the doorway. Cabanard waved his arms. The lantern moved slowly up and then down.

"All's well. Come on," Cabanard said, starting forward.

About a third of the way across the field, a black shape bounded at them. Cabanard called to it, and the dog, a hound that stood nearly to his waist, paused and then came to his side and sniffed his clothing and his hand. Cabanard laid a hand slowly on the great beast's head and scratched between and behind its ears. The dog's tail began to wag.

"This is Bolt, Cossrow's hunting dog. He recognizes the smell of his master on these clothes. Don't be afraid of him," Cabanard said.

"We don't all smell like his master," Orannan pointed out.

"He won't attack without the command."

That was some reassurance. Nevertheless, Orannan walked gingerly and kept a close eye on Bolt all the way to the house.

Cossrow's widow, a tall and sturdy woman named Evra, awaited them at the door. She led them into the house, shut the door behind them, and bolted it firmly. She lit another lantern and inspected her guests.

"Is it you that be storyteller?" she asked Orannan.

Orannan recalled the description repeated by Cabanard and

felt a momentary flush of anger at such quick recognition; but then, remembering what this woman had offered and the risk she ran in doing so, he smiled and said, "I am Orannan the teller of tales, lady, and I offer you my thanks for your kindness and courtesy."

"It is like a storyteller's his talk is," said Evra approvingly. "Do you have tales of the old times? Of the three brothers and the Stone Hand?"

"I do, lady. I know more tales of the brothers than any other storyteller in the north, and better ones."

"He speaks the truth, Evra," said Cabanard, nodding.

"You must tell us one this night. We will eat a proper meal, with soup and meat and nice pudding, and then you will tell us a fine tale."

"I will be honored, lady," said Orannan, bowing.

Turning to Stoggan, Evra said, "And you be the one who worked for the healer and the fool?"

"I am."

"Did he teach you healing?"

"He did not."

"A pity he did not. My hands do get stiff and sore these cold mornings. A healer could tell me what to do, but no healer ever passes this way."

"Is there any traffic this way at all, Evra?" Cabanard asked.

"Woodwards come by now and then, and Godomor from the near farmstead sends his boys over every ten days to offer their help to the poor widow." Evra gave a short, sharp laugh and grinned at them. "He be a widower himself, and he thinks now that Cossrow's gone, I be falling all over myself to marry him, and he to get some decent land and a good snug house at last. Silly old fool, him without a tooth in his head and bent over like a birch. As if he could ever be the man my Cossrow was!"

"Coss was the best. He brought us out of some bad spots."

"And you saved his life more than once. Many a time he said to me, 'I would not be sitting at this table now, love, but for the strength and loyalty of my friend Cabanard.' Happy I am, truly, to do good for you and your men in return."

"We appreciate it, Evra. I think it might be best, though, if we sleep in the barn, just in case another patrol comes past or a neighbor stops by."

"It's a great offense you've done Halssa, surely."

"Halssa seems to think so."

Evra looked at the three men and then stirred suddenly and said, "And here stand I, gaping and chattering, and you all starved and ready to drop. Sit at the table and let me get some food in front of you, now."

In a very short time, the three men were downing bowls of thick steaming soup. No sooner had they finished and sat back to sigh in comfortable repletion than Evra filled their empty bowls with savory stew. She watched with great satisfaction as they ate, and then she rose to bring a sweet pudding to the table. She took a bit of the pudding herself; then she cleared the table and laid a fresh log on the fire, against the autumn chill.

The three travelers stretched out their weary legs to the warmth. Orannan drew his chair closer to the fire, uncovered his harp, and struck a few exploratory chords. He winced at the sounds, tightened the strings, and tried again with better results. After a few trials, the harp was tuned to his liking.

"I will tell a tale of Colberane and how he found the beautiful Davasha in a land far away. Will that please you, lady?" he asked.

"It will. But I hope you will tell a tale of Ambescand before you go," Evra answered.

"I will, lady. I will tell a tale I told at Ennet's Hostel, in the Fastness, and made warriors weep for pride. But tonight, the tale of Davasha, for it is a tale as brief as it is beautiful, and I am too weary to tell a longer one."

Orannan brushed his fingers lightly over the strings, bringing forth soft sensuous chords of trembling beauty to set the mood for his tale. His voice was hushed and gentle, a sound to suit the mild warmth of the fire and the honeyed glow of lantern light on the wooden walls and the comforting kitchen aromas. His was no dry recital from the annals; he sang a sweet and poignant tale of first love. The tale was brief, as he had promised; but even so, Cabanard nodded off a score of times during the telling, and Stoggan's head sank to his chest in sound sleep.

"Get you to the barn, now," Evra said when the tale was done. "Bolt will keep good watch, and you may sleep as long as you wish."

They slept profoundly and dreamlessly until midday. Stoggan and Orannan rested through the day, while Evra cared for their travel-worn garments. Cabanard, with Evra's help, refreshed his memory of the bypaths and hidden ways of Long Wood.

That evening, Orannan told the promised tale of Ambescand, with all his own embellishments, and left his small audience moved beyond words. Evra wiped tears from her eyes and squeezed the breath from the storyteller with a hug when he was done. Cabanard, hand on his sword hilt, gazed into the fire, nodding. Even the taciturn Stoggan clapped the storyteller on the shoulder as he rose.

Early next morning, the three prepared to set out southward. Their appearance was already much changed. Cabanard wore the woodward's garments of his old commander; they hung with room to spare even on his burly frame. Slung at his back was a double-bit ax made to Cossrow's orders. It was a bit smaller and lighter than the common woodward's ax, more suited to use as a weapon than a tool. A long dagger hung from his belt, and he carried his sword in his hands.

"Hide it well, Evra," he said, holding the sword out to her. "I'll be back for it some day."

"I will cache it beneath the barn. You know the spot."

"See you wrap it carefully. It's a good blade," Cabanard said, not relinquishing his grip.

"Do you think I've forgotten how to keep a good weapon?"

"No, Evra. I trust you." He drew the sword from its plain leather-bound scabbard and looked fondly down on the wave-patterned steel. "Syragus made this. It's the work of forty days, and he was the best swordsmith of his time." He slammed the blade home and handed it to Evra, looking like a man abandoning his only child. "Let's be on our way," he said in a husky voice.

Orannan and Stoggan wore their own clothes, except for their traveling cloaks, which were old and well worn, dug from the bottom of an old chest. But their garments had been dyed the green of Long Wood. Orannan's harp, wrapped carefully as a swaddled infant, was cached in the house rafters, and as he walked, he seemed uncertain what to do with his empty hands.

"We should have brought more food, Cabanard," he said as the farmstead disappeared from sight behind them.

"We have enough for three days. Any more and we'd look suspicious. Remember, we're not strangers anymore, we're woodwards. We're home," Cabanard replied.

"But what if we run out of food?"

"Stoggan can buy some, or we can forage. No more talk now. Save your breath. We have to cover forty greatmarks a day, or we'll be traveling all winter."

On they marched, day after day. The Fool's Head fell behind them. They reached the southern limit of Long Wood, crossed the river, and started the dangerous passage of the open lands that lay between the foothills of the northern mountain range and the fringe of the great Southern Forest. To the west, beyond a horizon of pale gray, lay Mistlands.

At twilight, as they settled for the night in a sheltered hollow, Orannan looked to the west and said, "I wonder if Traissell escaped Halssa's men."

No one spoke for a time, and then Cabanard said, "We're safe enough as long as we stick to our story. Even if they come upon us, they'll probably just take our food and our purses and bluster at us for a bit, then go off. They're not looking for three woodwards."

"All the same, I prefer to have no dealings with them," said Orannan.

"Nor do I. So keep careful watch. You're on first turn."

They ate their plain meal, and Orannan took up his post at the crest of a low rise, while the others enfolded themselves in their traveling cloaks to sleep. Keeping watch here on the open grasslands was quite different from night watch in the forest, and Orannan found it unnerving. His imagination, always lively, began to run away with his common sense.

The moon was bright—Gleaners' Moon, they called it— and a north wind stirred the grass and low bushes and raised a murmur as of voices all around the hill. Orannan heard footfalls and whispers and saw shadowy skulking forms appear and disappear among the swaying grasses. His neck grew sore from sudden turns to look behind him and to all sides. He was not a particularly brave man even in the best of circumstances, and these surroundings undermined what small courage he possessed. He found them no less frightening for being imaginary.

When the hand closed over his mouth and the dagger pricked his throat, he nearly died of fright on the spot. He scarcely heard the hard voice that whispered, "One sound and I slit your throat."

He was flung face down to the ground, and a foot was planted in his back, between the shoulders. Expert hands ran over him, and his purses were plucked free. He heard muffled voices and the muted clink of coins, and then he was jerked to his feet.

He was surrounded by men dressed in dark bulky clothing, their faces stained with dust or soot to dull the reflection of moonlight. He took some slight encouragement from the fact that none of them appeared to be wearing Halssa's colors.

His arms were gripped firmly. A tall man stepped before him, raised a smoke-darkened blade, and pressed the tip into the hollow of Orannan's throat. "How many more of you? Speak the truth."

"Only two. No more."

"What are three travelers doing here?"

"Poor woodwards, seeking a new start in the south."

"Poor?" The man raised a fat purse and shook it in his face. "You have a strange notion of poverty."

"I carry the purse for all. That's everything we have. The others have nothing, nothing at all."

"We'll see for ourselves. Come along, you."

Orannan was dragged down into the hollow where his friends had been sleeping. The sudden darkness blinded him for a moment, but he soon distinguished a figure sprawled out with two men standing over him.

"Where's the other?" the tall man demanded.

"We saw no other," a voice replied.

The tall man turned to Orannan. "You said there were three of you."

"There are! He may have heard you and run off."

The tall man muttered angrily, "We'll get him. What did you find on this one?"

"A cheap trinket wrapped up like a treasure. A purse full of trash—daibas and half lunes and copper bits, and not many of those," said the man who had spoken before.

"Any food here?"

"Scraps. Not enough to give every man a decent mouthful."

The tall man stepped to the rim of the hollow. Outlined by the moon, he looked down on those within the shallow bowl. He stood as if in thought for a moment and then said, "All right, kill that one. We'll find the—"

With a loud grunt, he came hurtling forward into their midst and crashed to the ground, where he lay still. The men holding Orannan released him and drew their blades. A shadow slipped past him; there was a flash of moonlight on steel, a gurgling cry, and then uproar and utter confusion as the hunters found themselves not merely hunted but trapped and made a wild rush to escape. Orannan snatched up a blade and slashed wildly at a man scrabbling up the slope; he felt the blade strike resistance, and he heard a cry of pain, but the man kicked free and kept going, and he had no wish to pursue him.

"Orannan! Stoggan! Are you all right?" Cabanard's voice called.

"Yes! I'm here!" Orannan replied.

"Stoggan! Are you hurt?" Cabanard called again.

There was no reply. Cabanard went to where Stoggan lay. He turned him over.

"Did they hurt him?" Orannan asked.

"His throat's cut." Cabanard was silent for a time, except for a low grunt of surprise. Then he said, "Get yourself a good weapon. We'll move out now, toward Mistlands."

"Who were they, Cabanard? They didn't wear Halssa's colors," Orannan said as he searched the fallen leader for his purses.

"Nobody's men, just a band of robbers."

"I shouldn't think there'd be much for them to rob out here on the open grasslands."

"I don't know. Let's go, quick, before the rest get their courage back."

They moved out with as much speed as the light and the terrain permitted and did not stop until morning. When a low thicket showed on the horizon ahead, Cabanard said, "We'll rest there until midday and then turn south again."

"Why not go straight on to Mistlands?"

"Halssa's patrols are probably watching the borders. We're too close as it is, but we need a rest."

With daggers drawn, they made a cautious circuit of the thicket. Finding no sign of danger, Cabanard worked his way in. After a time, he emerged.

"No trace of anyone here for a long time. We should be safe."

"I'll take first watch, Cabanard. I don't think I could sleep right now."

"Thinking about Stoggan?"

Orannan hesitated and then reluctantly said, "Yes. Getting killed in your sleep like that . . . I wouldn't want to go that way."

"No. Tell me, what do you know about Stoggan?"

"No more than you do. He was Traissell's servant, that's all."

Cabanard reached into his shirt and drew out a silken cord about a half mark in length. "Have you ever seen one of these?" he asked.

Orannan studied the cord and showed a sudden expression of utter bewilderment. "It's a strangling cord! There's a fraternity of master thieves—"

"The Children of the Silence."

"That's right. That's the name I heard. I came to an inn once, and they had been there, had dispatched an entire caravan. There was a cord like this around the neck of one."

"When I saw how neatly Stoggan used his dagger, I knew he was no common servant, but I never suspected this. Why would a master thief become a healer's servant?"

"Hiding?"

"Planning something, more likely. If he'd been hiding, he'd have had something of value on him. But his purse was lean, and the only other thing he had was this cloak pin. I took it from the one who killed him." Cabanard held out the cloak pin for Orannan's inspection.

"Nice workmanship. Nothing valuable, though."

"Worth a couple of arkads, maybe. No more. And yet that robber said he had it all wrapped up like a treasure. A master thief knows value better than that." Cabanard tossed the cloak pin up and caught it. "Well, it may be no treasure, but it will serve. I lost my own clasp back in the hollow, and this will do nicely. It's a bit small—a woman's, I imagine—still, it will do the job," he said as he fastened the pin in place.

For just a moment, something plucked at Orannan's memory. Before he could pursue the thought, Cabanard's hand closed on his wrist.

"Someone's coming."

"How many?"

"Too many to fight. We'll head straight for Mistlands. It's the easiest way to lose them."

"What about Halssa's patrols?" Orannan asked.

"We have to take the chance."

They set off at a stooping run across the open grasslands. Cabanard led the way into a narrow dry ravine. They pounded on, out of sight of anyone above, forcing themselves to keep the pace despite aching muscles and fatigue and hunger and the raging fire in their lungs.

Cabanard rounded a turn in the path and nearly collided with a swordsman who had moved out of ambush just an instant too soon. He slipped the sword stroke and slammed his fist into the man's face. Snatching up the fallen blade, he began to scramble up the wall of the ravine. Orannan, having seen the encounter, was already at the top. Both men had seen Halssa's colors on the swordsman's sleeve, and now they heard the shouts from the ravine.

An arrow went wide of Cabanard, two marks to the left and low. Another hissed by close enough to hear. He dodged and ran on, gasping. The gray skies of Mistlands lay too far ahead. He could not last—neither of them could—and their enemies were closing in, Halssa's men nearest and the robbers behind them. An arrow or a sword stroke from behind, and it would all be over. Cabanard did not want to die that way. He looked for a place to make his final stand.

Far ahead, dark forms emerged from the gray curtain.

They came directly at him, skimming the ground, moving smoothly and freely, about chest-high to a man. He recognized the dark creatures of Mistlands and knew that this was truly the end. There were enemies on all sides. This battle would have no victors.

CHAPTER THIRTEEN

NORTHWARD ONCE AGAIN

Cabanard ran on. An arrow whispered very close to his ear. Others missed him by wider margins. He heard no footsteps near. His lungs were burning, and each step was like a blow, but Mistlands now lay within reach. He began to think that he might escape.

A black shape, like a shield seen edgewise, loomed before him, veered, and headed directly to intercept him. It glided smoothly about a half mark off the ground, its broad wings scarcely moving. Cabanard marked the point where their ways would cross and pressed on, ready for the clash. But when it was no more than two marks away, and he was set, sword cocked back to strike, the bog creature swerved sharply aside and upward to avoid him, and Cabanard gaped in astonishment at the sight of a human rider prone on the thing's back.

The first cries reached his ears, and as other creatures passed silently overhead and closed on his pursuers, the sounds of violent conflict swelled and rang on the cold, dank air. He heard the threatening clang of steel on steel, the shouts of rage and defiance, the screams of mortal anguish, and the indescribable death cries of the bog creatures—all blended in one hideous din.

Two of Halssa's men burst into sight, running headlong directly for him, bows in hand. Cabanard readied himself. Behind them a black shape rose and then swooped and dived for the runners. As the creature closed, the two fleeing guardsmen stopped, turned, and loosed a pair of arrows. The bog creature jerked in midair as if it had raced to the end of a tether. It wheeled end over end like a great dark cloak blowing in the wind, its long tentacles flailing wildly. Its rider went tumbling to the ground.

As the guardsmen made ready to close on the fallen rider, Cabanard moved in. The riders had spared him and attacked his enemies; that made them his friends, and here was a chance to repay them.

The guardsmen had thrown down their bows and drawn their swords to finish the rider. When Cabanard rushed upon them, sword poised to strike, free arm wrapped in his cloak, they were taken completely by surprise. He laid open a gash on one's skull with his first blow, and the man went sprawling and lay still. The other met his attack, and they exchanged hard blows. Then they parted and circled each other warily.

Cabanard's opponent was a big man, as strong as he and far less fatigued. Each blow that Cabanard parried sent a painful jolt up his arm, but he endured, letting the man exhaust himself. After one wild overhand slash that would have split him in two had it landed, Cabanard slipped his point under the man's chin, just piercing the tender flesh.

"Yield," he said, pressing home.

The man dropped his sword and held his open hands out to his sides. The two men stood facing one another, panting with exhaustion, and then Cabanard became aware of the silence. The battle was over. The other man, too, noticed the sudden stillness.

"Who won?" he gasped.

"Don't know."

"Who are you? Not Mistlander, not robber."

Cabanard merely shook his head. He was too exhausted to reply. Overhead, three bog creatures circled. He waved to them, and one bolted off toward Mistlands, while the others circled lazily over the battlefield. He heard someone approaching, loudly and clumsily, and signaled his prisoner to be silent. In a short time, a young man appeared, limping badly and supporting himself with the shaft of a broken pikestaff.

"You can rest safely here. I think your friends will be back for you," Cabanard said.

Mumbling thanks, the young man lowered himself gingerly to the ground and cradled his head on his arms. He was very pale.

"Are you badly hurt?" Cabanard asked.

"My leg."

"Broken?"

"Don't know. Hurts if I put weight on it."

With a prisoner to watch, an injured enemy nearby, and fugitives liable to appear at any moment, Cabanard could not devote time to the Mistlander. He tossed his cloak to the young man, reassured him with words, and waited.

Once again a bog creature circled overhead, and this time Cabanard could see that it was marking the place. Soon six men armed with pikestaffs appeared. He lowered his sword and greeted them in peace.

Two went at once to the side of their injured companion. Three others led the guardsmen off. The other, who appeared to be the leader, addressed Cabanard.

"Why were Halssa's men pursuing you?"

"I don't know. Ask them."

"I have asked you," the Mistlander said sternly.

"I've answered. I don't know."

One of the pair attending the injured Mistlander approached, bearing Cabanard's cloak. He and the man who had questioned Cabanard drew apart and spoke for a time in lowered voices. At last they separated, and Cabanard's questioner returned to hand him his cloak. Cabanard slung it over his shoulder.

"You attacked two men and kept them from harming one of ours. We owe you thanks," he said.

"It's no more than you did for me and my friend. If you hadn't come along, we were finished."

"We saved you by sheer chance," the Mistlander said, smiling. "Halssa's patrols have caused much disturbance on our borders. We decided to strike at them in force to let them know that their incursions could not be tolerated."

"I think you made your point. Is my friend safe?"

"There was another, dressed in the same fashion as you. He is being brought to us."

"Good. Thank you."

"Tell me, stranger, are you an enemy of Halssa?"

"All my friend and I want to do is make our way safely west, away from all this constant fighting."

The Mistlander smiled sympathetically. "Many seek to escape the present circumstances."

"We had hoped to cross Mistlands. Will you help us?"

"That we cannot do," said the Mistlander.

Cabanard felt as though a door had been slammed in his face, where moments before a broad vista had opened to the horizon. He looked at the other man, stunned, and asked, "But why not? What harm can it do you to help us?"

"The Pikemasters have decided. Mistlands is our sanctuary and will remain inviolate. Neither Halssa's forces nor his enemies nor those who flee him will enter. The years have been hard, stranger, and we will not risk all we have accomplished."

"Would it ruin everything if you allowed people to cross your lands?"

"In time it would. Already we find robbers and marauders and other violent men coming among us. To protect our own people and what we have built, we will admit no one."

Cabanard looked the Mistlander coldly in the eye. "Turning men back is no better than killing them. Between wandering bands of robbers, Halssa's patrols, lack of food, and the winter coming, there's small chance of our getting to a safe crossing."

The Mistlander raised his hand in a gesture of peace. "We are not without gratitude. We will give you food and warm clothing and an escort to a place of greater safety. But we cannot allow anyone to enter Mistlands."

The offer encouraged Cabanard. Orannan's arrival at that point restored his spirits completely. Four Mistlanders arrived with the storyteller, and Cabanard's questioner went apart with them, leaving the two friends alone.

"Halssa's combing the north for us," Orannan said anxiously, after making certain that no one could overhear him. "I heard them questioning the guardsmen, and they said they had orders to bring in an old healer and all in his party."

"Did they describe us?"

"No. 'A storyteller and a swordsman' was all they said. And a servant."

"Well, that's not us. Remember, we're woodwards, heading west to try for a new start."

"You helped one of them, didn't you? That means they'll guide us across Mistlands. We're safe now."

"Not yet. Mistlands is closed up as tight as the Headland. Nobody enters."

"What will we do, Cabanard?" Orannan blurted out in sudden terror.

"Take what we can get, I suppose. They offered food and warm clothes and an escort. That will help."

Orannan sighed like a lost soul. "I can't keep going much longer. I've been tired before and hungry, but I've never been this tired and this hungry and had an army hunting me, and robbers. Maybe you can take this, Cabanard, but I'm a storyteller, not a warrior."

"I'm not fond of it myself," said Cabanard, rubbing his shoulder. "Do you have any suggestions?"

Orannan shook his head desolately. "None."

They stood in silence, too weary to talk. Cabanard drew his cloak around him and fastened it. He was looking for a place to sit, when the Mistlanders' leader returned.

"You and your companion appear much fatigued," he said.

"We are. Hungry, too."

"We must camp here for the next two nights to care for our wounded. Stay with us. It will be safe. When we break camp, a party will guide you to the Southern Forest or Long Wood, as you choose."

The two friends agreed without hesitation. Within a short time they were seated comfortably by a low but very hot fire, drinking warmed wine and eating a stew that contained chunks of tender, juicy meat with an odd fishy taste to it. Cabanard recalled the fallen bog creature and asked no questions.

Whether out of courtesy or precaution, the Mistlanders did not require their guests to stand a turn on guard. With full bellies, a good fire, and no duties, Orannan and Cabanard rolled up in their cloaks and slept from sundown until the following midday. When they awoke, they found that three healers had come from Mistlands to tend the wounded. Cabanard, who had a soldier's practical knowledge of wounds and treatment, looked on with interest as they prepared to remove an arrow lodged in a man's chest. He would have considered such a wound fatal and put the man out of his suffering, but the Mistlands healers proceeded with unhurried confidence. First they brewed a herbal effusion for the injured man to drink. Scarcely had he finished the last drops before he was in a deep sleep. One of the healers then rubbed the skin around the injured area with a clear salve, and another, using a curious double-bladed instrument unknown to Cabanard, withdrew the arrow expertly. The man lay still, breathing evenly. The arrow came out smoothly, with little loss of blood.

Noticing Cabanard's interest, the healers invited him to assist them in setting the leg of the youth he had helped save, and he did so gladly. When all the Mistlanders had been treated, and Cabanard stood by the fireside, rubbing his shoulder, one of the healers offered to apply a salve and a fomentation to ease the soreness.

"I'll be glad to try it, healer, but I don't expect anything," he said, unfixing his cloak. "I've lived with this stiff shoulder for twenty years."

"Our medicines are very powerful. We follow the teaching of Staver the Healer."

"Staver Ironbrand? He was a swordsman."

"He was swordsman *and* healer and the last great mage of the north. Would that he were in our midst again."

Cabanard pulled off his shirt and sat by the fire as the healer directed. "There are legends that say he'll return when his people need him," he said.

"We do not believe such legends," said the healer, and Cabanard judged it best to let the conversation drop.

While Cabanard was occupied with the healers, Orannan circulated among the other Mistlanders, alert for any tales and stories they might tell around the fire. Although his fine harp was hidden in a farmhouse far to the north, and he had no prospect of touching it again for a long time, storytelling was his profession, and the opportunity to gather some new tales or rediscover forgotten old ones from the elusive Mistlanders was not to be lost.

When the three men nearest him fell silent, Orannan observed, "This was a fine victory. Your storytellers will make a good tale of it."

"They will, if any man remembers how," said one.

Orannan made no immediate response. He held out his palms to the welcome warmth of the fire, and after a time he asked casually, "Do you have no storytellers among you? We never hear the songs and stories of Mistlands."

"There's none to tell," said the Mistlander bitterly.

"But there'll be stories now. We have a victory to celebrate," said another.

"Are there no tales? No legends before today?" Orannan asked.

The man next to him said, "You forget how we came to be in Mistlands, stranger. Or perhaps you never knew. We did not come in triumph. Ask Sallers," he said, indicating the man on Orannan's other side. "He made the Long Journey, every step, and shed his blood a dozen times along the way."

Orannan turned to the Mistlander called Sallers. He was a lean, hard-looking man, as pale-skinned and weatherbeaten as his comrades. Orannan tried to judge his age but could only conclude that Sallers was something more than thirty but surely less than fifty winters old and that his years had been hard ones. His appearance and expression were not such as to encourage questions, but when Orannan hesitated, Sallers spoke.

"We'll remember this day surely, stranger," Sallers said, gazing into the fire. "It's the first victory for us since the day we left the High City to march against the Crystal Hills. They were great fighters, those white warriors. Forty of them held us off until the rest could smash the bridges behind them. They died to the last man, but there's many a song sung of that battle, and no man calls us the victors."

Orannan nodded. He knew the songs of the white legion's heroism well. He had sung them scores of times.

"So we headed home and walked into a siege," Sallers went on. "Every adventurer and mercenary and robber in the north had descended on the High City once we were gone. We tried to save our city. Four times we attacked them, and four times they broke the attack. After the fourth, there weren't enough of us left to try again. Nothing for it but to leave our homes behind and find a new one. We started west. Half the plain was burned black in front of us, and the rest was picked clean. People starved. We wintered in the mountains." He held up stump-fingered hands, with the top joints of four fingers missing. "I left those in the mountains. Two men out of every three died, but we didn't give up. We got to Long Wood in the spring. There was no welcome for us."

Sallers was still once again, looking into the fire, clenching and unclenching his maimed fingers. The other Mistlanders seemed locked each in his own bitter memories. Orannan felt the pain in the silence all around him. He was aware in a disjointed way of the turmoil that had befallen the north in the years after the overthrow of the last Vannenson ruler, but song and legend and rumor were different from the memories of a survivor. Sallers's halting account made the past come alive with a vividness Orannan the storyteller envied even as Orannan the man pitied the sufferers.

"We did things no man likes to remember, stranger. It was do them or die, and we wanted to live. The next winter we spent in Mistlands. Forty-one men, twenty-nine women, a handful of children," Sallers said. "They were from Long Wood, the women and children, all widows and orphans. They knew what might happen to a woman alone and to children. They chose Mistlands. When we came, nothing lived here but the bog creatures. We tamed them. We rebuilt the abandoned settlements. Mistlands is ours now, and no one will ever move us."

Cabanard, his shoulder covered with a cloth that gave off a sharp-scented steam, settled at Orannan's side. He appeared to have something on his mind, but he remained silent until the Mistlanders began to speak among themselves. Then he drew Orannan aside, where they could not be overheard.

"Tomorrow they return to Mistlands, and we have their promise of an escort to safety. Which way should we go?" he asked.

Without hesitation, Orannan replied, "Whichever is safest."

"If I knew, I wouldn't have had to ask. The Mistlanders think that the approaches to the Southern Forest are heavily patrolled. They don't know about Long Wood."

"Then I suppose we ought to try Long Wood."

"It looks that way, much as I hate to retrace my tracks again. We've gone north, then south, now to go north again . . . I feel trapped, as if someone has been manipulating me," Cabanard said uncomfortably. "There's something odd about all this."

"There is. Do you know, Cabanard, I just realized—when

KINGSBANE 133

they questioned the guardsman, and he told about the patrols being after the healer's party, he said nothing about the patrol we killed. It's as though that wasn't important at all."

"We know Halssa's after you."

"But the guard didn't mention me. That's the odd thing. He said, 'the old healer's party,' as if Halssa wanted all of us."

Cabanard gave a dry rasp of bitter laughter. "He'd better hurry. Half the party is dead. Maybe Traissell, too, by now."

Orannan shuddered. "Let's not talk about it."

"All right. Long Wood, then?"

"It's the only choice we have. Maybe we can hide out somewhere for the winter."

"We may have to. Snows can't be far off." Cabanard moved his shoulder and smiled at his comrade. "These Mistland healers are good. My shoulder hasn't felt this loose since I was a boy." He peeled off the cloth, now cool, and swung his arm freely, reaching high without the slightest uneasiness. "I think I'll work out with the ax for a while. I could use some practice. I can't expect to walk around Long Wood carrying a sword from one of Halssa's guards."

"Certainly not," Orannan murmured, shaking his head.

Cabanard had a good practice session, after which the Mistland healer who had treated his shoulder looked very pleased with himself. That night all slept soundly, without alarms. Just after daybreak, Cabanard and Orannan, in the company of four pikemen, set off to the northeast for the borders of Long Wood.

CHAPTER FOURTEEN

COLD PURSUIT

The innkeeper was a talkative man, and he found the solitary traveler to be a good listener. He meant to ask the young fellow, in the proper time, why he was traveling north alone at this season with a crippled leg and a crutch under his arm. There was a story in that, surely. But all in good time. Now it was the innkeeper's chance to relate the strange incidents of a few days previous, a story he had been bursting to tell to an unfamiliar ear.

"Now, when I heard the knock I was pleased. There's few travel these ways in the best of weather, and at this time of the year I sometimes go days on end without custom." The innkeeper was hunched forward on a three-legged stool, his big red-knuckled hands on his knees and a supremely earnest expression on his face. He raised one hand slowly and spread two pudgy fingers. "Two of them there was. The little one was all skin and bones, big bright eyes darting everywhere, and him hopping about like a finch. The sort of man who can slip a dagger into your ribs so smoothly you'll walk a half a greatmark before you fall dead. And the other. . . ."

The innkeeper paused dramatically. "There's men come to this inn who cut down trees as big around as this room; the woodwards of Long Wood are some of the biggest, strongest men I've ever seen. But this traveler could have picked up one of those men in each hand and thrown them out the door the way you and I would throw away an old boot. He was . . . well, massive like a boulder." Here the innkeeper let out a great breath and shook his head once more.

"Of course, I had no choice but to welcome them inside," he resumed. "I stepped over to bring in a few logs for the fire, and I just happened to glance over to the edge of the woods, and then I thought I was really done for. I caught a glimpse of three men slipping away, all carrying long pikes. And you know what that means. Mistlanders, come out of their bogs to raid Long Wood again after all these years of peace. I was sure of it. So, my friend," the innkeeper said, clapping his hands down on his knees and thrusting his head forward, "what do you think happened then?"

Brondin—for it was he who sat in the high-backed seat with his aching leg stretched out to the fire—took a sip of weak beer, put down his tankard, and said, "I know. They killed you and burned the inn to the ground."

The innkeeper gaped at him for a moment. Then, seeing the grin spread across Brondin's weary face, he burst into sputtering laughter and said, "Ah, you're too quick for me. You young fellows are altogether too quick for me. Killed me and burned the inn." He laughed again, longer and louder, and leaned over to tap the toe of Brondin's boot. "I tell you, my friend, I'm going to try that on the first of my neighbors who comes in. In truth, of course, they did nothing."

"Nothing?"

"Nothing whatsoever," the innkeeper said smugly, enjoying Brondin's obvious surprise. "The pikemen vanished, and the two at the door, well, not only did they not do anything nasty, but they were two of the pleasantest guests I've ever had stay at the inn. Later on, the little fellow told a story —well, bits and pieces of a story—of a great battle on the grasslands between Mistlands pikemen and guardsmen from the High City."

"The guardsmen were far from home."

"Ah, they be everywhere lately, even here in Long Wood," said the innkeeper in disgust. "They stopped at an inn off to the west some time back. Looking for an old healer and his companions, they were."

"Maybe Halssa's got a bellyache," Brondin suggested, grinning.

"From what I hear, it's the healer and his friends will have the bellyache if the guardsmen find them. It was said they are wanted badly, and it would not be wise for anyone to conceal them."

Brondin nodded thoughtfully and said, "I won't ask you

where you stand, innkeeper, but for my part, if this healer and his friends have made Halssa that angry, I'd give them my last pair of boots and the last daibas in my purse."

"There's none in Long Wood fond of Halssa, friend, nor fond of the usurpers he replaced. We be loyal to the Vannensons still."

"They were good rulers."

"They were, indeed." The innkeeper was silent, thinking; then he chuckled. "Now, this big burly fellow the other night was no friend of Halssa. After he'd had a bit to drink, he started to sing a song. His friend kept hushing him up, and he kept singing. A funny song it was, too, about Halssa and his sweet young bride."

"I thought the little fellow was the storyteller."

"Oh, he told about the battle, but neither one of them was a storyteller. The little fellow was insistent about that. Mind you, I think he would have been a decent one if he tried, but he must have told me twenty times that he had absolutely nothing to do with storytelling."

"It's amazing, isn't it, how people always deny their true talents?" Brondin said amiably. "Right now, I think I can display a rare talent for eating. I hope you'll not let me eat alone."

The innkeeper would think of no such thing. He gladly dined with Brondin and drank with him until well after dark, talking freely all the while. But his conversation revealed little more of value, if indeed he had given Brondin any information of value at all. Brondin was uncertain about that.

It was common knowledge by now that Halssa's men were looking for an old healer named Traissell and his servant and a swordsman and a storyteller who might be traveling with them. The travelers had not been found so far, and Halssa's men were encountering strong resistance in their search. That much was welcome news. But while it was comforting to know what had not happened, it was little help in learning where the cloak pin might be. Regaining the cloak pin was the important thing, and it seemed to Brondin to be growing more important every day.

From seemingly idle conversations like the one with the innkeeper, Brondin had learned a great deal. It was all rumor and hearsay, of course, but it was consistent; taken all together, it posed a bleak and bloody future for the north.

Halssa was deepening the harbor of the High City and building a camp to house an army from the east. Westerners were again coming north in small bands, as their people had done a generation ago. Whether these newcomers would support Halssa, join his enemies, or fight for their own interests, no one could be certain; but no man could doubt that their coming greatly increased the danger of war and a new age of fire and blood and gathering darkness in the north, with no victors but the raven, the wolf, and the worm. With the cloak pin to support his claim and to unite the warlords behind him. Brondin believed that he could force Halssa off the throne without resorting to open warfare. If it was necessary for peace, he would negotiate; he wanted peace for the north more than he wanted revenge. Others would criticize him for such a course, he knew, condemning it as weakness, but he felt that Balthid would forgive him. The north came first.

Before he left the inn next morning, Brondin had one last conversation with the innkeeper. A question had arisen in his mind, and he meant to have it answered. Something about those two curious visitors troubled him, and he found himself entertaining a wild hope.

"It didn't occur to me yesterday, but I believe I've seen that pair you spoke about," he said idly as he filled his pack with bread and cheese. "I remember particularly that the big fellow wore a cloak pin different from any I'd ever seen before. It was silver, shaped like a hand, with a big pale blue stone in the center. Did this man wear such a pin?"

"Now, that's odd," said the innkeeper. "I noticed his cloak pin myself and asked him about it. He just laughed and ignored the question, but . . . well, doesn't it seem strange to you that a great bear of a man would be wearing a cloak pin as small and delicate as a lady's? Gold and silver in it, nicely worked, and a ring of garnets. Odd, isn't it?"

Brondin struggled to keep his composure. He wanted to hug the innkeeper and set off at the greatest speed he could muster in pursuit of those two and the lost cloak pin. But he drew a deep breath and said dismissively, "Oh, perhaps it's a love token. Anyway, they headed north, did you say?"

"They did. Never said where they were going, but I saw them take the northern road."

"Then I may see them for myself one of these days."

"Perhaps you will. Good traveling, friend."

At almost the same moment, in the High City, Halssa was in a rage as the result of a message from his adviser. Karash-Kabey stood before him, solemn-faced, clutching the Doom-staff, his eyes fixed on the vacant air above Halssa's head.

"And how long has Brondin been missing from Balthid's Keep?" Halssa demanded. "Could your spy tell you that much?"

"Impossible to say precisely," the adviser responded in his deep, calm voice. "More than twelve days but not more than thirty-six, I am sure."

"In thirty-six days a man could be anywhere from the Cape of Mists to the Red Mountains. Even a puny cripple." Halssa growled, angered beyond his stock of words to express.

"I have one who can find him if my lord wishes."

Halssa looked up sharply. "The assassin?" His adviser responded with a slight nod, and Halssa said, "Do it. Send him out at once. And if anyone is with Brondin, he's to kill the lot of them! Every one, do you hear?"

"It shall be as you say."

"I should have done this the first time he got in my way. And don't bother telling me that you advised it," Halssa snapped, although his adviser showed no sign of speaking. "Well, I'm doing it now. And as soon as the first ship arrives, I'll lead an expedition against Balthid's Keep myself. Burn it to the ground and salt the ashes." Somewhat mollified by this resolution, he seated himself, looked up, and said, "So much for Brondin. Is there anything else your spy had to say?"

"Only that, my lord."

"Then go and send your assassin about his business. Tell him the quicker he is, the better my reward will be."

"My assassin requires no reward," said Karash-Kabey, and turned to make his stately way from the chamber.

Halssa looked after him and was on the verge of speaking, but he checked his tongue. There were questions he did not wish to put to this man, for he feared that he would sleep less well for knowing the answers.

Karash-Kabey descended a stair and then another and passed through a little-used door that led to another long staircase. Down he went, level after level below the palace, moving in long strides through the darkness as a man might walk a forest path under the midday sun. He came to a heavy oak door, which opened at the touch of his fingertips. As he entered, a light came to life overhead and began to glow, and a moist, dragging sound came from a far recess of the chamber.

"You have done well. One more task, and then we concentrate on the true work," said Karash-Kabey.

"Now I seek Brondin," came a rasping, inhuman voice from the dark corner.

"Yes. Find him and mark him. The other will follow."

"Other kill Brondin."

"Brondin and all with him. It is best that way, I think. Go."

Out of the shadows lurched a formless thing of an uncertain dark color. It moved and flowed, and its outline wavered and spread until it had achieved the lineaments of a great bird. Its back and the upper surfaces of its wings were a sooty black that drank the feeble light of the chamber and gave back no reflection; its undersurface was the gray of a winter sky. Turning upon Karash-Kabey eyes like embers and opening a hooked beak that was gray and smooth as polished stone, it said, *"I find Brondin, stay near until other come."*

It hobbled out the doorway into the dark corridor and there spread its wings with the muffled snap of a heavy cloak blown in a sudden gust of wind. With no further sound, it was gone.

Karash-Kabey took up a thing that appeared like a bundle of dried and blackened vines, twisted into the grotesque semblance of a gaunt and elongated human body. From a pouch around his neck he withdrew a single long white hair, which he wound thrice around the midsection of the dry black thing and fastened with an intricate knot, softly speaking an incantation as he worked.

He lay the thing on the stone floor in the center of the

chamber and began to inscribe a polygon to enclose it. At each angle, he drew a symbol. When this was done, and the polygon was complete except for one small break in the lines, he placed three candles equidistant around the twisted thing and set a fourth at its rootlike feet. He paused for a time to gather his strength and prepare himself, and then he lit the three candles and closed the figure.

He spoke a single word aloud, and the air around the fourth candle shimmered as if the candle were alight; but it burned with no visible flame. Instead, it drew to itself the light of the three, and as their light flowed inward, Karash-Kabey chanted in a tongue unheard on earth since before the rising of the mountains and the birth of the seas. His voice was not stilled until the thing stood before him, infused with demonic life, awaiting his command.

Brondin traveled steadily northward, and slowly he closed the gap between himself and the two travelers. They displayed neither the desperate haste of fugitives nor the stealth of thieves but moved at the sensible pace of the seasoned sojourner, covering the maximum distance each day without discomfort of exhaustion. Brondin could not make sense of this, but he welcomed it. He could keep up.

At a branch in the road he lost them. They had not stopped at the first inn he reached, and when the second innkeeper said that he had seen no travelers such as Brondin described, Brondin was ready to retrace his steps and take the other path. But he learned that the roads rejoined a day's travel farther on, and there, to his great relief, he picked up their track once more. They had been at the crossways inn only the day before.

Snow fell during the night, mantling fence posts and railings and covering the ground with an unbroken blanket of white. In the morning, the innkeeper announced that seven fingers' depth had fallen. It was not enough to concern oneself with in Long Wood, but there would be three times that much in the mountains and an end to traveling before long.

Brondin ate hurriedly, filled his pack, and moved on. His leg pained him constantly, and his shoulder ached, but he knew that he could not slacken his pace. He walked all that day and through the night with the aid of a small lantern.

Snow began to fall just at dawn, but he pressed on, desperate now to find his quarry before the ways became blocked.

That day, in the gray light of late afternoon, he limped painfully to a small inn at the southern tip of the Fool's Head. Wind swept across the open lake, chilling him and drilling the dry pellets of snow into his raw cheeks. The cheery warmth of the hearthside was like a deliverance. But far more welcome than the shelter and the benches and the aroma of the thick soup bubbling in a pot by the fire was the sight of the two men who sat warming their feet at the hob. One was a brisk, bright-eyed little man as slender and active as a youth; the other was a great bear of a man, big-fisted and thick-limbed, with grizzled hair and a weather-beaten face.

On pegs by the fire hung two cloaks, steaming in the heat. Brondin saw the glint of scarlet on one of the cloaks and sighed with relief. He hailed his fellow travelers as one would greet old friends.

CHAPTER FIFTEEN

THE OTHER

The innkeeper shook the wet flakes from his cloak and hung it beside the other three. He took up a stance before the newly fed fire, rubbing his red hands and pausing from time to time to blow on the fingertips. Properly warmed, he turned his back to the fire and addressed his three visitors.

"Five fingers of snow in the front yard and still falling," he announced, as if speaking of his own noteworthy accomplishment.

"If it keeps up, we may be here for a long time," said Orannan.

"It's too early for a big storm," Cabanard said confidently.

"Not any more, friend," the innkeeper said. "Five winters back, we had snow knee-deep on last day of Gleaning. Didn't see ground again until the middle part of Flowerdown." He ran his hands through his thinning hair, damp with melted snow, and rubbed them vigorously on his thighs to dry them. Cabanard mumbled sourly about northland winters, and the innkeeper cheerfully said, "Never used to be like this until the Nine Years' Winter. Now, none of you would remember those days—I don't, myself—but my father often spoke of them. He was only a boy then, about the age of my youngest, but he remembered. In all his days, up until the cold came, he never saw snow on the ground before Firstfrost, and it never stayed later than Lastfrost. The old names used to mean something then. Now they're more like a joke. Ought to change all the months' names so they make sense, that's what I say."

"Ought to change the weather. That's what I say," Cabanard muttered, and drained his tankard.

Brondin, too, emptied his tankard and signaled to the innkeeper to refill all three, inviting him to join them. As the man set about his task, Brondin said to the others, "I'm certainly glad I met you two. I'm not fond of solitary traveling, and in weather like this, well, I appreciate your letting me join you. I'll do my best not to slow you down."

"Nobody's going to walk fast in fresh snow," said Cabanard.

Orannan laughed and said to Brondin, "He'd try to walk fast if the snow were up to his chin. I'm glad you're coming along, my boy. With the two of us shouting at him, we may get him to keep a reasonable pace."

All three laughed at that, and Brondin's good spirits were unforced and unfeigned. He had found the cloak pin, and it seemed to him that neither the man who wore it nor his companion had the faintest idea of its significance. After a shared dinner and an evening's easy conversation, they had invited him to join them on their way to the Fastness. Once within the Fastness, among friends and supporters, Brondin foresaw no difficulty regaining the cloak pin.

For all his high hopes, Brondin was not blind to the possible dangers. These two were the swordsman and the storyteller Halssa sought, and that made it far more dangerous to travel in their company than to make his way alone. If they were indeed thieves, they were likely to consider him a potential victim; but he considered that unlikely. Despite his youth, Brondin had had experience in judging men. He was not always correct in his judgments, but he had felt an immediate liking for these two, and his liking grew as he learned more about them.

It was plain to him that they were not who, or what, they claimed to be. When they addressed each other or spoke of themselves, they used the names awkwardly, and Brondin, himself under a false name, recognized the sign. The very awkwardness they displayed was reassuring; clearly, they were not accustomed to traveling under false names.

Brondin was certain that the smaller one had never cut down a tree in his life and that the other had gained his skill with an ax on the battlefield. The big man had the ways of Henorik and the other western adventurers who had followed Balthid. He was slow-seeming, but his eyes missed nothing. His manner was friendly, but he kept his ax in easy reach and all entrances in clear view, and he let no one pass behind him.

Whoever they were, whatever their true destination and purpose, Brondin knew that he could not let them out of his sight. He was pleased to see them drinking so freely and glad that the snow was still falling. No one would slip away tonight. When their host returned with four brimming tankards and began to recite grim tales of frozen travelers, Brondin stretched his feet out to the fire and listened contentedly.

When they arose in the morning, the snow had stopped. The sky was bright blue, without a spot of cloud. All was utterly silent and still, and in the cold crisp air, every snow-mantled branch stood out with magical clarity. Distance, motion, and time itself seemed to have been suspended.

The three travelers filled their packs and put extra food in every available pouch, pocket, and fold of clothing. The innkeeper smiled at what seemed to be excessive caution, since they would easily reach the next inn by nightfall; but they had not told him their true plan. They intended to cross the river near there and then make their way north along the mountain trails. That route involved six days—possibly seven—of hard traveling, but the likelihood of encountering one of Halssa's patrols or a band of brigands on these trails was small.

Cabanard led the way, and they walked until midmorning with no sound but their labored breathing and sniffing and the squeal and crunch of dry powdery snow underfoot. At a narrow trail, branching off sharply, Cabanard turned eastward and finally called a halt at the edge of the trees. Without speaking, he pointed to the foot of the rocky slope, about a greatmark distant, where the narrow ford lay.

"Not frozen yet," Cabanard said. "We have to cross at the ford."

"Any chance someone is watching?" Brondin asked.

"Always that chance. I'll go first and see if it's clear on the other side." Cabanard made his way through the ankle-deep snow slowly and warily, looking in all directions. He fixed his gaze upward for a moment, and Brondin looked up to see what had caught his interest. He had just a glimpse of a pale-bellied bird soaring overhead on motionless wings;

then the bird wheeled and dropped from sight. A hawk, Brondin thought. It was hard to be sure with the sun in his eyes.

He returned his attention to Cabanard, now crossing the river, and watched him make his way up the far slope and disappear into the rocks. A little while later Cabanard emerged, ax in hand, and signaled for them to cross.

A gusty wind had risen in the river valley, and Brondin had a hard time crossing the slippery rocks under its buffeting. When he slipped a second time, narrowly avoiding a fall, Orannan lent his support. Together they made the crossing easily.

"So far we're in luck," Cabanard said, greeting them. "No sign of anyone here recently, and this wind will cover our tracks by afternoon."

"It may freeze us before that," Orannan said miserably, pulling his cloak closely around him.

"Not if we keep moving," said Cabanard, turning and leading the way into the mountains.

They worked their way about three greatmarks east, until they came upon a narrow trail; then they turned north. The wind currents in the twisted mountain passages were erratic. They walked for long stretches without feeling the slightest breeze and then suddenly rounded a curve in the trail and walked into a blast of snow-charged icy wind that plucked the breath from their lungs. In some places the way was clear, scoured to the naked rock, while in others they had to struggle through deep drifts.

Gray clouds gathered on the first afternoon, and the wind rose. They trudged on for three more days with threatening skies overhead and the sun never brighter than a distant candle behind a sheet of horn. At night, they slept in clefts and rude shelters among the rocks, with no fire to warm them.

By morning of their fourth day in the mountains, Brondin's leg had come to feel like a rod of cold iron jammed into its raw socket. He set his teeth, fixed his mind on the cloak pin, and forced himself on. They were halfway there, but he feared that he could not endure until they reached the Fastness.

Just after midday, the clouds broke and the wind died. As

if to compound their good fortune, Cabanard called a halt. While they rested in the warm sun, he announced that this night, at least, they might be able to enjoy a fire.

"There's a grove of evergreens around a spring about six greatmarks ahead. I've camped there before. Good shelter and plenty of firewood. We'll be there before dark easily," he announced.

"What if someone's already there?" Orannan asked.

"Either they make us welcome, or we throw them out into the snow. I mean to be warm tonight."

Brondin nodded vigorously in assent. He did not much want to fight anyone at the moment, but he would have battered his way through a small army to sit by a fire.

Cabanard suddenly shielded his eyes and pointed upward. "There's that bird again. I think it's waiting to make a meal of us."

"I saw it when we crossed the ford," Brondin said, when he recognized the gray shape.

"It's been following us since we left the inn."

Orannan frowned and said gloomily, "It's a bad sign, a carrion bird following us."

"I'd call it a good sign," Cabanard corrected him. "If it's been following us, that means there's no one else nearby, and our way is clear."

Orannan took reluctant comfort from that suggestion, and they resumed their march in better spirits. The sun was still above the mountains when Cabanard led them through a narrow defile and they found themselves looking up at a sloping wall of deep green. There, on a south-facing hillside sheltered from the winds, a grove of evergreens had sprung up and survived. Those nearest, at the lower end of the slope, towered some ten or twelve marks high. The sight of them was as welcome to the travelers as it was surprising.

By sunset, they had set up camp and were settled around a cheerful fire, all cold and discomfort forgotten, dining on hard bread and cheese and dry salted meat as if they were banqueting on dainties. Brondin lay with his bad leg nearest the fire, basking in the healing heat. Orannan sat cross-legged, facing the flame with his eyes closed and a half smile of pleasure on his face, like an ecstatic worshiper. Cabanard, after laying a log on the blaze with architectural precision, unfastened his cloak and seated himself on a fallen trunk. He spread out the cloak before the fire near his feet, tossing the cloak pin carelessly upon it. Brondin saw this and winced, but he said nothing.

Brondin lay back, pillowing his head on his pack, and fell into a light, dreamless sleep. He awoke in the night, with the stars brilliant overhead and the warmth of the fire at his side, feeling contented and comfortable. Yawning and stretching, he flexed his knee cautiously. The anticipated stab of pain did not come. He rubbed the leg, probing the tender spots where poorly knit bones created pockets of pain, and found that the fire had baked out much of the soreness and stiffness. His leg felt better than it had for a long time.

He propped himself on his elbows and looked around. Close to the fire, rolled up in his cloak, Cabanard was snoring regularly. The fire had sunk by this time, and Brondin pulled himself to his feet to feed it.

He lifted the thick chunks easily, with no discernible strain on his leg, and laid them carefully on the fire. As the flames rose, crackling loudly in the stillness, Orannan sat up, rubbing his eyes.

"Sorry if I woke you. The fire was getting low," Brondin said.

Orannan yawned and then climbed to his feet, rubbing his neck and rolling his head from side to side. "Stiff," he said. "Must have rolled too far from the fire."

"It's a good fire. I'll hate to leave it."

"Three more days and we'll be sleeping in the Fastness. That's what Cabanard said."

The fire had caught, and the flames were rising between the two men. Brondin settled down once more, rolling himself snugly in his cloak, and was just drifting off to sleep when he heard Orannan's voice but could not distinguish the words. He raised his head and heard Orannan say, "Yes, that's what it is. Someone's coming."

At the words, Cabanard came wide awake, and his hand went for the ax. Brondin reached for his dagger but did not draw it. He rose, letting his cloak fall away, and as he rose, he saw a very tall figure dressed in a dark robe moving smoothly toward the fire. Orannan, on the opposite side of the fire from his companions and nearest the newcomer, extended his arm in welcome. "There's room by the fire, traveler. Come and warm your bones and take—"

His words turned into a choked cry as the stranger's hands shot out and clamped around his throat, and he was lifted from the ground. As Brondin drew his dagger, he saw Cabanard, ax upraised, dash to the far side of the fire to close with the towering figure.

The intruder was even taller than it had first appeared, nearly a mark in height, enshrouded from head to foot in a dark robe, with a cowl pulled forward to conceal its features. It made no sound and seemed oblivious to the gashes Orannan was inflicting on its forearms. Hands extended straight before it, the intruder held Orannan off the ground in a rigid grip, as steady as if it held a bundle of rags instead of a wildly hacking, kicking, slashing man. It was as unheeding of Cabanard's attack as it was of his friend's struggles.

Cabanard struck a powerful overhand blow at the attacker's shoulder. It landed squarely on the collarbone and drove deep into the breast. It had no effect whatsoever. Jerking the ax free, Cabanard struck again, bringing the ax upward, crashing into the rib cage and sinking to the heart, lodging the axhead tightly in the wound. As Cabanard struggled to pull his weapon loose, the creature, as if first aware of his efforts, struck him one sweeping blow that knocked him sprawling.

By now Brondin was on the attack. He drove his dagger into the creature's throat, thrusting upward with all his strength and then driving a second hard blow home before the hooded face even turned toward him. The creature flung aside Orannan's limp form and stretched out its hands to clutch at Brondin. The hands were dark, with long, supple fingers, and Brondin shuddered as they brushed his face. They felt like the legs of a spider. He stared into the shrouded face; there was nothing within that cowl but darkness.

Cabanard returned to the attack. Seizing a long chunk of wood, he landed a blow on the creature's head that would have crushed the skull of a giant. The thing did not even turn. With the ax still lodged in its ribs, it started forward in a smooth, gliding motion, its spidery fingers outstretched for Brondin's throat.

Brondin tried to sidestep, missed his footing, and went sprawling on the trampled muddy ground. He scrambled to his feet, and before the thing could turn, got to the opposite side of the fire. Whatever this monstrous thing was, it was clearly after him. It seemed to be invulnerable, but he hoped that if he could hold it off for a time, he and Cabanard might be able to overcome it by their combined efforts.

He stood his ground, dagger extended before him, waiting for the thing to move one way or the other so that he could move correspondingly and keep the fire between them. Instead, the creature paused only for an instant and then strode forward into the chest-high flames, scattering burning brands and embers as its hands groped for Brondin.

Brondin staggered back in horror. His heel tangled in Cabanard's cloak, and once again he fell. The dagger flew from his hand and vanished in the surrounding dark. As the grip closed on his throat, his searching hand fell on the cloak pin. Instinctively, he thrust it into his attacker's forearm and raked it toward him.

At the touch of the cloak pin, an inhuman shriek rent the air, and the grip on Brondin's throat loosened. He was released. The thing stood over him, its robes smoldering from the passage through the flames, its long arms flung up as if in agonized lament. Brondin struck out again with the cloak pin, puncturing its leg, and the thing shrank back. Climbing to his feet, dodging the wildly flailing arms, Brondin pursued the attacker relentlessly, thrusting and raking and tearing at the thing as it writhed and screamed.

Cabanard, meanwhile, had taken up his makeshift club once more and was dealing great blows. They fell unnoticed on the thing's head and shoulders; all its fear was for the cloak pin that flashed like a golden dagger in the fire glow, wrenching forth an unearthly cry each time it struck home.

The thing crumpled and fell. Brondin flung himself astride it, driving blow after blow into its chest, until at last it lay silent and motionless. The ax handle protruded from its ribs; it had taken a score of crushing blows from Cabanard and had been torn and pierced by the cloak pin until its dark robe lay in tatters; yet not one drop of blood had it shed.

Brondin climbed unsteadily to his feet and stood panting for breath. He looked down on the fallen creature, lying with an arm and shoulder in the fire, its robe burning and smoking.

"What was it?" Cabanard asked.

"I don't know. Nothing human."

Cabanard knelt and drew aside the cowl to reveal a head devoid of all human features. It was simply an elongated dark burl, deeply rutted, with no trace of humanity on it. With a grunt of disgust, he replaced the cowl. He rose and looked squarely at Brondin.

"It appeared to me that this thing was after you."

"I think it was," Brondin said. "As soon as I came near it, it went for me."

"Why?"

"I don't know. Let's see to your friend."

Orannan's throat was lacerated and badly bruised, and he found it painful to swallow, but the assurance that his attacker was dead and the sight of its body did much to restore him.

Cabanard dragged the carcass to one side, built up the fire, and then said, "I think we'd better talk, son. If something like that comes after you, and you kill it with a cloak pin, you're no common traveler." His manner was not threatening, but it was clear that he meant to know.

"I'm not. But neither are you two."

Cabanard looked a bit surprised by his remark, but after a moment he smiled and nodded. "Maybe it's time for all of us to say who we are. There's something I want to know first, though. Is Halssa your friend or your enemy?"

"Halssa had my father killed, and he's tried to have me killed, too. If I didn't know he had no magic, I'd say he sent this thing after me. He would if he could, I'm sure."

"Why does Halssa hate you so much?"

"The blood of rightful rulers is in my veins, and Halssa has usurped my place. I mean to get it back, and he knows I do. I'm Brondin, son of Balthid and Dolsaina: Brondin of Balthid's Keep, and Halssa's dearest enemy."

With a cry of joy, Cabanard sprang to his feet. "You're Balthid's boy! I should have recognized you right away!" He laughed and threw his arms around the astonished Brondin. Then he held Brondin at arm's length and studied his features, nodding in apparent satisfaction. "That's Balthid's nose, yes, and Balthid's chin. Oh, yes." He peered closer and said, "Your eyes are green. You got that from your mother, did you?"

"I did."

"Well, you got your fighting spirit from your father, that's plain enough. Oh, Balthid would have been pleased to see you tear into that thing with only a cloak pin in your hand. You did your father proud, my boy."

"Did you know him well?"

Cabanard laughed and repeated, "Did I know . . . ?" before bursting into renewed laughter. "I came east with Balthid when I was younger than you! He led me into my very first battle. Did he never speak of Cabanard?"

"He did, indeed!" Brondin cried. "You were one of the Iron Hundred. You saved his life at the last battle near Southmark, before he settled at Balthid's Keep."

"He'd saved mine often enough, son. If he hadn't taken me east with him, I'd have been hanged before the year was out." Cabanard shook his head and murmured, "Balthid's son." He chuckled, rubbed his shoulder, and shook his head, as if still unable to believe that this encounter had taken place.

Orannan, clearing his throat, said hoarsely, "And my name is Orannan. I'm Orannan the teller of tales. You may have heard of me."

"I heard you tell of the battle of the Stone Hand and the death of Colberane," Brondin said at once. "I was only a boy. We were visiting someone. I can't remember who or where, but I remember your tale well."

"You do?"

"I could never forget it. I've heard the annals and sometimes recited them, but the way you told it, I almost felt as if I were there. When you described the giant gray men bursting out of the ground . . . and the coming of the dragon . . . and the white legion!"

"That was always one of my best tales," Orannan said.

"When we get to the Fastness, I hope you'll tell it again."

"Oh, I shall, my friend, I certainly shall," said Orannan, greatly pleased.

"Tell me, Brondin," Cabanard asked, "why is the master

of Balthid's Keep traveling about the north in winter, with no guards, not even a sword at his side, when Halssa's bent on killing you?"

"That's a fair question. I was looking for this," Brondin replied, holding up the cloak pin.

He told them the whole story, beginning with the day he first learned of the theft. They listened, fascinated, and then told him of their own adventures and the finding of the cloak pin on Stoggan's body.

"I knew there was something . . . some legend . . . I just couldn't remember," Orannan said.

"Well, now we all know a lot more," said Cabanard.

"More, but not enough," Brondin said. "I'd like to know whether Stoggan was working for Halssa or someone else or just for himself. And I wish I knew who sent that assassin and whether another will follow this one."

"Halssa's no sorcerer, but I've heard stories about his adviser," Orannan said.

"So have I. Never believed them, but now. . . ." Brondin glanced at the still, dark form lying near them. "I guess the magic isn't dead, after all."

"I think you hold some powerful magic in your hand," Cabanard said, pointing to the cloak pin. "It destroyed that creature. Magic against magic."

"We all fought it."

Cabanard shook his head. "I struck it two killing blows with the ax, and a score more with that log, and it didn't even notice me. Orannan nearly severed its wrist, but it hung on. It didn't show any reaction until you jabbed it with the cloak pin."

"Yes. Well, in that case, we'd better get to the Fastness as quickly as we can. Now that the cloak pin has shown its power, there may be more attempts to take it."

First light was rising in the east by this time. They readied themselves for the trail, and when they turned their attention to the body of the night attacker, they marveled and shuddered at the sight it presented to them. All human semblance was gone. It lay like a bundle of dry blackened sticks wound in moldy rags, and a faint stench of decay hung over it, mixed with the acrid smell of burnt cloth. They dragged it to the fire and flung it on; then they fed the flames until they rose high overhead and the heat drove them back. Only when the fire was sinking and all trace of the thing was reduced to indistinguishable embers did they set out for the Fastness.

CHAPTER SIXTEEN

CAUGHT IN A WEB OF STONE

The sun had scarcely passed the mountaintops when the sky rapidly clouded over, and soon a dry powdery snow began to fall. In the windless passages, it caused the travelers little difficulty; but when it was whipped up and whirled in all directions by a sudden gust, the snow became an obscuring, shifting wall of whiteness that slowed their progress to one cautious step, and a pause, and another groping step, until they could once more see the way before them.

By afternoon they had covered little more than twenty greatmarks, and the effort had exhausted them. Brondin's leg was aching once again; Orannan staggered, collapsed twice, and then walked unsteadily; even Cabanard plodded with weary, dragging steps. They slept that night in an alcove, sheltered from the worst of the wind but chilled to the bone by the relentless cold.

In the morning, Orannan was shivering uncontrollably and could scarcely stay on his feet. With the help of his companions, he forced himself on until midday, but at last he sank down and could go no farther.

"His head is burning, and his body is cold," Cabanard said after a quick examination. "It's the winter sickness."

"Can he go on?"

"Not for at least a day. It makes a man weak as water. He needs rest in a warm place," Cabanard said, glancing at the barren, windswept stone all around them.

"Could we get him to the Fastness? They could treat him properly there."

"At our best speed, we might get to the Fastness by tomorrow. Carrying him would add at least another day, if we could do it and not be caught by a patrol. And by then, even the healers at the Fastness might not be able to help him. We have to find shelter here."

"It's a bad place."

"The worst. Halssa's men are thick as flies in this part of the mountains." Cabanard sighed and began to strip off his excess baggage, tossing it by the side of the road. "Help me move him over here by these rocks," he said. "Pile all this around him to break the wind a little. I'll scout up ahead."

Brondin stooped awkwardly over his sick companion, arranging all their packs into a low windbreak. Orannan was shivering incessantly. His teeth chattered, and his face was pale. He half opened his red-rimmed eyes, licked his dry lips, and said in a croaking voice, "I'm sorry. Too weak . . . cold."

"We all need a rest, Orannan. Cabanard's looking for a place where we can lie up for a day or two, maybe build a fire."

"Cold," said Orannan faintly, shaking from head to foot.

The sky began to clear. As the first full rays of sunlight touched him, Brondin moved Orannan into the warmth and spread his own cloak over the sick man. He leaned back against a rock, easing the weight on his leg, and gazed idly up at the rocky slopes on either side of the path. They were as barren as the blade of a knife: stony wastes with no trace of life on them. His eyes swept back and forth over the desolation of gray and white, and then they lit on a spot of black. About halfway up the eastern slope was a ledge covered with a tumble of loose rock, and in the middle of the rock was what appeared to be the opening of a cave.

Brondin shielded his eyes, peered hard at the black spot, and became convinced that he had found the shelter they sought. The sun would fall on that slope all afternoon, and they could close up the opening and trap the warmth for the night, sealing out the wind. It was high up and would be a difficult climb, although not impossible. The ledge would make a fine observation point.

As he studied the spot, a motion in the sky caught his attention. The bird that had followed them from the inn followed them still. It dipped and circled and then rose in an ever-widening spiral. Suddenly it shot northward like an arrow.

Orannan cried out and began to thrash about, shouting words and phrases that made no sense to Brondin. As soon as he lay quietly once again, Brondin pulled the cloaks back around him and rearranged the packs. It was clear that Orannan was very sick. He could scarcely be expected to recover in a single day.

At the sound of running footsteps, Brondin drew his dagger and readied himself. It was Cabanard, breathless and exhausted.

"Ran all the way," he said between deep gasping breaths. "Full patrol . . . up the trail. Coming this way."

Brondin pointed to the ledge. "I think that's a cave. Have we time to reach it?"

Cabanard looked up and said, "Let's go. Take the packs. I'll carry Orannan."

The way was made doubly difficult for each man by his burden and by the urgency of flight. They were only a mark below the ledge when a cry arose from the trail, and an instant later an arrow struck sparks from the rock a half mark wide of Brondin.

Cold made the bowmen's fingers clumsy. Three more arrows clattered uselessly against the rocks, and then Brondin was sprawled on the ledge, his hands extended to haul Cabanard and Orannan to safety.

The opening was sizable, and once Cabanard had stowed Orannan safely inside, he returned to the ledge and stretched out beside Brondin to look down on their pursuers.

"What do you think they'll do?" Brondin asked.

"Probably set up a guard here to seal us in and then wait for us to run out of food and water."

"Is the cave deep?"

"Didn't bother to look."

"I have a lantern in my pack," Brondin said. "I'll go in and see how far back it goes."

He emerged a short time later, looking gloomy. "It's only about four marks deep; then it looks as though it's collapsed."

"Could we clear it?"

"Depends on how much rock fell and how much time we have."

Cabanard nodded. "I'll go in and look. You keep an eye

KINGSBANE 157

on the patrol. Shove a rock over the edge now and then so
they don't get comfortable."

Cabanard drew back and reentered the cave. Brondin kept
watch, and when five of the patrol clustered together, he
hurled a rock the size of a man's head directly into their
midst, hitting one on the foot. A dozen arrows hissed by him
in angry and futile retaliation. After that, the patrol kept out
of sight. Brondin rolled a rock over the edge from time to
time, but had no further success.

Toward dusk, he saw two men starting to make their way
up the opposite slope. They were archers, and they carried
full quivers. He worked his way back from the edge and
entered the cave.

Cabanard had cleared away a considerable number of
rocks, and his face gleamed with perspiration in the lantern's
beam. When Brondin advised him of the patrol's latest move,
he said, "That means they plan to come in. There were six
bowmen in that patrol. The two on the opposite slope will
keep us pinned in here so the others can get to the ledge.
Then they'll just work their way in step by step and let off
an arrow at anything that moves."

"What can we do?"

"Not much, unless we can get through these rocks. They
probably won't do anything until it's light, but I'm not sure
that's enough time."

"If we both worked at it, we'd have a better chance."

"One of us has to keep watch. I don't think they'll try
anything in the dark, but I could be wrong."

"Then you keep watch for a while. I'll come out when I'm
tired," Brondin said. "I've got a bad leg, Cabanard, but I'm
not a weakling." Without waiting for Cabanard's response,
he pushed past him and set to work.

They worked through the night in turns, until Brondin
broke through to the far side of the rockfall. By removing
all the smaller rocks, they had made a narrow tunnel just
big enough to crawl through. The rest of the rocks were too
huge for their combined strength; but as they worked, it had
become clear to them both that this was not a random pile
of fallen rock. The roof was firm. All the boulders had been
brought into the cave and placed carefully, and the inter-

stices had been filled with smaller stones until the cave was solidly blocked for about six marks' distance.

When they saw, beyond the blockage, a cave descending to the limits of the lantern's beams, they knew that they had chanced upon one of the old escape tunnels from the Fastness, sealed to prevent the escape of the Lool in the dark times. The Lool no longer prowled the tunnels; they were spared that horror, but the way to the Fastness through the tunnels might be long and tortuous, and their food and water —and most important, the oil for the lantern—were low.

They hauled Orannan through the narrow tunnel and laid him down, securely wrapped in all three cloaks. This done, they doused the lantern and sat down to rest.

"I think we ought to stay right here until Orannan can walk," said Cabanard. "It's not so cold, and we can take turns resting until we're ready to move on."

"What if they come in after us?"

"I don't think any man's fool enough to crawl through there in the dark. If one of them is, we'll get ourselves a bow and some arrows. More likely, they'll seal us in."

"We don't have much choice, do we?"

"If you hadn't noticed the cave, we wouldn't even be alive by now. We're way ahead," said Cabanard. "Do you mind taking the first turn at watch? I'm tired."

Brondin was exhausted, but he agreed without hesitation. Cabanard needed rest more than he. In a short time, Cabanard's regular breathing gave way to low snoring.

Seated in the darkness, Brondin strained to keep awake and alert. He thought of all that had befallen him since that day in the treasure room of Balthid's Keep, when his fingers had sought the cloak pin and closed on emptiness. He had escaped the traps of enemies and the betrayal of false friends, destroyed a monstrous creature that even a tough old campaigner like Cabanard could not overcome, pressed on despite all hardships, and regained the cloak pin. He reached into his shirt, where he had placed it for safekeeping, and its warm smooth touch reassured him. The way had been hard, and the way ahead might be harder still, but he would endure and prevail. Even now, with an enemy at his back and a legend-haunted path into darkness his only escape, Brondin felt that he was not fleeing but rather approaching some unknown goal; that whatever he had done thus far was only a prelude—his great task lay before him.

Then he shook his head and smiled at his own soaring fantasies. It was all very well to dream of glory, but the truth of things was sobering. He was a cripple, a hunted man, a would-be leader whose followers were far away. Even if he made it safely back to Balthid's Keep with the cloak pin in his possession, those who wished to mock him and deny his claim would find reason to do so, and those who had been loyal to him would remain loyal. His advisers had known this all along and had tried to tell him. That was the way of people, and it would not change for a legend and a bit of jewelry.

Yet the cloak pin had destroyed the demonic thing that came upon them; Brondin knew that as surely as he knew the pain in his leg. His had been the wielding hand, but the power was in the cloak pin. The creature had shrieked and known its doom at the first touch. There was magic in all this, surely—magic to summon such a thing and bring it upon him, and magic in its destruction. Whatever men might say, the magic was not gone from the northern lands.

A distant voice and the grating of stone on stone brought him instantly out of his reverie. A glimmer of light shone at the far end of the narrow tunnel through which they had passed, and the voice came again, louder and clearer this time, though muffled, as if the speaker were shouting into a cauldron.

He heard Cabanard stir and then felt a firm grip on his wrist. "Don't show your face, or you may get an arrow in the eye. Answer if you like, but keep hidden," Cabanard said in a subdued voice.

"You in there! Fugitives!" the voice cried again.

"What do you want?" Brondin responded.

"Come out, all three of you. Come out now, and you won't be harmed in any way."

"Who are you, and what do you want with us?"

"We serve Halssa, King in the High City. We seek information about men who plot against our master."

Brondin heard Cabanard's low laughter near at hand. "Halssa's learned how to be a ruler: see a plot everywhere you look."

"What shall I tell them, Cabanard?"

"Nothing useful."

Brondin waited a moment. The voice called to them again, and he responded. "Halssa's men never come this far west."

"We're in pursuit of our master's enemies. If you give us useful information, you'll be well rewarded."

"You can't fool us. You're nothing but a gang of robbers," Brondin shouted.

There was no immediate response. After a time, a new voice addressed them, saying, "One of you can come out and see for himself that we wear Halssa's colors. We give you our word. We won't try to hold him. It's daylight out here. You can see us plainly."

"Thieves! Robbers!" Brondin cried with a convincing show of righteous rage. "You won't take us with a trick like that!"

Cabanard laughed. "That's good. That'll get them all riled up," he said approvingly.

"It won't get us out of here."

"Your father led me out of worse places than this, lad. We'll get out, never fear."

The confidence in Cabanard's voice was welcome, even though Brondin could not bring himself to share it. He knew that any escape from this cave depended more on sheer good fortune than on his own or his friends' ability.

"You in there! Hear this!" shouted the original speaker. "We are Halssa's men. You can believe that or not. If you don't come out right now, we'll seal you in. You can die believing whatever you like."

Neither Brondin nor Cabanard replied. They waited silently for what seemed a very long time, and then they heard the first rock being jammed into place. The grating and jarring of stone on stone went on, ever more muffled, until it was no more than a faint and faraway rasp sensed as much by vibration as by sound.

Then came a silence broken only by their own breathing and the weak moaning and muttering of Orannan. Brondin could hear himself swallow.

"Time for a look around," said Cabanard as casually as if he were about to inspect a room at an unfamiliar inn. "I have a few candle stubs. We'll use them and save the lantern." He struck sparks from his flint and steel and coaxed into life a tiny flame, from which he lit a candle about as long as his thumb. The first thing he did was inspect Orannan.

"He's having bad dreams, but at least he's sleeping. Stopped shivering, too. He'll be ready to travel on before long."

"Do you really believe this will lead us to the Fastness?" Brondin asked.

"If the old stories are true, it will."

He returned long afterward, triumphantly bearing a fragment of a torch. It was a treasure more valuable, under the circumstances, than a chest of jewels. The torch was ancient, dusty, dry, and brittle as an icicle under his touch, and it burned with the eagerness of straw. But it was easily ignited, and its momentary warmth and brilliance were welcome.

By the time Orannan felt strong enough to walk, their light supply was down to two short candle stubs plus Brondin's lantern. They judged the oil supply to be sufficient for two days' low burning. Their food, cut to half rations, would last them three days. Cabanard was confident that they would be under the heart of the Fastness in a single day of walking.

Cabanard led the way, with Orannan following close behind him and Brondin bringing up the rear. Their progress was easier than it had been since they had left the last inn, and except for the eerie swoop and reach of shadows and the hollow echoing of every sound, it was almost pleasant. The surface underfoot was smooth and level, the temperature cool without severity. The way ran straight for a long distance, with a downward slope so gentle as to be barely perceptible. It curved left and then sharply right, leveled for a short way, and then descended steadily for what must have been three full greatmarks before again leveling off.

They walked on in silence. The echoes made talking difficult and unpleasant, and so there was no conversation along the way. The first time they spoke was when Cabanard stopped and raised the lantern over a heap of bones. They were human bones, clean and white as if they had been boiled, jumbled together carelessly. They could not have fallen that way by themselves, but there was no sign of another's presence.

"The Lool got this poor fellow," Orannan said.

"How can you tell?" Brondin asked.

"The Lool guarded these tunnels, ate everyone who set foot in them, until Staver Ironbrand destroyed it."

"What did it look like, Orannan?"

"No one knows. Big, I suppose. Fast. Ferocious."

"No chance the Lool might have escaped, is there? I'd hate to turn a corner and . . . it's dead for certain, isn't it?"

"The Lool is dead, no question about it."

"How?"

Orannan scratched his head and shrugged. "I've heard different stories," he said. "According to one, Ironbrand turned himself into a dragon. According to another, he became a great white wolf. Whatever he became, it was too much for the Lool."

"How did Ironbrand get out? Do the stories tell that?" Cabanard asked.

"Magic."

Cabanard grunted, lowered the lantern, and stepped out. They walked on, silent again, and came at last to a point where the smooth stone underfoot gave way to spongy dirt, humped and mounded into uneven hillocks. Above them, the roof of the cave arched to heights lost in shadow. Cabanard turned to his companions with a look of triumph on his weary features.

"We're under the Fastness. All we have to do now is find the way up," he said.

"There's only one way—a well that opens in a room at the very center of the innermost tower. That's how the forces of the Scarlet Ordred took the Fastness. I know the story well," said Orannan.

"Does the story give directions?"

"No. It just says the well is at the center, that's all."

Cabanard sighed and said, "Stories never tell the important things."

They stepped forth once more. The going was hard for Brondin on the slippery, yielding ground, but he kept up with the others. They wandered aimlessly. Cabanard's efforts to keep a straight track to the center were thwarted by the undulating surface. They came upon heaps of brittle bones with dispiriting frequency. When Brondin commented on the grim sight, Cabanard assured him that the bones were a good sign.

"The more bones, the closer we are to the well," he said. "The old masters used to throw their prisoners down, and the Lool waited just below for his meal. Isn't that right, storyteller?"

"That's what the stories say," Orannan assured him.

At the top of one rise, the ground did not fall away on the other side but sloped steadily upward as far as the lantern could reveal. Cabanard hurried forward, and the light glinted off a field of bones, lying as thick as shells on a sea strand.

"This is it! The well! We've found it!" he cried exultantly. He ran to the crest of the slope, his feet crunching the brittle bones.

He stopped, raised the lantern, and looked up. Slowly, he let the lantern drop to his side. Orannan reached him first. He took the lantern, directed its light upward, and groaned. As Brondin struggled to rejoin them, he heard Orannan say the single word, "Blocked."

CHAPTER SEVENTEEN

WHEN THE SUN
SHINES UNDERGROUND

Three massive metal bars crossed the well opening about a mark up from the point where it curved into the roof of the cavern. They were anchored firmly into the wall at either side. Upon them, great slabs of stone had been laid and closely fitted. On top of those slabs, in all likelihood, was piled more stone to the top of the well, sealing off the tunnels forever. The three companions stared up at the end of their hopes. One by one, they lowered their eyes in despair and sank to the ground in silence.

After a time, Cabanard took up the lantern and directed its feeble beams around them. "There's wood all over the place," he said.

"What good will that do us now?" Brondin responded.

"More good than sitting in the muck and feeling sorry for ourselves. Come on, let's make a fire so we can take a proper look at things."

The wood was all finished lumber, trimmed and smoothed, with holes where pegs had once been driven. They quickly gathered enough for a small fire. When it was burning brightly, they could see a great supply scattered about.

"They must have used a lot of scaffolding to get those bars in place," Brondin said.

"Lucky for us they left all this wood down here," said Cabanard, pulling a heavy beam close to the fire and seating himself on it.

"What's lucky about it? We can't eat wood," Orannan said crossly.

"If we can see, maybe we can find a way out," said Cabanard, unruffled. "According to everything I've ever heard, there are fourteen tunnels leading from this cave. We know

164

one of them is sealed, so we can't go back the way we came. That leaves thirteen."

"Some of them are still blocked."

Cabanard shrugged. "Some aren't. We have to take our chances."

Orannan followed Cabanard to where a stack of long beams lay, and they set to work. Brondin went off by himself. He came upon the remains of several torches, two of them scarcely used. He brought his findings back to the fireside and went out again with one of the torches in hand, searching the ground closely. If the workmen had left behind torches and scaffolding, they might also have left lanterns and oil, perhaps even a water bottle. It was worth the seeking.

At the bottom of the central rise he walked around one hummock, climbed another, and surveyed the surroundings, with the torch held high over his head. Something glinted mirror-bright in the distant shadows. Such a reflection was most likely to come from a manmade object, and Brondin made the best speed he could over the soft ground in which his crutch sank at every step. The closer he came, the more brightly the thing gleamed. Reaching it at last, he looked closely and then stepped back, awed by the sight. Before him, half buried in the dank earth, was a golden breastplate. From its size and its ornate design, it could only be the breastplate of Korang the Warmaker.

Brondin knew the story of Ironbrand well. He had always believed it true, but this tangible evidence of its truth brought a lump to his throat and made his heart beat faster. As he gazed down on it, he recalled the testing of Staver, his ancestor, and felt hope rising within him.

He jammed his torch into the ground and tugged at the breastplate. It came free easily, and he laid it flat and began to brush away the dirt with his fingers. There were dents that must have been the work of the Iron Angel and a long furrow scored along the ribs by that fabled blade of deliverance.

As he wiped the last smudges from the golden surface, he heard the sound of his name echoing through the deep recesses. He made his way to the top of the rise and waved his torch back and forth, shouting, "Cabanard! Orannan! Come see what I've found!"

A light bobbed toward him, and he soon could make out

the figures of his friends approaching. With a final wave of the torch, he retreated over the brow of the hummock. Thrusting the torch into the ground before the breastplate, he stepped behind it and raised it erect for them to see.

They arrived together and reacted as one, crying out in surprise and throwing up a hand to shield their eyes from the dazzling golden glare of reflected torchlight. Brondin cried, "It's the breastplate of Korang! It was flung down here when the Fastness fell!"

Still squinting, Orannan came closer and stretched out his hand to touch the breastplate gingerly. "It looks just the way the legends say it should," he murmured.

"Look there and there," Brondin said, pointing eagerly. "Those are the marks of the Iron Angel."

Orannan glanced up, wide-eyed. He said nothing but crouched to inspect the markings more closely.

"Cabanard, come and look," Brondin called. "This is too big even for you. Korang must have been a giant."

Cabanard did not reply. He stood, torch raised, his eyes fixed on a point a few marks distant. He ran toward it, past his uncomprehending friends, skidding and sliding down the slope. Once on the spot, he stopped, tugged at something buried, and at last raised aloft a sword and scabbard. Jewels and gold glinted from beneath the covering of muck, and a leather belt fell away in rotted bits as Cabanard flourished the magnificent weapon.

"Korang's sword! Look at it!" he cried exultantly. "What a piece of work!"

He brought it to where the others stood and quickly cleaned away the surface dirt. The sword seemed to grow as its brightness increased. Stood on end, it came to Cabanard's chin. Even his big hands had ample room to grip it and some to spare.

When he drew it from the scabbard, the blade flashed as if newly forged. Cabanard stepped clear of the others and swung the sword in an arc. It cut through the air with the low hollow hum of a wind in the forest.

"Beautiful," he murmured. "With a sword like this, I'll never run from Halssa's patrols again." He cut the air with three more passes before sheathing the blade. "I saw something shine, but I wasn't sure. It blinded me for a bit. It was like looking into the sun—that bright. Wasn't it, Orannan?"

The storyteller nodded and said, "Yes, just like. . . ." He fell silent, frowned, and then asked Cabanard, "Do you remember what Janneret said just before he died?"

"The healer's friend?"

"Yes. He said something about the sun shining underground. We'd find something when the sun shines underground. Don't you remember?"

"It was all gibberish to me. I don't remember any of it."

Orannan pressed his fists against his temples in an effort to recall the prophecy. His memory, honed by long practice, served him well. " 'Three will find what may be found when the sun shines underground.' That's it. And it's come true."

"What else did he say? Can you remember?" Brondin asked.

"He said that two would go early to their graves, and it happened. Daike and Stoggan were killed."

"Janneret died, too. That makes three," Cabanard pointed out.

Orannan dismissed the objection with a gesture. "He meant Daike and Stoggan. Remember, he said, 'One will speak and then be still.' That was his prophecy for himself. It came out just as he said."

"Is that all he said?"

"There was more. One would fight, and one would burn, and one would bleed. And one would steal and another save. I can't recall exactly how he put it. He only said it once, and it took us all by surprise. He'd never spoken before."

"Try to remember, Orannan. Did he say anything that might have been about a way out of this place?"

"I don't think so."

Cabanard said sourly, "If he did, we'll only understand it after we're out. That's always the way with prophecies. Let's stop talking and find some more torches."

Cabanard's words brought them back to the reality of their position. With less than two days' rations left, they had no time to spare. If they followed one false trail and were forced to backtrack, they might not have the strength to go on.

They found no oil but enough torches to give them six

days' light, keeping Brondin's lantern for a last resort. Back at the fireside, they took a skimpy meal and a short rest before setting forth to seek their escape.

After about a half day's walking, they noticed that the high roof was beginning to curve downward and the walls to narrow. Soon they were once again enclosed in a stone shaft, with a firm surface underfoot. The tunnel rose for a short way and then leveled. It continued to run level, curving and recurving, for about another half day's walking, and then it forked. One branch led upward, the other down.

Cabanard stopped, turned to Brondin, and asked, "Which way?"

"They must both lead out."

"They might."

Brondin looked first at one dark opening, then at the other. There was nothing to choose between them but whether he preferred to proceed uphill or downhill. He scratched his head and then dug into his purse and took out a daiba.

"If it shows dunes, we go uphill. Agreed?" he asked. When they nodded, he sent the coin spinning upward. It fell at Cabanard's feet.

"Tree," the swordsman said. "We go down."

They had walked only a short way when they came upon a heap of bones. After a glance, they studied them closely with fascination and a growing uneasiness. What had appeared at first sight to be human bones were different from any they had seen before. They looked like the remains of a human being compressed to half its height and twice its width. The arm and leg bones were short and very thick. The dome of the skull was like a broad, shallow bowl, inverted over a protruding jaw. The eye sockets were narrow and elongated, with heavy ridges like protective arches over them.

"A delver," Orannan murmured fearfully.

"What's that?" Cabanard asked.

"An ancient legend. I never thought it might be true." Orannan rose from his knees and moved away from the bones. "Long ago—incredibly long ago, before men learned how to count time—the Fastness was raised here in these mountains by an unknown race of builders. One story says that they were magicians who summoned up a legion of strong, stunted creatures from beneath the ground to cut and carry and place the stone, then imprisoned them beneath the Fastness when the work was done. Another says that the delvers were an older race, living here when men came. They were driven into hiding by the builders, but they creep up from time to time to steal children or do harm to men. I always thought it was just a story, but those are the bones of a delver."

"One heap of bones doesn't make all the old stories true," said Cabanard. "Come on."

"No, no further. If there are delvers below, we'll be killed. They're stronger than three men and terribly cruel. They'll tear us to pieces and eat us."

Cabanard unsheathed the great sword of Korang. "Nobody's going to tear us apart while I have this in my hands, I promise you."

"Let's not make any hasty decisions," Brondin said. He gripped his crutch firmly and stooped to take up one of the delver leg bones. The bone, at its narrowest point, was thicker than his forearm; his fingers did not meet around it. Taking it in both hands, he snapped it in two. "These bones are ancient. I never could have broken that if it hadn't been old and dried out."

"But what does that tell us about the rest of the delvers?" Orannan asked.

"Maybe the Lool got them all. Maybe they fled so far below to escape him that they'll never know we're in these tunnels."

"The Lool has been dead a long time. I think we ought to backtrack and take the other tunnel," said Orannan.

"Why should we run? We can fight our way through anything," Cabanard said.

"That's not what you said at Riverroad Camp. I remember you saying that when the odds are against you, you run. Fighting is the last resort."

"I didn't have this blade in my hands when I talked like that."

Brondin looked at Cabanard and saw an expression on the swordsman's face that he had not seen there before. Cabanard stood in a silent crouch, as if ready for battle, with Korang's sword extended before him. In his other hand he held a torch high, and by its light he glanced from one of his friends to the other, suspicious and alert. Orannan, who also carried a torch, shrank back a step from that threatening gaze. Brondin moved closer, and Cabanard tensed.

"Put the sword down, Cabanard. Please, for all our sakes, put it down, now, quickly," Brondin said.

Cabanard bared his teeth, but Brondin came on, and when he stood within arm's length, he raised his hands slowly and laid them on Cabanard's shoulders. "You trusted my father. Now trust me, Cabanard. Lay down the sword," Brondin said, fixing his eyes on the swordsman's.

The sword of Korang clattered to the stone floor, and as it struck, Cabanard gave a start and opened his eyes wide, like a man abruptly awakened. He shuddered, dropped the torch, and raised both hands to rub his eyes. Behind him, Brondin heard Orannan give a great sigh of relief.

"Are you all right now? Feel like yourself again?" Brondin asked.

"Yes. I wanted . . . just wanted to fight . . . kill someone."

"What happened?" Orannan asked, moving closer and taking up the fallen torch.

"It's the sword. The spirit of Korang clings to it still, and if a man takes it up, Korang's magic begins to work in him. He was called Warmaker because his special magic was to rouse men to war and violence. That's why Cabanard wanted to fight our way out."

Cabanard seated himself on the floor of the tunnel and leaned back, rubbing his brow with one hand. "I think I would have used that blade on you two if you had tried to make me turn back. It was an awful feeling. I knew all along that you were my friends, but that didn't matter. The only important thing was to use the blade."

"Let's leave it here and go back to the other tunnel," Orannan said, looking fearfully at the golden scabbard and the silver blade that gleamed in the light of the torches.

"I don't think we can leave it," Brondin said. "If what you heard was a true prophecy, we were meant to find that blade. We can't run away from it."

"But if it changes a man, how are we going to take it with us?"

"I'll carry it," Brondin said. "I think the cloak pin will

protect me. If it doesn't, and the sword of Korang works on
me, it will be easier for you to get away from me than for
me to run from either of you. Whatever this accursed blade
does, I'm sure it won't cure my leg."

"Take it, Brondin. I don't want to touch it again," said
Cabanard.

"I don't want to touch it, either. But I think one of us
must."

Orannan had seated himself by Cabanard. Brondin, too,
sank down to rest, and by mutual tacit consent they remained
there for a time, regaining their strength for the upward
climb that might prove to be their last chance of escape.
Brondin still felt hopeful, but even he was sobered by the
new perils that seemed to rise out of nowhere. The delvers,
if such creatures still roamed this dark labyrinth, would be
a dreadful enemy. But they, at least, could be faced and
fought. The magic of a long-dead sorcerer, lingering like
some ageless poison to work evil on future generations, was
a terrifying thing.

Brondin turned his head and looked upon the sword of
Korang, lying between him and Cabanard. He laid a hand
on the cloak pin fastened at his shoulder and clutched it
firmly. It had saved him from magic once, and he trusted
it to help him again.

Orannan suddenly sat up, taut and attentive. "Listen.
Down there," he said in a hushed voice.

The others did his bidding, scarcely breathing in the fixity
of their attention. No sound came.

"I know I heard something. Like a stone scraping along
the floor of the tunnel," Orannan said.

"If something is coming up this tunnel, let's not wait for
it to get any closer," Cabanard said, rising and taking up
one of the torches.

Brondin drew himself erect and leaned over to pick up
the sword of Korang. Cabanard watched him closely as he
raised it in both hands.

"Do you feel different?" Cabanard asked.

"No. I want to get out of here as fast as I can. I don't
want to fight anyone, just escape," Brondin said, sheathing
the blade.

"Listen! There it is again!" Orannan cried.

This time they all heard the faint sound from the dark depths of the tunnel. Cabanard took his half-burned torch, drew it back until the flame was perilously close to his face, and then hurled it like a blazing javelin into the darkness. It skipped twice, with a spray of sparks, until it came to rest and flared up again. In the light, something moved, scuttling out of the glare.

"There's something down there, and it doesn't like light," said Cabanard, igniting a fresh torch. "That may hold it back for a time, but we'd better hurry."

They made their way as fast as they could to the fork where the other tunnel opened, and then they started up. Brondin was hardly aware of the pain in his leg as he hobbled on at a speed he had never thought himself capable of sustaining, least of all with a giant sword on his shoulder. Panting, they pressed on without a pause. Brondin's lungs were burning; his head throbbed with every gasping breath; but now the sounds of pursuit could be heard behind them, and there was no possibility of rest.

The air grew steadily cooler, until it was chilly enough to sting their straining throats with every breath. They drew their cloaks closer. The tunnel sloped sharply upward, and they struggled on, dizzy from hunger and near collapse from exhaustion. But the upward grade was short. The tunnel soon leveled and then sloped slightly downward. The air was cold now, and a current made the torches flutter and murmur.

Then Orannan, who led the way, gave a single cry of despair and let his torch fall. He sank to his knees beside it, covering his face with his hands. When Brondin reached the spot, he snatched up the torch, raised it, and saw the light fall on a wall of closely packed stone.

With a roar of rage and frustration, Brondin flung down the torch and let the sword of Korang clatter to the ground. He lurched forward, seized a rock, and pulled with all his strength. The crutch slipped from under his arm, and he fell backward, still clutching the stone.

It came free. The whole face crumbled and fell, and when the dust had blown away, Brondin lay less than half a mark from the tunnel mouth, looking up at the first light of the dawn sky.

CHAPTER EIGHTEEN

THE LAST ESCAPE

"It's a good thing you pulled that rock and didn't push it," Cabanard said, looking down the sheer face of the cliff to the shadows below. "It must be more than a hundred marks to the bottom."

Brondin, standing beside him, nodded. He studied the narrow ledge that extended to the left of the opening. "I wonder how far we have to walk along that," he said.

"We'll find out soon enough. Can you manage with the sword slung at your back?"

"I think so."

"You won't be able to use the crutch."

"I can walk without it. The crutch just takes the weight off my leg so I can move faster."

"We won't be moving fast along that." Cabanard took a final look at the ledge and then drew back into the tunnel. "We may as well finish our food here. The less we carry, the easier it will be."

Orannan looked down the tunnel apprehensively. "What about the delvers?"

"They won't come any closer while there's light."

Orannan stayed near the opening and ate standing up. The others took full advantage of the opportunity to rest. Despite the bright sunlight of morning, the cold made it impossible to sit for long, and they were soon ready to move forth.

The ledge was narrow; it was just possible for a man to place his feet side by side. For as far as they could see, it ran straight along the sheer rock face, and it seemed to be clear of snow and ice. Below them was a straight drop. Across the canyon, the skyline was about eight or ten marks above the level of the ledge, running straight as a taut bowstring.

Cabanard led the way. Orannan followed, and Brondin took up the rear. They had barely set foot on the ledge before they felt the full power of the wind that roared down the narrow canyon from the north. It numbed their exposed faces and worked its way into gloves and through cloaks, chilling them to the marrow. It tugged at their clothes and pushed at their bodies. It slackened and then suddenly intensified, forcing them constantly to adjust to its force. At its fiercest, it left them gasping helplessly, with faces burrowed deep into their cloaks in desperate search for breath.

Pausing briefly at every sheltered spot, they worked their way along at a slow crawl. When the sun was overhead, they found a deep recess and gladly plunged within, where the air, though bitter cold, was still.

"That wind is going to kill us," Orannan said. "We'll all be blown off the ledge in one of those gusts."

Brondin, furiously rubbing his gloved hands together, merely nodded, and Cabanard said, "If our hands and feet get numb enough, it won't take a wind."

"How much farther can this ledge go on?" Orannan asked plaintively. "We've gone ten greatmarks at the very least, and—"

"Not more than two," Cabanard corrected him.

"All right, two. And there's no sign of an end."

"It can't be far. This is an escape route. Anyone using it would want to get clear in a hurry."

They started off once again, and in a very short time Brondin saw Orannan gesturing excitedly toward the skyline. Turning his head cautiously, Brondin saw figures on the ridge; at first there were only two, but then a number of others appeared at once. At this distance, about thirty or forty marks, he could not make out what they were doing, only that they were moving about rapidly. He could not tell whether they had seen him and his friends.

That uncertainty was soon resolved. Three of the figures sank down, and three arrows arced across the canyon in quick succession. The wind carried them far off the mark, but the archers' intentions had been made quite clear.

The next three arrows came closer. Brondin saw more of the figures kneel, and then a volley of arrows came at them. But a sudden gust swept these away, and they dropped harmlessly into the shadowed depths. Despite his grim situation, Brondin smiled, remembering their fear that the wind might kill them. Now it appeared that only the wind would save them.

Orannan had pulled some distance away, and Brondin drove himself to close the interval. Without the crutch to distribute his weight, his leg was working harder. The pain was great, and he was tiring fast.

Suddenly, the wind died. With its howling and blustering stilled, an eerie silence filled the canyon. Then the arrows came thicker than ever, and Brondin almost despaired. Halssa's archers were good. At this range, with no wind to thwart their aim, they would be deadly.

He heard an arrow clink into the wall just above him and clatter to the ledge. Another struck less than arm's length ahead, stinging his face with chips of stone. He heard arrows striking all around him, and it came to him that the wind might help to kill them after all, more deadly in its absence than in its full force.

Brondin felt a sharp stab of pain in his leg and a tug at his hood. He reached back and touched the shaft of an arrow hanging at his back, caught in the fold of his hood. He jerked it free and flung it from him, and at that instant, as if a blessing had been conferred on the three fugitives, a blast of wind roared down the canyon. Its wailing and wuthering and the pattering of the dry pellets of snow it bore sounded to their ears like the soft voice of a beloved comforter.

No more arrows came. When they reached the end of the ledge and squirmed through the narrow notch that brought them at last to the ground, the three fugitives looked back and saw no trace of the opposite ridge through the curtain of snow.

Brondin reached around to take the crutch he had slung at his back, next to the sword of Korang. As he moved, he felt a pressure on his leg. Looking down, he saw the shaft of an arrow protruding from his thigh, the head deep in the fleshy part of his bad leg, the shaft caught in his cloak. He felt suddenly weak, and before he could reach out for support, he staggered and fell.

"What's wrong?" Orannan cried, alarmed.

"He's hit," Cabanard said, hurrying to Brondin's side. He knelt and drew aside the cloak to reveal the arrow.

"I'm all right. I can go on," Brondin said.

"If you can, that's the best thing to do. I can get that out, but you'll lose a lot of blood. Better to wait and find a healer when we reach the Fastness," Cabanard said.

"Help me up. Once I have the crutch to lean on, I'll be able to walk."

"Are you sure?"

"This leg has always been my weakness. An arrow doesn't make it that much worse."

Cabanard led the way westward, trusting that he would soon cross one of the main trails to the Fastness. Once again they wound through narrow defiles, with sheer walls of sloping rock rising on either hand and a cold wind buffeting them like an invisible icy flood, drawing the warmth and the very life from their bodies. The snow fell heavily for a time and then diminished. The wind dropped, and visibility improved.

Cabanard stopped abruptly and crouched to inspect a dark object that lay in their path. The others closed around it and watched as Cabanard brushed the snow from a boot. Orannan lent his assistance, and soon they had uncovered a frozen body. It lay on its side, sword in one hand, the other hand clawing forward. The teeth were bared in an angry grimace, but the eyes were shut as peacefully as a sleeper's.

"His name is Shallender. He was one of my best men," Brondin said.

Cabanard tugged the stiffened cloak away from the body. "He took a lot of killing," he said at the sight of the man's wounds. "Any one of these would stop most men."

"What was he doing here, Brondin? Looking for you?"

"When I learned that Halssa was after a party of travelers, I sent my men out to follow his patrols and seize any prisoners they'd taken. Shallender's men must have run into a patrol."

"Must have been beaten, or they wouldn't have left his body," Cabanard said.

"Maybe. Or maybe he was ambushed, and they didn't know where to look."

"That's possible," Cabanard said, rising stiffly. "We can't do anything for him, so let's keep moving."

"Do you know where we're going?" Orannan asked.

"If we keep heading west, we're bound to cross a trail."

"But are we still heading west? We've been turning and winding through these mountains since morning. I'm all mixed up. We can't see the sun. We could be heading right back to the canyon, Cabanard!"

"I don't think we are. Come on," Cabanard said, turning his back on Orannan and stepping off.

Brondin fell in behind the storyteller. He was weak from hunger and fatigue and loss of blood. At each step, a few more drops seeped out. He could not feel the arrow in his leg, but he knew that the blood would keep coming until it was removed and the wound closed. If they could reach the Fastness, all would be well.

About a greatmark farther on, they came upon two bodies lying within a few marks of each other. Both wore Halssa's colors, and both had fallen to bowmen. The arrows projecting from them bore three green bands on the shaft.

"Your men got even for Shallender," Cabanard said. When Brondin only nodded, he went on. "They may have come out on top, after all. Maybe they're waiting for you at the Fastness."

The wind had died by this time, but now the snow began to fall thickly in flakes the size of a man's thumbnail. At once their range of vision closed in, and all around them was only a great featureless whiteness, slowly and gently covering everything it touched. As they pressed on, the flakes clung to their boots and filled every fold of their cloaks.

Brondin had no sensation in his feet or fingers. A dull pulse beat in his leg at every step, but he could not feel the steel lodged in his flesh, and for long intervals he forgot the wound completely. His thoughts were jumbled. He pictured his men waiting anxiously for his arrival at the Fastness and wondered what story they would tell of their encounter in the snow. He imagined their expressions when he told them that all was now well, that the campaign against Halssa could begin in earnest, and when he told the story of his own journey and his adventures—the struggle with the night demon, the flight from the delvers, the sword of Korang. At the thought of the great blade, he reached behind himself to assure himself that it still hung securely at his back, and the sudden motion caused him to lose his balance and fall forward.

He lay stunned for a moment and then pulled himself slowly to his feet. The sword was safe. He drew his cloak tightly around himself and started forward. The footprints of his friends were filling in quickly; he had lain there for only an instant, he was sure, but already the track was faint. He hurried forward, peering into the whiteness, unable to see a trace of Orannan.

Pressing on, he came to a fork and followed one branch until he realized that there were no footprints before him. He turned and retraced his steps; then he took the other path. Gasping now, light-headed and blinded by the snow, he limped on through the ever-rising drifts.

He found himself lying prone. He groped for his crutch but could not lay his hand on it. Something pressed heavily against his back, holding him down. He started to rise, but his numb hands slid out from under him. It did not seem to be so cold as it had been, and he felt very tired. Something urged him to rest for a time and regain his strength; at the same time, he knew that he must not give in, must force himself to rise and struggle on until all strength and will were gone.

He lifted his head and called his friends' names, but his voice was weak. No one would hear him. He had to save himself or die.

Again he propped himself up, and again he sank down into the soft snow. He was too weak, too tired to try again. Drawing the cloak over him, his hand tightly closed on the cloak pin, he closed his eyes and surrendered to sleep.

CHAPTER NINETEEN

THE WORK PROGRESSES

*While bold men spoke of battle, and placed their faith
  in arms,*
*One walked among them silent, untouched by war's
  alarms:*
*A man who came from nowhere to serve a new-won
  throne,*
Drawn to a deep of darkness by a power locked in stone.
And other men who traveled across the northern lands
*Were senseless of the destiny that closed them in her
  hands. . . .*

From *The Last Deed of Ambescand*

Halssa glared at his adviser but did not speak. Karash-Kabey met his eyes calmly and stood in patient silence, waiting, his hands clasped loosely around the Doomstaff.

"So your assassin failed," Halssa said at last.

"Brondin escaped him, my lord."

"Not only did Brondin escape your infallible assassin, he disappeared. Vanished. You admit you have no idea where he is."

"He goes northward. He will be found, my lord."

"He has been found. He's been found and finished. I've just received word," Halssa said with a narrow smile of triumph. When his adviser showed no reaction to this news, he went on. "One of my patrols came on him and two others near the Fastness. They trapped him in a cave and sealed him in. They're guarding the entrance just in case he tries to dig his way out. In the spring, they'll go in and drag out what's left. When Brondin's head hangs over the western gate, maybe things will be quiet."

"Did they see him clearly, my lord?"

"Clear enough. They saw the crutch slung at his back."

"A man may carry a crutch and not be Brondin of Balthid's Keep, my lord."

Halssa shook his head slowly. "Not this time. I can't believe that the mountains are full of crippled travelers who run at the sight of my patrols. No, Brondin's trapped now, and I'm rid of him."

"Let us hope your men find him when they enter the cave."

Halssa laughed. "He won't disappear from them the way he did from your assassin. My guards may not be learned men, but they get the job done."

"A cave may have more than one opening, my lord," Karash-Kabey pointed out coolly.

Halssa pondered that for a time, frowned, and said, "That won't help him. My men say he carried no torches and a very slender pack. If he doesn't go mad in the darkness or break his neck, he'll starve to death."

"It appears, then, that my lord is fortunate."

"Now I can pull back my outer guard and strengthen the city's defenses. With Brondin gone, there's little danger of an uprising, but a show of strength never hurts. It's force that put me on this throne, and it's force that will keep me here. I came close to forgetting that, but I'll remember it in the future," Halssa said decisively. He turned to Karash-Kabey and added, "You've advised me well in some matters. I've never hesitated to admit it. You know that. But when it comes to tracking an enemy down and disposing of him, I'm the expert. I need seek no advice in such matters, and in the future I won't."

Karash-Kabey acknowledged the rebuke with a nod but did not speak. Halssa dismissed him, and he left the chamber at his customary pace, stately and unhurried, like a man beyond all ordinary human concerns. Mockery or praise, rebuke or reward, all seemed matters of equal indifference to him.

He descended the lightless ways to his private chamber beneath the palace. Once secure within, he summoned the shapeless being that served him. It dragged and scraped its way to the edge of the shadows and halted there, a darker bulk against the darkness.

"I will hear again what happened when the other came

upon Brondin and his companions. Tell me what you saw and omit nothing," said Karash-Kabey.

"I did not see all. I remained hidden, as you commanded."

"I am aware of that. Tell me all you saw."

The creature began to speak in a grating voice whose pitch and tone and timbre varied from phrase to phrase, and sometimes from one word to the next, without ever losing its unnatural and inhuman quality. It went on with its account until the point at which it had returned to the chamber. Karash-Kabey listened all the while with lowered head and closed eyes; he did not speak again until the thing was silent.

"Brondin alone destroyed the other. His companions had no part in it. Is that correct?" he asked.

"They fought, but their weapons had no effect."

"What weapons did Brondin use?"

"First he struck with his dagger. It did not wound. The other knocked him to the ground, and Brondin took something from the ground and struck. The other screamed a death scream."

"What did he take from the ground?"

"Could not see."

"Not a sword or any kind of weapon?"

"No weapon. Something small."

"Could it have been a cloak pin?"

"Brondin wore no cloak. Only thin one wore cloak."

"Was it bright like metal, or dull like stone?"

"Was bright."

Karash-Kabey was silent for a time, deep in thought. This matter was far more serious than he had made known to Halssa, and it disturbed him. His assassin demon, a thing of magic, had been destroyed by an ordinary mortal. Such a thing should have been impossible.

Brondin knew no magic; of this Karash-Kabey was certain. Yet somehow, in his moment of greatest need, his groping hand had fallen on an object of sufficient power to overcome a thing immune to all weapons of ordinary men. It was too great a coincidence to accept.

The other two could have had nothing to do with it. They were creatures of no consequence, a brute and a teller of tales. The key to the mystery lay in Brondin.

Karash-Kabey knew the legends of the cloak pin that had

been passed down to the daughters of the ruling family since the time of Ambescand and had become a treasure of the Vannensons. He knew its early provenance, long before it had been placed on the breast of the first Ciantha, although he could not learn its origin. It had been in the presence of great power and might yield up its power when held by the rightful possessor. But it had been stolen from Brondin; his spy had heard the words from Brondin's own lips and could not doubt their accuracy. Could Brondin have regained the pin somehow? It was unlikely. If he had, would he have left it lying carelessly on the ground in a time of peril? Would he not rather have kept it close on his person, safely concealed?

It was all a great mystery, and it had come at a time when Karash-Kabey wanted no distraction. His plans were close to fruition. Before summer returned to the northland, all would be in place, and he would have at his command power such as no man had ever possessed before him. To be so close and then to have disturbing questions raised in his mind was intolerable.

He rose and paced the floor slowly, weighing the problem and examining all facets. His assassin demon had been destroyed by means of magic. The cloak pin was a possible but unlikely weapon. If Brondin had in fact been given some other magic weapon when his life was surely lost, then he was being used by a rival, an enemy of Karash-Kabey. There was no other reasonable possibility. And therein rose a new and disturbing mystery, for no living soul knew of Karash-Kabey's plan. Others had once shared his secret, but they had faltered and been destroyed, and now he alone knew. Who, then, could oppose him?

He had to know more before he could decide on a course of action. Brondin might be a threat no longer, but that was not certain; he could not accept unquestioned the boasting of Halssa. Recalling Halssa's contemptuous manner and condescending words, he furrowed his brow and then smiled a thin, mirthless smile. A time was approaching when Halssa would regret his discourtesies, but that was a concern for another day. Now he must put his mind to rest about Brondin.

"You will return to the mountains when your work here

is done," he commanded his servant. "Enter the cave where Brondin is said to be trapped and seek him out. I must know if he lives."

"*Is he to die?*"

"Yes, but not by you. You are to take no risks. I still have need of you."

"*I am ready.*"

"The barge is full. Guide it to the cave on Slill and then bring the stone to me."

The formless servant croaked a reply. It moved out of the darkness, its outline flowing and shifting, and rose on two stumpy legs that melted at once into four. Its form stabilized. A headless broad-backed thing, it stalked at a rolling gait from the chamber to begin its task.

CHAPTER TWENTY

THE LADY OF LASTHAVEN

> *And while the blades were whetted, and anvils rang*
> *aloud,*
> *And plot with plot encountered, and rumor stirred the*
> *crowd,*
> *And hopes were raised and shattered, and plans un-*
> *made and made,*
> *Deep in the silent mountains, where stranger never*
> *strayed,*
> *A child grew into womanhood in a valley far away,*
> *Unmindful of her danger and the part she was to*
> *play. . . .*
>
> From *The Last Deed of Ambescand*

Brondin opened his eyes to the bright light of a winter morning. He was lying in a soft bed, with a comforter pulled up to his chin. The air of the little room was pleasantly warmed by a fire that crackled and muttered in the shallow fireplace that took up much of one wall. Beyond the window at his side, a clear blue sky shone through a delicate lacework of naked branches.

Calm and stillness pervaded the atmosphere, and Brondin sensed that he was safe, even though he had no idea where he was, how he had arrived, or how long he had been there. His clothing lay neatly folded on a low stool near the fire, and his cloak hung from a peg on the wall behind them. The cloak pin was clearly visible, fixed in the cloak. The sword of Korang stood in the corner nearby, and his crutch was beside it. Reassured, Brondin sank back into a light half-sleep.

When he came fully awake, he was conscious of a great hunger. He sat up, examined his hands, and ran his fingertips over his face. The cold had done him no damage. Throwing the covers aside, he saw that his leg had been treated and bandaged. It was stiff and still tender, but there was no pain from the extraction of the arrow. The work had been done by expert hands and had been done some days ago. He had slept for a long time.

The warmth and coziness of the room lulled Brondin's hunger and concern into a pleasant languor. He lay back, pulled the covers up to his chest, laced his fingers behind his head, and looked over the little room to learn what he could.

It was small, simply furnished, and spotlessly clean, and Brondin judged it to be one of many such rooms in a large and prosperous house. Certainly it was not part of an inn—much too clean and quiet for that—nor was it a room in a humble cottage. The carvings on the mantelpiece and door, the elaborate bedstead, and the bright design painted on the ceiling were the work of master craftsmen, not rude artisans. The window was glass of the finest quality; he could see outside without distortion. And since he saw branches and treetops, he knew that he was not in the Fastness. The bed was big and very comfortable, and the bedclothes were soft and white and had a mild, pleasant fragrance. At a sudden suspicion, he sniffed cautiously at his arm and hand and discovered the same fragrance. He had been bathed thoroughly, and he had no memory of it.

With this knowledge, he felt compelled to rise; he had been helpless, indeed, oblivious, for too long. However solicitous his host might be, Brondin did not like the feeling of such passivity. He swung his legs over the side of the bed, planted his feet firmly on the cool smooth boards, and with the aid of the bedpost pulled himself to his feet. He felt a twinge of pain in his injured thigh, but it subsided, and no blood appeared on the bandage. He stood a bit unsteadily, lightheaded from hunger. The air was cool on his bare skin but not uncomfortable.

He limped to the stool where his clothes lay and took them up. They, too, had been washed and were comfortably warm from the fire. His cloak had been brushed and his boots scraped clean of mud and thoroughly greased. Slowly, clumsily, he pulled on breeches and boots, drew his shirt over his head, and then, leaving his tunic on the stool, went to the door. It was unfastened.

He opened it cautiously and peered out. He was in a long hall with closed doors on both sides. At one end of the hall was a staircase, and he could hear faint sounds of activity rising from below. He reentered the room, closing the door softly behind him, and finished dressing. For a moment, he thought of removing the cloak pin and carrying it with him, but he finally deemed that an unnecessary precaution. Cloak, cloak pin, and sword could remain there. Whoever his hosts were, they certainly were not looters. He fitted the crutch under his arm and made his way down the stairs.

At the second landing, he stopped to inspect the hall from which the staircase rose. It extended the full length of the house, some nine or ten marks, and was about half that wide. Three fireplaces filled the great space with warmth and light and struck flashes from the polished surface of the long table that stood in the center. Brondin thought of the hall at Balthid's Keep and felt a pang of longing for his home. This hall was a bit larger, perhaps, but it was not as splendid to his eyes.

A man dressed in a plain gray robe stepped from the shadows at the side of the nearest fireplace and raised a hand in greeting. "Welcome to Lasthaven, Brondin. Come and dine, and I'll tell you all."

"Are my friends safe?" Brondin asked at once.

"They're safe and contented and well fed. I never saw anyone with an appetite like those two, though I imagine you'll be able to match them. They told me what you've been through. Come, sit down," said the man in gray.

He was about Brondin's height, slender, with a thick thatch of iron-gray hair. Over his left eye he wore a dark patch. With his good eye, he closely studied Brondin's approach. When Brondin reached the table, he started forward to assist him, but Brondin waved him off.

"I can manage."

"That's good. You're walking well. Any pain?"

"My leg is a little stiff, but it doesn't hurt. Who removed the arrow?"

"I did. I'm a healer." The gray-haired man seated himself opposite Brondin and rang a small silver bell. "I have a great deal to tell you, and I'm sure you have questions for me, but first of all you must eat. It's been nearly three days since you've come here, and you've done nothing but sip water."

"I do feel a bit weak," Brondin admitted.

"We can't have that. You'll be needing all your strength before long," the healer said, smiling.

Something tugged at Brondin's memory, but before he could capture the elusive notion, a servant arrived, bearing a tray. On it were a round loaf of dark bread about the size to fit in a man's cupped hands, and a steaming bowl.

"For the time being, just bread and soup. If you try to eat too much all at once, you'll get sick. I let your friends eat all they wanted, and they each got a bellyache," said the healer.

Brondin nodded and reached for the bread. It was warm and delicious. The soup was a meat soup, thick and rich enough to be called a stew. He had to force himself to eat slowly, but even so, the meal was quickly over. He mopped up the last traces of soup with the last crust, popped the bread into his mouth, and leaned back in his chair, contented but still hungry.

"That's enough for now. In a little while we'll have a hot meat pie, but in the meantime I want to talk to you," the healer said.

Brondin swallowed the last morsel and said, "I'd like to know where I am and how I came here. The last thing I remember clearly is losing my way in the snow and falling."

"A party of our men came upon your friends, searching for you, and when they found you, they took all three of you here."

"Where is 'here'?"

"This is Lasthaven."

"You mentioned that already. It doesn't tell me much."

"No, I suppose not," the healer conceded. "Do you know the account of the death of the last of the Vannensons to rule in the High City?"

"Stiragos had the misfortune to rule when the Long Winter came upon the north. The people wanted to blame their suffering on someone, and when a cabal of nobles conspired against poor Stiragos, the people were eager to support them. He was deposed and slain, and so were his wife and children. The nobles seized power and ruled as the Council of Thirty-nine until they began to kill one another off. Not long after that, the High City fell."

"That is the accepted story," the healer said.

Brondin leaned forward and looked at him sharply. "But it isn't the true one. Is that what you're saying?"

"There is one inaccuracy. The wife of Stiragos did not die."

"Eudotia lived? What became of her?"

"She was badly wounded and nearly mad from grief. Her husband and children had been slain before her eyes, and she herself was stabbed and left for dead. But some of her servants and many of Stiragos's bodyguard remained loyal. They brought her to safety, and when she was able to travel, they took her here."

"Why here?"

"Eudotia had a cousin living here, a woman named Palician. They'd never met. Palician's mother had married a man from here and simply vanished from sight. Only Eudotia knew where she was, and she had never told anyone. When Eudotia came and brought about a hundred exiles with her, the newcomers took to calling the valley Lasthaven, and the name stayed."

"Eudotia had another cousin."

"Yes, I know of your mother. And I know of the cloak pin."

Brondin's head snapped up, and he pointed across the table. "You're Traissell the healer. It was your servant who stole the cloak pin!" he cried angrily.

Traissell raised his hands in a pacific gesture. He shook his head, with a pained expression on his face. "Please, please, my boy. You're rushing to conclusions. Your cloak pin was stolen by a master thief who called himself Stoggan. That was certainly not his name, but it's the name he gave me when he asked to become my servant. I imagine he was on his way north, making his escape from Balthid's Keep, when we met."

"Why did you take on a thief as your servant?"

Traissell raised his eyebrow and said drily, "He did not introduce himself as a thief. He told me a very credible tale of being pursued by the sons of a tyrannical landowner he'd killed to avenge his family."

"Did you believe him?"

"I had reservations, but I didn't think it prudent to call him a liar. Besides, a servant is always helpful."

"Are you telling me that you had nothing to do with the theft of the cloak pin?"

Traissell ignored the question. "I see you've regained it," he said.

"It was sheer chance. Cabanard picked it up when Stoggan was killed, and later I met Cabanard and Orannan."

"And was that, too, sheer chance?"

"I was looking for them, it's true. But it was plain good fortune that I found them."

Traissell smiled a knowing, mocking smile that Brondin found disquieting. He said, "Sheer chance. Plain good fortune, you call it."

"Do you have a better name for it? It certainly wasn't planned," Brondin said irritably.

Still smiling, Traissell said, "You didn't plan it. That doesn't mean it wasn't planned."

"Who planned it, then? And why?"

Traissell shrugged. "We may never know what power lies behind all this, but we may be able to figure out why it was done. Let's examine what happened. Because the cloak pin was stolen, you left Balthid's Keep alone. Would you have done that if there had been no theft?"

"Certainly not."

"Entirely alone, you found Cabanard and Orannan, something Halssa's patrols and your best men could not do. And when you found them, these two fugitives, who would naturally suspect any stranger, accepted you as a companion. Another bit of good luck."

"We were going to the same place, and three travelers are safer than two. And I'm sure a cripple doesn't strike people as dangerous."

"You may not be as fast as some men, Brondin, but you look powerful enough to be dangerous. I think even Cabanard might hesitate to cross you. In any event, you were more powerful than the murdering thing that came upon you in the night."

"It was the cloak pin killed that monster, not my strength."

Again Traissell smiled that knowing smile. "Ah, yes, the cloak pin. How fortunate for you that Cabanard had found it and that you just happened to lay your hand on the cloak pin at the moment when it was the only weapon that could save your life. And how very fortunate you were to find the cave just when Halssa's men were closing in, and to break through into the tunnel, and to escape the delvers and the archers, and to be found by men from Lasthaven and brought here. All sheer chance, was it, Brondin? Do you really think so?"

Brondin leaned back and studied the healer narrowly. "When you put it all together that way, it doesn't sound much like chance. It's almost as though someone wanted to bring me here. But why? What's here for me?"

"There's someone you must meet. Her name is Ciantha."

"Ciantha? That's a Vannenson name."

"She's a Vannenson, like you. You and she are to marry," Traissell said matter-of-factly.

"Marry? You're mad, Traissell!" Brondin cried.

"I'm saner than you are, my boy. I see things as they are and as they must be. You and Ciantha will marry. You have no choice, either of you," Traissell said. As Brondin started up, his face set in anger, the healer made a calming gesture and explained. "It won't take place until you're both safe in the High City, so there'll be plenty of time to get acquainted. She's a very comely girl, Brondin. Intelligent, brave—you're fortunate."

"When I rule in the High City, I'll seek out a wife for myself."

"That's exactly what we must avoid. Do that, and there might not be peace in the north for the next three generations. Besides, no one else would do for either of you."

"Maybe we can decide that better than you," Brondin snapped.

"Go on and decide, then. Your families are equal, and your claims are equal. If either of you married anyone else, you'd be choosing to marry beneath you. You must marry Ciantha. You owe it to your ancestors, Brondin; to the people of the north, who deserve peace and proper governing; to all your descendants, who must not bear lesser blood. And Ciantha has no choice but to marry you," Traissell said. He spoke without heat, as if he were explaining an involved puzzle to a child.

Brondin had no illusions about marriage. For a man or woman in his position, marriage was not a matter of affection but of calculation, with the judgment and advice of wise elders taking precedence over private feelings. A youngest son with no prospects, a dowerless daughter, a commoner might marry as they pleased; those with the responsibility of lands, followers, and armies married as prudence and policy dictated. It was the price of birth, and one paid it without complaint.

But it was one thing to be ruled by one's advisers and quite another to sit across from a stranger in a strange hall and be ordered about like a boy. Brondin was not ready to accept Traissell's calm, assured advice without question.

"You speak as though you had some interest in this marriage," he said.

"I do, and I'm willing to explain. I want you to understand and agree freely, Brondin. And I want you to stay put and not jump about. You don't want that wound opening."

"What I want is an explanation."

"Very well. Your mother's mother was cousin to Eudotia, and on the basis of that relationship, you claim the rightful rule of the High City and all the north. Is that not so?"

"It is."

"Ciantha is of exactly the same descent, through Palician. Do you see now why you must marry?"

Brondin nodded thoughtfully. "If either of us were to seize power, the other would always be a threat."

"Precisely. Oh, I suppose one of you could kill the other, but fortunately your minds don't work that way. A good thing, too. That sort of behavior gives people nasty ideas. Once start assassinating, and there's no end to it."

"Am I to take that as a promise of my safety here?"

"Of course you're safe here," Traissell said indignantly. "These are not the days of Duarin, my friend."

"It occurs to me that I carry the cloak pin of the first Ciantha, and a woman who claims the right to rule would be most eager to obtain it. And since I'm here in her stronghold, I might—"

Brondin stopped abruptly at the sound of a slight movement at his back. He turned quickly, his hand dropping to the hilt of his dagger. At the sight of the woman who stood near him, he flushed slightly and then drew himself up slowly and gave a deep bow.

She was small of frame and pale of complexion. Hair the color of glowing embers hung in two thick plaits on her breast, reaching to her hips, and her eyes flashed a pale green in the firelight. She smiled and gestured for him to take his seat.

"You're not alone here, Brondin. My people will follow you as they follow me. And I will take the cloak pin from you only on our wedding day," she said in a voice at once soft and strong.

"If I spoke unjustly, I apologize, lady. I've had too many surprises for one day, and so much is puzzling still." He returned her smile and reached out to take her hand. "Of all the surprises, you're surely the best."

Traissell cleared his throat and waved Ciantha to the place at Brondin's side. When she was seated and Brondin was seated beside her, the healer settled into the chair facing them. To Ciantha he said, "I came here in the early days of Yellowleaf, unknown to anyone, and told you that a man of Vannenson blood would soon come to Lasthaven and would bring the cloak pin of authority with him. You trusted me, and these things have come to pass. And you, Brondin," he continued, turning his eye on the young man, "though you've known me a very short time, must be aware that you can trust me. I took no advantage of your helplessness, and I healed your wound with all my skill."

Ciantha nodded to acknowledge his words. Brondin hesitated a moment and then said, "What you say is true, but it's . . . it's like one of the old tales, Traissell. I can't help thinking there's a trick to it."

"Stop suspecting those who would do you good. If we wished you ill, you'd be dead by now or on your way to the High City in chains. Be sensible, Brondin."

"Sensible? What's sensible about this? I collapse in a snowstorm, and I wake up in a fine safe house where a stranger tells me I'm to marry a woman of high blood. The woman appears, and she's beautiful. This is a dream, Traissell!"

"Most men would enjoy such a dream. If you think it's all too good, hear me out."

Brondin nodded. "Speak on."

"I must ask for your trust in a far graver matter. In the spring, when the roads are open, we must go to the High City, where the two of you will confront the enemy."

"That's what I had planned to do and will do. But why must Ciantha join the battle?" Brondin asked.

"You misunderstand me. I do not speak of armies, Brondin, nor do I speak of battle as you know it."

In an even voice, Ciantha asked, "Do you mean that the two of us must confront Halssa alone? You've never spoken of this before."

"The enemy is not Halssa. Halssa is a mere man, a war-lord and an adventurer. He can be overcome by force of arms. The enemy is his adviser, Karash-Kabey, a sorcerer of great power and great ambition. He represents the gravest danger to face the northland, to threaten all lands and all peoples, since the days of the Stone Hand. No army can defeat him."

Ciantha and Brondin exchanged an apprehensive look and reached out to clasp each other's hands, seeking and giving reassurance. Brondin turned to Traissell and in a hushed voice asked, "A sorcerer? Are you certain?"

"The thing that stalked you in the night was not of the natural world. It was an assassin demon. Karash-Kabey learned of such things in the east. He has sent them against other enemies. Tell me, Brondin, did a dark bird fly overhead before the demon came?"

"Yes, it did. It seemed to be following us."

"It was the Gohl-Sadhi, serving spirit of Karash-Kabey. It is a formless thing, capable of being turned into any shape. As a great bird, it spies on the enemies of Karash-Kabey."

"Then I've already faced sorcery," said Brondin.

"And overcome, with the cloak pin to protect you," Traissell added.

"But can the cloak pin protect us from Karash-Kabey and his power?" Ciantha asked.

"I believe it can. We must trust that something will protect you, because you must face him. There is no one else. You alone bear the blood of the great liberators of the past—of Ambescand and Ciantha and the sons of Vannen. Twice before, when the dark power threatened the northlands, your ancestors rose up to drive it back. Now your turn has come."

"But they had power!" Ciantha protested. "We're not sorcerers. We know no magic. The magic is gone from the north!"

"The power was sent to them when the need came. We must trust that it will be given to you."

"How can we be sure?" Brondin asked.

"You can't make bargains with your destiny, son. Even kings and wizards can't do that. You do what you must and hope for the best. There's no other way."

"And if we fail?"

"Then there is no hope at all, for anyone, ever again. Evil will pour forth into the world once more," Traissell replied. All three were silent for a time, and then the healer smiled. "We have until spring to prepare ourselves, and the most important thing is to build up our strength. It's time for that meat pie, Brondin," he said, taking up the silver bell.

And in a moment, the horror lifted and the world was the old world once more—until the spring.

CHAPTER TWENTY-ONE

HIGH SANCTUARY

Lasthaven was only four days' travel from the Fastness and twenty-four from the High City, but it was as remote from those places as if it lay at the bottom of the sea. Set like a bowl into the mountains, ringed with sheer peaks that served as palisades against intrusion, it was linked to the outside by a single narrow path that coiled up the mountainsides, invisible to observers below. A narrow pass in which a dozen men could hold back an army was the only breach in the mountain wall.

No one had ever come upon Lasthaven by chance; no map existed to guide a traveler to it. Yet in this legend-haunted land, tales were told in the inns and taverns, wherever wanderers met, of a lost domain where life went on as it had in ancient days, unchanged since the time of magic and mystery before the coming of Ambescand. There, it was said, a race of people worked and lived and dressed in the old way; their speech contained archaic words and turns of phrase, and their purses held coins from the time of the Old Kingdom, still as bright and unworn as if they had been newly struck.

Brondin and his companions had heard all these tales and done their share of wondering. Now they found themselves in the fabled place, treated as honored guests.

Cabanard, after the first few days of rest and recuperation, had struck up a wary acquaintance with the training master of the small defense force. In a very short time, he had become the unofficial training master, and the training master had become his assistant and eager pupil. Cabanard's experience and his skill with all the weapons in the armory made a deep impression on the men who would soon be leaving Lasthaven to fight their first battle. They listened with

rapt attention to his every word, and Cabanard basked in
their recognition.

Orannan felt like a man who has stumbled upon a treasure.
Not only had he found an audience to whom every song and
story in his repertoire was new, he had come upon a store-
house of fresh material to add to his stock. Night after night
he sat by the fire in the great hall and held the long table
spellbound with his tales. He visited the homes of the common folk and listened to their charms and fables, and he
heard the soldiers' marching songs and bawdy catches, match-
ing them story for story and tale for tale.

He was most popular with the children, and this surprised
him, for Orannan seldom encountered children in the places
where he performed and had a cautious view of their potential for careful listening. But one sunny afternoon he found
himself facing a semicircle of silent, attentive small faces.

He was in the kitchen of the great house, where he had
been reciting an old rhyme made up of fanciful recipes for
imaginary delicacies, to the great delight of the kitchen
workers. The children had slipped in one by one, and the
staff, preoccupied with listening, had not shooed them off. By
the time Orannan reached the final verses, which told how to
prepare and serve a dessert made of cloud flour and wind-
fruit sweetened with raindust and thunderseeds, a dozen children of assorted ages and sizes were in the audience.

Amid the adults' laughter and shouts of approval, one tall
boy stepped forward and looked up at Orannan hopefully.
The storyteller swept the group with a glance and then fixed
his eyes on the tall boy.

"Please, Master Orannan, will you tell us a tale of outside?"
the boy asked nervously.

"Well," said Orannan, clearing his throat and rubbing his
neck with light fingertips, "it will have to be very short.
Have to save my voice, you know."

"Oh, yes, Master Orannan. Whatever you say."

"And there must be a fair exchange. When I've done, one
of you will have to sing a song or tell a tale in return."

They glanced at one another in a thrill of panic. A high
voice from the crowd piped, "Zoley's the best singer of us,
Master Orannan." At once, others took up the cry. The tall

boy turned to glare at them and then looked up at Orannan once again, smiling faintly.

"And you're Zoley, I assume."

"I am, Master Orannan."

"Is it true you're the best singer of this whole lot?"

Zoley straightened and said, "Best singer in Lasthaven is what people say."

"Do they, indeed? Well, I have a treat in store." Orannan took up a small harp, and as he tuned it, he said, "I'll sing a very short song about the Fool's Eye. Do you know where that is?"

Twelve heads shook in the negative.

"You've heard of Staver Ironbrand and his brothers, haven't you?" Orannan asked severely, and all heads nodded. "Well, the Fool's Eye is an island in a lake called the Fool's Head, and the Vannensons had a great adventure there. I may tell you of it another day but not now. It's very long."

"We like long stories, Master Orannan," Zoley assured him.

Orannan rubbed his throat and shook his head. "Another time." He busied himself with the harp and then looked up suddenly and said, "I hope you're not easily frightened."

They assured him that they were not. But they whispered and drew closer to one another as Orannan raised the harp and began to sing.

> *"Who strikes a flame on the Fool's Eye*
> *Makes waters churn and waves run high,*
> *Blots the light from out the sky,*
> *Makes the wind and water vie*
> *With deathly howl and awful cry—*
> *Watery death is ever nigh*
> *When fire burns on the Fool's Eye."*

He let the final note fade, repeated the last two lines in a lower voice, and then repeated them once more in a whisper barely audible to his nearest listener. In the silence he looked around the half circle of wide-eyed faces, fixing each for a moment with solemn gaze. At last he said, "And that's my song. Now I must hear yours. What shall it be?"

A babble of shrill voices shouted suggestions, and Orannan

had to hold up his hands to still the uproar. Pointing to the girl who stood at his immediate left, he said, "We will make our suggestions in an orderly fashion and allow Zoley to choose his song. You first, my dear."

"The tale of Achalla and the blind girl, Master Orannan," said the child with an awkward, eager bow.

As they moved around the semicircle, Orannan's wonder grew. One by one, these children called for tales of the long-forgotten northern gods: gentle Achalla, the healer and comforter; Ylveret, the giver and taker of life; Wrothag, the blustering giant who wielded the frost ax; Gundobad the fair, and jesting Malasir, and wise Niss. Orannan knew these names and had heard a few fragmentary tales about them, but nothing like what the children's words suggested. Except for a few scattered pockets of believers, the old gods lived no more in the world beyond Lasthaven, and no one spoke of them. But in the minds of these children, they were as alive and familiar as the neighbors. To Orannan it was as if a whole new treasure had been heaped upon the riches he had already gathered.

When all had spoken, Zoley announced his choice. He would sing of Wrothag's contest with the sea giants. He took up a rigid stance, hands tightly clenched at his sides, feet together, and began to sing. His voice, though untrained, was good. His song was a marvel of beauty and force and subtle effects, and Orannan was more impressed the more he listened. If this song was typical of the songs and tales of the old gods to be found there, he was indeed in luck.

When Zoley finished, he bowed his head, red-faced, and accepted the praise of his friends and the kitchen workers. When Orannan clapped him on the back and addressed him as a fellow storyteller, the boy's face lit up. And when Ciantha and Brondin appeared to add their plaudits to the rest, Zoley was close to bursting with pride.

"Why don't we all meet here tomorrow to exchange more songs and stories?" Orannan suggested, and the children agreed enthusiastically.

"Come every day, if you like. Makes the work go easier," said the chief cook.

"We shall. It will be great fun. But now you'd best be getting home," Orannan said to the children. Collaring Zoley, he added, "Take good care of your voice, do you hear? No shouting or screaming like the other children. You've been given a gift, and you must protect it."

"I will, I promise. Will you teach me how to play harp, Master Orannan?"

"Perhaps. We'll talk about that tomorrow."

"And to juggle?"

"Certainly not," Orannan said, drawing himself up righteously. "If you wish to be a juggler, my boy, you'll have to learn from a clown. I am an artist, not a clown. Now, I want no more talk of juggling. You be here tomorrow, ready to learn the harp."

When the children were gone, Orannan said, "The people of Lasthaven have a great love of song, Lady Ciantha. And they've kept some fine old tales and songs alive."

"This valley was settled before the time of Ambescand. The north was troubled in those days, too, and people came here seeking a safe haven. They believed in the old gods then, and we of the valley still believe, though all outside have turned from them," Ciantha said.

"Not all," Brondin corrected her. "At Balthid's Keep we still honor their names."

"But what do the others believe? What gods do they worship?"

"None. They say that the gods failed them in their greatest need, and they will worship nothing."

Ciantha shook her head, and her expression was troubled. "How can people worship nothing? Surely evil must come of that."

"Certainly, much evil came upon the north after the old gods were abandoned. But whether that was the cause is hard to say."

She turned to Brondin, frankly curious now, and said, "Your father was a westerner, yet he and his men accepted the gods of the north. Did they have none to worship in the west?"

"They left them behind." Brondin reflected a moment and then smiled. "Balthid once said to me, 'A wise man honors the gods of the country,' and I guess that's what they did. A lot of my father's fighting men had the frost ax tattooed on their shoulders. They said it brought them the protection of Wrothag."

"Did it?" Orannan asked.

"They believed it did."

Ciantha said, "You sound doubtful. What do you believe, Brondin? You say that you honor the old gods' names, but do you believe in them?"

"I think I believe that something guides us. I believe that very firmly since speaking with Traissell and meeting you. But whether the gods we name are the only power over us, I cannot say. I sometimes think that the gods we know have gods of their own, and they fear and worship their gods as we do ours."

"And do they doubt, too?"

Brondin laughed and took her hand. "Perhaps they do."

Orannan saw the way they looked at each other and understood his presence to be superfluous. He excused himself and went apart to rehearse Zoley's song in his memory.

Ciantha and Brondin scarcely noticed his departure. They had taken to spending most of their time together, and it was obvious to all who saw them that it would require no sorcery, no prophecy, no political imperative to force them to marry. They had been at perfect ease with each other within minutes of their first meeting. Ease had turned to fondness and then to love before their first parting.

For Brondin, who had grown up surrounded by fighting men and martial values in a place that was more fortress than home, the mere presence of Ciantha was like a visitation from another world, where grace and beauty and tenderness had replaced the harsh regimen of constant vigilance. Her every word, every changing expression, every motion attested to a life he had never imagined possible, and the thought that he was to share that life made him weak with joy and wonder.

Ciantha was equally love-struck. Brondin, the man from the unknown outer world, had brought new life into the quiet valley. She scarcely noticed his weak leg, so enthralled was she by his quick mind, his tenderness to her, his courage in the face of dangers beyond human power. She had heard from both Cabanard and Orannan of his slaying of the assassin demon and his decisive action with the sword of

Korang. Now the prospect of leaving Lasthaven, which once had filled her with dread, was of no concern. Wherever her destiny might lead her, whatever horrors she might face, she would be safe with Brondin by her side. She believed that absolutely.

Snow Moon came, and the people of Lasthaven celebrated the ancient feast marking the death and rebirth of the year. The snows fell and deepened, and then the still silent days of fiercest cold were upon them. It seemed that the white grip of winter would never loosen.

But the day came when the channels down the mountainsides were full of racing water, and the ground broke through its white mantle to display a defiant scattering of green. The snow shrank back upon itself, and suddenly all was astir in the high valley.

Some went to the fields to begin working the soil for planting, as they had done every spring in memory, but many prepared to leave the valley. Couriers, their messages committed to memory, set forth for Balthid's Keep and the strongholds of Brondin's allies to give word of Brondin's safety and the time of the assault on the High City. Archers and swordsmen, trained under Cabanard's critical eye, readied their weapons for the long march. And at the end of one bright and busy day, Traissell informed Ciantha and Brondin that they were to make ready to leave in two days' time.

Their party numbered only six. A tall, rangy man named Imdall, who seldom spoke and never smiled, was to guide them through the mountains. Cabanard insisted on coming, in case they ran into more trouble than Brondin could handle alone, and a loyal servant of Ciantha's, a burly man named Emerax, joined them for added protection.

They left at first light, and by late afternoon they had reached the base of the mountain. That night they camped in a shallow cave and lit no fire. The moon, near full, was bright enough for their purposes, and they wished to give no indication of their presence.

Two uneventful days passed. They saw no one and no sign of life. Traissell constantly searched the sky. He would not say what he sought, but it occurred to Brondin that it might be the Gohl-Sadhi, the spy of his enemy.

At the third night's camp, Brondin pressed him, and Traissell admitted that he had guessed correctly. "I may be concerned over nothing. As far as Halssa knows, you're dead," he said. "But I think Karash-Kabey will want to make certain. After all, you destroyed his assassin demon. That makes you someone to worry about."

"Do you think he might send another of those things?" Brondin asked.

"If he learns who you and Ciantha are and what we're about to do, he may send an army of them. You're the only ones who really threaten him."

Brondin was silent for a time, and then he shook his head gloomily. "I could fight off another of those things, maybe two or even three, but an army of them, and me with only the cloak pin for a weapon . . . I don't see how I can, Traissell."

"Let's think about it. There has to be a way."

They spoke no more about it, but after a time the healer gathered up his traveling cloak, searched out a seam, and worried away at the cloth until he had worked free three long tough threads. He braided them and jerked them sharply to test their strength. Satisfied, he turned to Brondin and said, "Let me have the sword and the cloak pin."

Taking the braided cord, he bound the cloak pin securely to the hilt of Korang's sword, just above the crosspiece. The garnets and gold wire of the cloak pin blended with the trappings of the sword so well as to be almost invisible.

"There," Traissell said, inspecting his handiwork. "Now, if Karash-Kabey has learned about the cloak pin and prepared his creature to be wary of it, you'll give the thing a surprise."

"Do you really think it will come?"

"We'd be foolish not to prepare for it. And with this sword, you're ready for as many as he sends."

From that point, their marching order was different. Imdall still led the way, but Brondin walked close behind him. At a short interval came Cabanard and Ciantha, with Traissell close behind them and Emerax guarding the rear. Two more days passed with no sign of life on the trail or overhead, and their spirits rose. The little settlement of Riverbend was less than two days ahead. Brondin had friends there, and they would be able to rest in safety for a day or two before traveling on.

The next day, in midmorning, everything changed. As they rounded a bend in the trail, a tall hooded figure rose from the rocks and lunged at Imdall. The guide, taken by surprise, shouted a warning and drew his dagger. The attacker, without a sound, took him by the throat, shook him as a dog shakes a rat, and flung him aside. Hands outstretched, it came at Brondin.

Brondin threw his crutch aside, set his feet, and waited. This situation required no agility, only determination. He raised the sword and gritted his teeth; when the thing came within reach of his blade, he brought it up and over his head to shear down at the base of the creature's neck. At the touch of the blade, the attacker stopped, shuddered, and emitted an unearthly shriek that echoed and reechoed through the mountain passes. Brondin hacked again and again, oblivious to the flailing talons that raked his face and arms. As the assassin demon shrank and withered under his blows, he saw another coming toward him, long black fingers extended for his throat. He struck at it, and it, too, shrieked in its death agony and shrank back from the annihilating power of his sword.

When the second assassin demon lay like a wreckage of charred sticks and torn rags at his feet, and Brondin, panting and half blinded by the blood streaming down his face, leaned on his sword and looked blankly down on his victims, a cry came from the rear of their little column. Brondin turned quickly, and a taloned wing tip missed his face by a hair. A dark winged shape passed close overhead and soared upward. The Gohl-Sadhi had joined the struggle. Brondin wiped the blood from his eyes and readied himself for the flying creature's next attack.

The thing pivoted on a wing tip and came at him out of the sun. Its shape changed as it flew. Its claws extended, and hooked barbs erupted from the joints of its wings, which grew long and leathery. Its face lost all semblance of a bird's and became a great gaping maw surrounded by blood-red eyes. As it descended, Brondin drew back his sword; and then a bright shaft, like a javelin of light, came from behind Brondin and struck the thing head-on.

The Gohl-Sadhi seemed to burst apart at the impact. It

spun wildly and fell to the ground, where it lay thrashing and uttering horrible sounds. Brondin turned away from the sight, sickened. The Gohl-Sadhi was squirming and writhing, flowing from one unearthly hideous shape to another, a manic and uncontrolled pool of life whirling through a kaleidoscope of forms to the last metamorphosis: extinction. When at last it ceased to churn, it was a clear and colorless substance, neither solid nor liquid, slowly dissipating into nothingness.

Cabanard was the first to find voice. "What was it?" he asked hoarsely.

"It is the spawn of chaos, substance without form, being without life. Karash-Kabey summoned it forth to serve him," the healer said, watching the thing shrink away.

"What could kill such a thing? Did you do it, Traissell?"

"It would take magic to destroy the Gohl-Sadhi. The power of the cloak pin must have struck it down."

Brondin shook his head, mystified. "I did nothing. A bolt of light came past me and tore it from the air before I touched it."

"Yes. Like a spear of light. It passed over me, too," said Cabanard.

"Maybe we've got better protection than we know," said the healer. He looked closely at Brondin's blood-streaked face. "Are you hurt badly?"

"I'll be all right. See to Imdall and Emerax."

Brondin's injuries were minor. Ciantha cleaned the blood from his forehead and arm and applied a salve from Traissell's pack, and soon he was ready to travel on. Imdall and Emerax were not so fortunate. The guide was unconscious, with a bloody gash at the back of his skull and long bruises on his throat. Blood trickled from his ears and nostrils. Emerax was conscious but in great pain. The Gohl-Sadhi had struck him down from behind and sent him hurtling into the rocks by the roadside. His right arm and several ribs appeared to be broken, and his hip was dislocated.

Cabanard and Brondin made the injured men as comfortable as they could and covered them with their own cloaks for extra warmth. Traissell, after examining them closely, drew the others aside.

"Imdall mustn't be moved, and we can't leave him here. Is there anyone at the settlement who can read?" he asked.

When Brondin assured him that there was, he drew a fine brush and a tiny bottle of ink from his pack and ordered Cabanard to hold out his arm. On the swordsman's thick forearm he drew rows of markings. "That's what I'll need," he said. "You must press on and reach the settlement this day. Send them back here at once with all the things I've named. I'll stay here and do what I can for Imdall and Emerax."

"But we have no guide."

"The trail leads straight from here."

"All right, then, we won't get ourselves lost. But when will you join us, Traissell?"

"You can't wait for me. One day's rest at Riverbend, and then you'll have to leave for the High City."

"We can't go on without you, Traissell! We don't know where to find Karash-Kabey or what to do when we confront him!" Brondin cried.

Even as Brondin spoke, Traissell was drawing a piece of folded vellum from his pack. He laid it against a sloping rock and opened it to reveal a detailed plan of the palace. With a gaunt finger, he indicated one chamber.

"You must go here. Follow this tunnel—it's one of the old storm drains—and it will take you to the proper level," he said, tracing a path for them. "Do you have a lantern and plenty of oil? It will be dark down there."

"We'll find it. But what do we do once we're there, Traissell? Will we find Karash-Kabey?"

"I only know you must go there if he's to be stopped. And you must hurry to arrive before the assault. There's a chance you might be able to avert the battle if you defeat Halssa's wizard. And if you don't, he may be able to bring some terrible weapons to bear on your friends."

"More of those demons?"

"Probably. And worse things."

Brondin shuddered from revulsion as much as from remembered horror. "Then I must go. But I'll enter the city alone. There's no reason to place Ciantha in such danger."

"I must go! I will go!" Ciantha cried angrily.

"But we don't know what awaits us. Why risk both our lives?"

"Ciantha must go with you," the healer said. "She has the

Vannenson blood, as you do. And that is your greatest weapon."

"And I'm coming, too," said Cabanard. Before Brondin could voice his protest, he added, "I can't stop one of those demons, but I can handle anything human that carries a weapon. You can't fight off a patrol by yourself, Brondin."

Brondin looked at Ciantha's set, angry face and at the quietly determined Cabanard, standing with folded arms and awaiting his reply. Reluctantly, he nodded. He took Ciantha in his arms and reached out to clasp Cabanard's hand. "I'm glad to have your help. I just don't want to lose either of you."

"You won't," they said in unison.

CHAPTER TWENTY-TWO

TO THE PLACE OF RECKONING

They reached the settlement at Riverbend that night. Once the rescue party was on the way with the materials Traissell had requested, the three travelers surrendered to their weariness and slept until well into the morning.

All that day, Brondin listened to news of the alliance. Once he had put the bits of information together, the picture was encouraging. Ciantha's couriers had spread their message swiftly. His own men, led by Henorik, were already on the march north, where the armies were to gather on the plain before the High City on the last day of Earlygreen.

Parhender was still mouthing ambitious threats, but he had not acted. It was now clear to Brondin that talk was as much as anyone could expect from such a man, and he wondered how he ever could have thought otherwise. Parhender had the desire to be dangerous, but not the will. He was a born follower with the pride of a conqueror. He would not be helpful, but he was no threat.

Zathias had died early in the month of Gleaning, but his son Zantorne was of their number. He was younger than Brondin and eager to prove himself on the field. A powerful new ally, Moorook of Red Hill, had joined them and added seven score bowmen and nearly as many swordsmen to the army of assault. Stallicho and Witigense had settled their quarrel and fixed their peace by a marriage of their children. Now they were closer friends than before. Other men, petty landholders and warlords, were sending smaller contingents to the plain.

Halssa had injured too many people too many times in his reign. The forces of retribution were gathering now, and he could not stop them. There would be battles and many deaths, and blood and fire would again redden the High City, unless

Ciantha and Brondin could somehow prevent the clash of armies.

Brondin heard one bit of news that he kept to himself. Green Hall now stood abandoned, and no traveler would approach within five greatmarks of it. The master of Green Hall, one Domitane, had awakened all within its walls one winter night with his screams of terror. The chief guard, Ivermay, found his master cowering in a corner of the sleeping chamber, a jellied huddle of quivering flesh, quite out of his senses.

Domitane died that day, gibbering to his last breath of a dark bird that turned into a many-armed beast, a flapping cloak, a pool of darkness, and other things. By nightfall, Green Hall was empty.

That night Brondin lay long awake, his mind too bestirred for sleep. The full responsibility of his position was clear to him as it had never been before, and he felt crushed beneath it. He could not prevent the suffering of innocents in the siege of the High City or protect them from the fury that would surely follow its fall. Perhaps if he marched at the head of his army, he would feel worthy of his men's risks and capable of holding their battle-roused passions in check; but that could never be. The very thought of himself hobbling along, bobbing and stumbling, sword in his hand and crutch tucked beneath his arm, was ludicrous. He gave in to a bitter self-mocking laugh and stared out at the stars. He would never lead men as his father had.

But then, he asked himself, had Balthid or any man now living done such deeds as he? Three times he had faced demons from some dark place beyond his imagining; he had fought them, and he had overcome. He bore with him, in his very blood, a power to withstand the power of evil sorcery, for he had wielded the sword of Korang, immune to its warping influence. Such deeds placed him in the company of Ambescand and the sons of Vannen. He pondered this for a moment and then shook his head and laughed again as he pictured himself a puffed-up dwarf strutting among giants. His accomplishments were the result of luck, not of his own greatness. Those men were a different breed.

He wished that he might possess for a time the trait he so

often scorned in others: the ability to believe wholeheartedly in his own importance, despite all the worldly proof of his insignificance. Halssa had this gift; so did Parhender and most of the warlords and landholders and petty chiefs Brondin had dealt with in his short life as a ruler. He had seen men who were leaders of a half dozen ragged hungry ruffians and who swaggered like emperors. Such self-deception could —and usually did—drive men to folly and destruction, but it could also raise them to greatness. Surely, he told himself, surely Ambescand, Colberane, Staver, and Ordred had known from the outset that they were special men with gifts above all others, marked for a higher destiny. Such men could never have doubted their own abilities. But he, who shared their blood, did not share their certainty. Ciantha, he was sure, enjoyed it in full measure; but not he.

If he were certain of his mission, it might be possible to feel confidence; but he was walking into the unknown. He and Ciantha knew only that they must seek out and enter a chamber deep below the palace and confront Karash-Kabey face to face somewhere in the High City. Whether the sorcerer would be awaiting them—perhaps in that very chamber, armed with awful magic—they did not know. They might find themselves pent in some underground cell with an assassin demon or some worse horror. And they were placing themselves in this peril on nothing more than the word of a one-eyed old healer who had appeared in their lives from nowhere and taken complete charge of them.

Brondin sat up and perched on the edge of the narrow bed, his face buried in his hands. In the stillness that blanketed Riverbend, he could almost hear his imagination working. Thought was eroding his will and courage, undermining what little confidence he possessed. He must not think, but do. He must go boldly into the darkness and act as the moment required. It was a time for blind trust, and he found that he could not trust where he did not understand. He fell back on the bed and at last drifted into a troubled sleep full of phantoms and shadowy menace.

Rain was falling when the three left the settlement in the early light. It fell all day and for most of the days and nights of their eastward journey. Winter was over at last, and the melting snow and spring rains turned the plain into a sea of soft, clinging mud. The paths and byways were soon concealed under sheets of wind-furrowed water, but the main roads, hard-packed by generations of wayfarers, rose high and firm above the brimming ditches on either side.

They decided to spend their nights at an inn when an inn could be found, just as ordinary travelers would do. For the curious, they had a simple story: Cabanard was on his way to the High City to open a training school for caravan guards and any others who wished to learn skill with weapons; Ciantha and Brondin, his son and daughter, were his helpers. When pressed for details, they displayed the sword of Korang —a gift from a grateful western warlord, they said—and further questions were abandoned in admiration of the great blade.

One chill damp evening, before a bright blaze in a snug little inn, they dined in the company of two traders who were on their way to the Fastness. The traders were less concerned with where the three were going than with where they had been. They questioned them closely about the mountain trails.

"What about robbers?" one asked.

"We encountered none and saw sign of none," Cabanard assured them.

The traders exchanged an incredulous glance, and one said, "That's very strange. We've heard that they were more active than ever now that Halssa's pulled back his patrols."

"Why did he do that? Is there trouble in the city?" Brondin asked.

"Halssa seems to think so. I've heard talk of an army of his enemies planning to lay siege to the city. Mind you, I've seen nothing, and all I know is what I've heard. It might be a lot of empty talk."

"Is that why you're leaving the city?" Ciantha asked.

The trader hesitated for a moment, glanced at his partner, and then said, "In part, it is. Oh, we have business to do at the Fastness, a good deal of it. We had hoped to go there as part of a caravan, but we've heard of none forming. It's impossible to get guards. If a man's capable of bearing arms, he's not permitted to leave the city."

"If we were a few years younger, we wouldn't have gotten out ourselves," his partner said.

"To be honest with you, stranger," said the first trader, addressing Cabanard, "I'd be reluctant to bring my family into the High City just now."

"It sounds as if there'd be plenty of business for us."

"A city under siege is no place to be. Especially for a young lady."

"I can take care of myself," Ciantha said confidently.

"Perhaps you can, but sometimes. . . ." The trader hesitated as if it pained him to speak but then went on. "I was in the city when it fell to the brigands and adventurers. I was only a boy then, but I fought, and I still carry the scars. Everyone fought. And when the city fell, some terrible things were done. If I'd had a daughter, I think I would have killed her myself before I let those men get their hands on her."

Cabanard said irritably, "From what I've heard, there were terrible things done on both sides. And the Council of Thirty-nine had made a lot of people suffer during their time in power."

The trader held up his hands. "I'm not defending the council, my friends. They deposed Stiragos and killed him and his family. Stiragos was not a great king, but he was a lawful king and a decent man, and he deserved no such fate. Perhaps the fall of the High City was an act of justice. I only say that if there's to be a siege, I prefer to be far away."

The traders soon excused themselves to confer apart. Brondin rose and limped to the fireside. He stood so that the warmth fell full on his bad leg, and he gazed gloomily into the flames. His leg was paining him severely, the ordinary ache of cold damp weather aggravated by the renewed strain of travel. Ciantha came to his side.

"It sounds bad in the High City," she said.

"It will be worse if we fail. It won't matter which side wins; people will suffer all the same. They're our people, Ciantha, all of them, on both sides. We have to end this before the fighting begins."

"We will," Ciantha said.

"I wish I had your confidence," Brondin said, gazing bleakly into the fire. She took his hand, and when he looked into her eyes, he saw there a question that she could not bring herself to speak aloud. He laid his other hand over hers and, shaking his head, said, "I'm not afraid, really. It's the uncertainty. If we had a definite task before us, no matter how hard or dangerous it might be, at least we'd know what's expected of us. As it is, I feel like a tool in the hands of some power I can't even imagine."

"I do, too. But I remember a story about Ambescand." She smiled up at him and drew him to a stool near the fire. When he was seated, she stood behind him, her hands on his shoulders, and said, "My mother told it to me when I was very small. I don't remember every detail, but I remember her telling me that even Ambescand didn't know his true mission until the last days of his life, when he forged the blades of liberation."

"I never heard any such story."

"Well, that's what my mother told me, Brondin. She said that it was only at the sacred forge, in his final days, that all was made plain to Ambescand. Everything fell into place, like stones being brought together to make a tower, and he saw the true purpose and direction of his life, all of it, from the very beginning to that moment."

"But that's only a story for children, Ciantha. Can you really believe that Ambescand lived his entire life in ignorance? Think of what he did, of all he accomplished. Was that the life of a man blundering in the dark?"

"No, it wasn't like that. I'm not putting it clearly, Brondin. There was a reason for everything Ambescand did. But all the events of his life were leading him to one great deed, and he didn't know that until the moment came. It was much the same with the sons of Vannen. When they left the Headland, they didn't dream that they would one day confront the power of the Stone Hand and vanquish the Cairnlord forever. But when the moment came, they knew."

Brondin reached up and laid his hand on hers. Turning, he looked up into her face and said, "It may be true, Ciantha, but am I a man like Ambescand or the sons of Vannen? You're worthy of the name you bear, but I'm not a warrior, not a healer, certainly not a wizard."

"You hold yourself in low esteem, Brondin."

"I don't think so. I know the things I can do and the

things I can't. Wishes won't make me into something I'm not. I try to see things as they really are."

"No man sees things as they really are. When you set out from Balthid's Keep, did you imagine the things you'd see and do in the days to come? Did you dream of overcoming demons or wielding the blade of Korang?" Brondin made no reply. She leaned lower and said softly, "Did you dream you might find me?"

Brondin pulled himself to his feet and looked down on her lovingly. "In truth, Ciantha, your words would make a man out of me. I'm no more certain than I ever was and every bit as ignorant of what lies ahead, but you turn my thoughts to other things. You give me hope."

"Nothing more?"

"Much more. I care for you far more than I care for myself, Ciantha, and I want you with me always. But when I think of the danger that may await—"

She raised her hand to his lips to silence him. "I must go with you, Brondin. There is no alternative for us. We'll do what we must do, and when the need comes, the strength will come. We must believe that. And when our work is done, we'll have our life together."

The morning was gloomy and chilly, and the world lay drowned in a swirling milky mist, but no rain was falling as they left the inn, and none fell during the gray day. They passed that night in a barn, dry but cold, and the following night at a dreary inn, where they sat late before a small but welcome fire, with no company but a single sniffling, coughing innkeeper. On the next day, in the middle of the morning, they reached the dry channel leading from the abandoned storm drain.

They followed it until the afternoon. For a time, they walked along the bank, but as they moved ever closer to the High City, they decided that it was more prudent to descend to the channel bed itself, a mark and more below them, and thus remain out of sight. The mist had thinned somewhat, but it still lay on the ground, obscuring vision. They might easily walk into a patrol without warning if they remained above.

They came at last to a round orifice nearly a mark in

diameter, set into a slope. Here the streambed ended. The mouth of the storm drain was guarded by a curtain of metal bars, each one the thickness of a child's wrist, set at intervals of about a hand's length.

Cabanard and Brondin inspected the bars. Cabanard tugged hard at one, but it was firm. He glanced at Brondin, who nodded. They laid their things aside and, removing their cloaks, wrapped them around two adjoining bars to form protective pads over the rasplike rusted metal.

They took up a stance facing one another. Each took a firm grip on one bar and set his foot against the other. Brondin found it painful to rest all his weight on his bad leg, but there was no way to avoid it. Piercing this barrier would require all the combined strength and leverage that he and Cabanard could exert.

At the word, they strained against the bars, each pulling with all his might while his foot pushed in support of his partner's efforts. The bars creaked. Dry mortar crumbled and fell from the sockets, and the bars yielded slightly. At their second effort, the bars gave a bit more, but still not enough to admit even the slender Ciantha.

They leaned against the grating, taking in great gulps of air. Cabanard rubbed his shoulder, kneading his broad fingers hard into the muscle.

"How's your leg holding up?" he asked.

Brondin, still panting from exertion, did not answer at once. His response, when it came, was fragmentary. "Leg's all right. It's the arms. Feel like they're going to come right out of the sockets."

"Mine, too."

"But it's working."

"This time we'll do it," said Cabanard, flexing his hands.

They set themselves, gripped, and pulled with all their strength. Again, dry mortar sifted down, this time mixed with chips of stone. The bars groaned and slowly bowed until the space between them was the length of a full forearm, elbow to fingertips. The first barrier was breached.

The interior of the storm drain was dark and cool, but it was dry. Once inside, Brondin and Cabanard sprawled on the curving floor to rest their aching muscles, while Ciantha kindled a flame with the tinderbox. When torch and lantern were both alight, they folded their damp and mud-stained traveling cloaks and laid them aside. Taking only their remaining food and water and their weapons, they set off into the darkness. Cabanard led the way by torchlight, with Ciantha close behind. Brondin followed with the lantern.

The light of the entrance winked out as the storm drain rose and then leveled, and they walked on with wavering shadows before and behind. The way was straight and the surface smooth, and they made good speed to their first objective. Cabanard held the torch high, and all three gathered to look upward to a small round grating set directly overhead.

"Just big enough to let us through and small enough for us to move," said Cabanard.

"Unless it's barred," Brondin said.

"Traissell didn't seem to think it would be. Maybe he has friends in the city who cleared the way."

"But why?"

Cabanard shrugged. "I don't know. But so far, we've been guided well. I was in the city for a time, and all the grates I ever saw or heard of were so big, it took two men with tackle to move them. I don't know how Traissell found out about this one, but I'm glad he did. We can move it."

Brondin set himself under the grate. Taking his crutch, he placed the crosspiece against one of the bars and strained upward. The grating moved slightly.

"Will the crutch take the strain?" Cabanard asked.

"It's a single piece of oak. It can take anything."

Cabanard took a grip on the crutch. Together they thrust upward and then quickly to the side as the grating rose. It clattered and rang on the stone, and then the silence returned.

"I'll go up first," said Brondin.

Cabanard did not question the decision. He stooped, and Brondin stepped from his knee to his back and then straightened to grip the rim of the opening. Ciantha handed him the lantern and his crutch. Placing them above, he pulled himself up and out of sight.

Brondin found himself in a corridor that extended at right angles to the storm drain. It was slightly narrowed—he could almost touch the walls with his arms outstretched—but much higher, with a vaulted ceiling. The floor was flat. A shallow channel ran along the base of each wall to carry off the seepage, but the channels were dry. He heard no sound but the rustle of his own motion.

A coldness came over him; not a coldness of the body but a chill that touched his soul, as if he had entered a place from which mortal men had long been absent and were not welcome. Cabanard's shout from below jarred him from his uneasy mood.

"I'm all right," he called down. "It's eerie up here, but I see no danger."

He knelt and, bracing himself with one hand, reached down to draw Ciantha up to him. Cabanard came up next. Brondin, still kneeling, glanced at the grating and then at Cabanard.

"What do you think? Should we replace it?"

"Better leave the way open. We may want to get out in a hurry."

"What about guards?" Ciantha asked.

"The guards never come to these levels."

"Then we'll leave it open. Let's check the map and then be off. It's cold just sitting here," Brondin said.

According to the map, they were on the proper level. The chamber lay about three greatmarks away, at the end of a tangled skein of turns and counterturns. The map appeared to show other routes, simpler and more direct, but they kept to the way marked out, aware that passages unguarded by men might be under the care of more dangerous guardians.

The feeling of cold and depression grew in each of them as they closed on the appointed chamber. They did not speak of it to one another. For a long time, they did not speak at all; the hollow echo of their voices in that stone corridor was not a reassuring sound. But as they made turn after turn, Brondin, who now led the way, found Ciantha walking ever more closely behind him. Finally she came to his side, took the lantern from him, and slipped her hand into his.

"We're nearly there," Brondin said, his voice hushed.

"I'm cold, Brondin," she whispered. "There's something about the air here . . . the stillness. I'm afraid."

"There's magic close by. I can feel it," Cabanard said, and his deep voice set the echoes chattering to one another.

"I feel something, too. I felt it as soon as I came through the opening," Brondin confessed.

"So did I," said Ciantha.

Cabanard added, "Me, too. I didn't want to say anything."

They looked at one another uneasily. Their pace faltered just for a moment, but then Brondin stepped out doggedly, and the regular tap of his crutch on the stone rang in a faster tempo. Ciantha hurried at his side, and Cabanard, torch held high, followed close behind.

They rounded the final corner, and ahead of them they saw a faint glow. As they approached, they saw that it came through a wide doorway, as if a low fire were burning deep within the chamber beyond.

At the entrance, Brondin waved the others back while he stepped within to study the place. The light came from a single cresset that hung from a chain whose upper end vanished into darkness. It burned with a faint flame that was barely light enough to assure Brondin that the chamber was empty. He turned and bade Ciantha and Cabanard join him. The instant they reached his side, the air grew bright. There came a rumbling sound, and the entrance was gone. With astonished eyes, they looked on a stone wall that showed no hint of an opening.

Turning, they received a second shock. Beneath the flaring cresset stood a tall man, white-haired and dressed all in black. In his hand was a staff with a crystal tip that caught and held the light.

"At last you come to me," he said. His voice was soft and mild, yet it held a note of triumph. "Now, together, we will bring this work to its conclusion."

CHAPTER TWENTY-THREE

THE COMING OF THE MASTER

"Who are you? And what work do you speak of?" Brondin demanded of the still figure.

"The men of the city call me Karash-Kabey. Here in this chamber I will complete a work begun before the stars had names, and you will assist me."

"You'll get no help from us."

"No willing help perhaps, yet the help I need, you will provide. You have already given more. I would have been satisfied with a few drops of your blood. Now I have you both, the flesh and blood and soul of the enemy delivered into my hands."

"And what do you think you'll do with us?" Ciantha asked.

"You will be the sacrifice I offer in proof of my pledge," said Karash-Kabey.

He spoke no further word and made no motion. Only the crystal at the tip of his staff flickered faintly, and at that instant a light began to shine in the chamber, waxing steadily until all was as bright as day and the contents of the chamber stood revealed. Behind Karash-Kabey, on a dais, stood a hive-shaped mound of gray stones the height of a tall man. Thrust into it so deeply that only a bare hand's breadth of blade and the handle could be seen was a sword with a crosspiece in the form of a pair of wings.

"What has this to do with Halssa?" Brondin asked.

"Halssa does not matter. Your fate is here."

"A sacrifice to a pile of stones? I think not, wizard," said Brondin, reaching behind him to draw his own sword.

Ignoring the threatening gesture, Karash-Kabey said, "It is the resting place of a power older than the race of men. I will make that power mine forever."

Brondin felt Ciantha's touch on his shoulder. "No mere

218

pile of stones, Brondin," she whispered. "A cairn. The Cairnlord's near. It's the Cairnlord's power he seeks. It must be."

"Then that blade must be the Iron Angel," Brondin said in a voice hushed with wonder.

"It is, Brondin. I can feel the certainty in my bones. And if he tampers with it, Staver's work might be undone! The Cairnlord might be loosed on the world again, with no one to resist its power this time!" Ciantha said.

"The power was checked and scattered, thought to be lost forever. But I learned where the Stone Hand lay. I searched out the cairn and rebuilt it, and as it took shape, the power and the essence of the Cairnlord revived and grew ever stronger, inhering within the stone, restrained only by the presence of the Iron Angel."

"That's why you urged the harbor work!" Brondin cried. "You weren't serving Halssa; you were using him to regain the cairn!"

"I served the Cairnlord, and soon the Cairnlord will serve me. We will become one when its power pours forth from that stone prison and flows into me, transfigures me."

"Set that thing free, and it will destroy you," said Ciantha.

"Two things the Cairnlord desires beyond all others," the wizard went on as if she had not spoken, "and they are release and revenge. I offer both. It need only promise to serve me, and I will set it free and deliver the children of its enemy into its power." He raised his hand to point at them. "You are the final ingredient in the magic."

Brondin raised his sword and started for him. Karash-Kabey dipped his staff; the crystal flashed, and Brondin's crutch burst apart, shattered soundlessly into splinters. Brondin fell heavily to the floor, unable to break his fall. With a groan of rage and pain, he hurled the blade at the sorcerer, who struck it aside carelessly with his staff.

Cabanard darted forward, snatched up the blade at a dead run, and hurled himself on Karash-Kabey with the sword raised overhead, poised for a two-handed blow that would shear the man in half. As he brought the sword down, it slowed and halted in midair, as if it had encountered some invisible barrier. The big swordsman's arms bulged and knotted with the strain. Veins stood out on his forehead, and his knuckles whitened with his effort; but the blade was immobilized as if it had been in the hands of a statue.

Karash-Kabey reached up to touch the blade with the crystal stone of his staff. The sword glowed in a sudden flare of brilliant light, and Cabanard cried out in agony. He dropped the sword and staggered back, moaning, while white smoke rose from his charred and ruined hands.

"Provoke me no further, or you will suffer greatly before I allow you to die," said the wizard.

Brondin pulled himself to his feet with Ciantha's help. He did not release her arm. "Do as he says. We have no power to resist him."

"But we must stop him!"

Brondin shook his head helplessly. "How can we stop a sorcerer? We've been betrayed, Ciantha. We listened to Traissell and believed him, like a pair of foolish children."

"I can't believe that he betrayed us."

"I don't want to believe it, but it seems plain. He directed us here, even insisted that you come along. If you hadn't, there'd still be someone of our line surviving even if the Cairnlord killed me. But this way, the family dies. There'll be no one to resist the Cairnlord, no one who even knows it's free until too late," Brondin said. He took her in his arms, and as she pressed her head to his chest, he leaned down to whisper, "When I get the chance, I'll attack. Use your dagger on him then. Whatever he does to me, use your dagger and get him. He must be stopped."

They went to Cabanard's side. The swordsman's weathered face was contorted in pain. He lay on his back, his hands like raw, singed claws at his side. He breathed in deep, slow, shuddering breaths.

Leaning on Ciantha's arm, Brondin knelt stiffly at his side. "I'm sorry, Cabanard. Truly, I'm sorry," he said.

Cabanard turned his head to look at him through pain-bleared slits. "Not your doing," he gasped.

"I shouldn't have brought you here. Not you, not Ciantha."

"We came by choice."

Brondin laid his hand on his friend's shoulder. He had no words adequate to his feelings and could only hope that Cabanard understood.

Climbing to his feet, he faced Karash-Kabey, who stood a

scant mark away. The sword of Korang lay at the wizard's feet, but the cloak pin was gone, fallen when the white heat of enchantment had burned the bindings loose as it seared Cabanard's hands. Even with the cloak pin fastened to it, the sword had yielded to the will of Karash-Kabey. Brondin felt a great desolation of spirit at the hopelessness of their situation and the futility of his plan. Unarmed, devoid of magic, he could not dream of defeating a wizard of such power. Yet he must try.

He took a step forward, stooped as if to reach for the fallen blade, and then sprang at the wizard's throat with outstretched hands, hoping to catch him by surprise. He did not. He saw the glowing crystal on the staff swing to meet him, and he felt a sudden terrible blow, like a hammer landing full force at once on every part of his body, within and without.

He did not know how long he lay stunned. When he began to regain his senses, he was aware of nothing but pain. His flesh burned as if he lay packed in hot coals. All his bones seemed shattered; tendons and sinews felt torn asunder.

He heard screams. Faintly they came at first, then clearly. He wondered whether they were his own screams and was sure that they must be, since no one could bear in silence such pain as his. But he gradually realized that he was not crying out. He was beyond even that relief. The sound was outside him.

He opened his eyes and raised his head slightly. Pain lanced through him, and he thought for an instant that his head would burst apart. When his vision cleared, he saw Ciantha. She was huddled against the wall, crouching, hands raised as if to ward off a blow, and she was shrieking like the condemned who howl forever in the darkest corridors of Shagghya. Karash-Kabey stood over her, his open hand extended, not touching her or even coming near; yet Brondin could sense the pain and terror pouring forth from his fingertips like a scalding spray on flesh and spirit.

Brondin let his head sink back. He could do nothing for Ciantha, and he could not bear to look on helplessly. He wanted only to die and end his pain. He remembered the times he had felt the aching of his leg and thought in his innocence that he knew something of pain. Those pale shadows of true agony had been so little painful that he would now count the man blessed who had only to endure a lifetime of such trifles. Remembering, he felt an insane mirth rise in him, and his laughter brought with it agony, and the agony wrenched forth more laughter until he passed out.

When he awoke again, his head was clear. The pain remained. The chamber was silent.

Slowly he raised his head. Ciantha lay crumpled by the wall, unmoving. He could not see Cabanard. Karash-Kabey stood by the cairn, his eyes fixed on the Iron Angel. In a small black pot on either side of the wizard and at his back a low flame burned steadily. He was speaking in a low monotone, and Brondin could not distinguish the words. His hands traced intricate figures in the air.

Brondin could not long endure the added pain of holding up his head. He lay back, gasping and staring at the darkness overhead, and sank into the pain of despair. He had failed in every way. He and his friends were doomed, the woman he loved was to die a wretched death, and soon the power of evil would flow like a dark tide over all the earth. When he and Ciantha had died whatever monstrous death the Cairn-lord chose to inflict on them, there would be no one left to stand against the old enemy. All the courage and sacrifice, all the bold deeds and the long struggle of Ambescand and the sons of Vannen and Ciantha would be obliterated, forgotten, rendered worthless by the failure of the last of their line.

And at the very brink of desolation came the thought, *All this may be so, but I am not dead yet. The struggle is not over.*

He lifted his head again to watch the wizard. Karash-Kabey was silent, poised motionless before the cairn, arms extended and head thrown back. He breathed deeply, slowly, three successive breaths. Then he spoke a word aloud and closed his hands on the hilt of the Iron Angel.

For a moment he gripped it, straining. Then his back arched; his eyes bulged, and he emitted a low gurgling cry, a sound wrung from him as much by surprise and fear as by pain. Brondin watched, astonished, this sudden reversal, as Karash-Kabey tore free from the Iron Angel, reeled back blindly like a drunken man in helpless flight, and collapsed.

For a time he lay whimpering like a beaten dog; then he was silent.

Now there was hope. Brondin steeled himself against the pain and tried to rise. Three times he fell back, dazed by the currents of agony that raced through him at the least effort. On the fourth attempt, he pulled himself to his hands and knees.

He was no longer fully sane, and there was a remote corner of his mind that perceived this. His thoughts were like images moving over the jumbled shards of a broken mirror: fragmentary, disordered, and fleeting. Before everything else, dominating by its intensity, was pain. There was hate, and love for his friends and followers, and shame for his failure, and pride, and fear, and a great anger, and a longing for peace.

He started to creep forward to the cairn and collapsed. No longer able to rise, he dragged himself across the stone floor, teeth clenched, blazing eyes fixed on the sword hilt. With the Iron Angel in his hands, he would be powerless no longer. Its touch had blasted Karash-Kabey into helplessness, and it alone could destroy the sorcerer and end the danger. The Iron Angel would be his deliverance and his victory.

The distance to the base of the dais seemed endless, but at last he made it. There he stopped. The platform on which the cairn stood rose a half mark from the floor. Brondin gripped the edge, tried to draw himself up, and failed. If there had been steps to the dais, he might have crawled up, but he had seen none. His strength was gone, and his will was not enough. He beat his fist on the stone, almost weeping in his rage and frustration, and then a shadow fell over him. Karash-Kabey stood on the dais, looking down. His face was ashen, glistening with perspiration, but his expression was as calm as ever.

"It appears that not all can touch the Iron Angel unharmed," said the sorcerer.

"Then you've failed," Brondin murmured, unable to look up.

"I have been delayed, nothing more. You will draw the blade for me, and I will succeed."

"You will never succeed," said a commanding voice close at Brondin's back.

"You!" Karash-Kabey cried.

"Yes, it's I. Not dead, nor mad."

Brondin recognized the voice but could not believe what he heard. Slowly, painfully, he turned his head and saw Traissell standing almost within his reach. But it was a different Traissell from the old healer he had known. Now he wore a soft pale robe that glowed with its own inwoven brightness; his eye patch was gone, and a jewel-like light glittered in the socket so long concealed. Strength and serenity came from him; and with the knowledge that Traissell was not their betrayer but their rescuer, Brondin felt his own strength renewed. He forced himself to his knees, and as he paused, gasping, Traissell laid gentle hands on his temples. At the touch, Brondin felt the pain flow from him like an evil flood receding.

"You are free with your power," Karash-Kabey said.

"I use my power as it should be used—a lesson you never learned."

"I learned from you all that I needed."

"You never learned control. You were my failure," said Traissell.

Karash-Kabey uttered a small mirthless laugh. "You measure failure in a curious way. I alone unearthed the great secret. It was you and the others who rejected it and turned on me. I overcame you all. I alone sought out the cairn and rebuilt it, stone by stone. And when I have annihilated you, I will unlock the cairn and become one with the power of the Cairnlord."

"You've lived with your own lies for so long, I suppose you believe them by now," Traissell said, and his voice was sad but patient. He turned to Brondin. "You, at least, will hear the truth. This creature was once my pupil. We dwelt in a land unknown in the north, and our names were not the names you know. I can scarcely remember them myself. It was many mortal lifetimes ago."

"Too many, perhaps," Karash-Kabey observed. "You were an old man when I was an apprentice. Now I am at the peak of my power, and you? It must require all your magic simply to keep from crumbling into dust."

Traissell smiled and shook his head. "Do you think I stopped learning on the day you broke the circle? I had my own two eyes then. Have you forgotten? An eye is a terrible price to pay, but it bought me valuable magic." Laying his hand on Brondin's shoulder, Traissell continued. "He and I and five of his fellow pupils belonged to a keeping-circle, working and studying together, preparing for a life of service to our people. One day we became aware of a great struggle going on in the world, a confrontation between good and evil magic of such magnitude that the power of both sides was consumed and a portion of the world was drained of all magic. When I sought further knowledge of this struggle, I found the way veiled. I deemed it wisest to look no deeper."

Traissell turned to cast the light of that glittering inhuman eye on Karash-Kabey, who faced it unflinchingly. "But he chose to seek further," said Traissell with a sigh. "Slowly, patiently, in deepest secrecy, he unraveled the tangled skein and learned that a being incredibly ancient, steeped in evil, had been overmastered by a mage with an enchanted blade. The locus of this being's power was a mound of stone. The mage had bound it to its locus forever by thrusting the blade into the stone and plunging all beneath the sea. And now my pupil proposed that our circle seek out the cairn and release the evil being in exchange for its power. And we refused him."

"You feared the power I offered you," Karash-Kabey said contemptuously. "You were content to spend your lives healing, protecting the borders, and enriching the harvests—the magic of apprentices and crones."

"Such was the work we were sworn to," Traissell said to Brondin. "Our countrymen relied on us. When he urged us to abandon our vows, we rejected him. But he won his brother and another poor misguided pupil to his side. When the rest of us denounced them, they attacked us. Of our circle, only he and his brother and I survived, and our land was blighted for a generation."

Traissell's voice had grown hushed, and he fell silent as if pondering his own words. Brondin glanced around and saw Ciantha kneeling upright, rubbing her eyes like one emerging from an evil sleep. He longed to go to her side, but Traissell held him firmly, as much by his story as by the firm hand on his shoulder.

"They left me near death—far nearer death than life—and

when I recovered, they were gone. That is when my search began." Traissell raised his head. "I've lost all track of years and distances . . . even of names. I've been so many men in so many lands. But at last I found the brother. He was a half-wit, living in a pigsty."

"He turned on me. He said we had wronged you and our people. He would have gone back and begged forgiveness. I emptied his mind," said Karash-Kabey.

"Enough remained of him to lead me to you. Here it must end."

"Here you end, old master. I will have a new beginning."

"But what of us?" Brondin cried. "Why are we here? We have no part in your conflict."

"I drew you here as an offering to the Cairnlord," Karash-Kabey said.

Brondin turned to Traissell. The elder wizard said, "That may be so. I can only tell you that I knew you and Ciantha must be with me at the final meeting."

"And Cabanard?"

"I knew there would be a third. I never saw his face," Traissell replied.

While Traissell's attention was diverted, Karash-Kabey moved quickly to take up the Doomstaff. At Brondin's warning cry, Traissell flung up his hands, palms outward. His opponent on the dais, seeing him ready, held off his attack.

"You will not stop me," said Karash-Kabey.

"I must."

"So for all your talk of healing and forgiveness, it comes at last to revenge. You disappoint me, old master."

"I seek no revenge. You're still my pupil, still like a son to me. I want to stop you before you destroy yourself utterly."

"No!" Karash-Kabey cried, enraged.

"Turn away from this now and return with me. With your magic, you can do great good and atone—"

Again, Karash-Kabey cried, "No!" He gripped his staff and raised it high, and the crystal head flashed brightly. The air grew thick, charged with a force that chilled Brondin's spirit even as it burned his flesh and sent him staggering back as if from a blow. He lay paralyzed by fear and wonder as the clash of magics broke before him.

The atmosphere of the chamber came to life. Brondin sensed unimaginable things swooping and stalking all around him and through him, pouncing and struggling and dissolving to re-form and renew the attack. He felt like a man suspended in the calm center of a maelstrom, unmoving at the still heart of a whirling cone of destruction, untouched in the midst of titanic energies that collided with the shock of mountains meeting headlong and falling back, only to spring to the combat anew.

Amid the tumult of these unseen powers, Traissell and Karash-Kabey stood taut and erect, rapt in concentration, the poles of the forces that rang and crackled and ripped through the charmed arena of their combat. Traissell still held his hands before his chest, palms out. His opponent gripped his staff tightly and held it across his body like a man preparing for a bout with quarterstaves. Only in the sheen of their skin, the throbbing of the temple veins, and the shudders and sudden starts that shook their bodies could the ferocity of the struggle be seen.

Brondin thought of Ciantha. He wanted to go to her, shelter her, protect her from the invisible storm that raged there, but he could not so much as turn to look at her. He could feel himself slipping away, being drawn into the churning currents of magic, and he could not resist. Bereft of even the protective cloak pin, he had no shield for body or mind. His will was dissolving, his senses blending and changing, his mind cracking into fragments that flew from him like leaves before an autumn storm. In this contest, he was of no more consequence than an insect on a field where armies meet in the shock of war, as helpless, as ignorant, as much a prey to blind chance.

And yet he was meant to be here—he and Ciantha and a third as their companion. Traissell's words rang through his consciousness clear as a note from a war horn. He was needed. He had a role to play, work to do.

While Brondin struggled to regain mastery of his mind and will, the greater struggle intensified. Wild light flashed from Traissell's eye and was met by brilliant bursts from the Doomstaff. Both men were streaming with perspiration; blood trickled from the corners of Traissell's mouth and from his opponent's nostrils. They wavered like men driven beyond endurance, exhausted and drained of all strength. Still the war went on.

Then the blood burst from Karash-Kabey's nostrils and lips in a bright flow. He fell heavily forward on the dais, still clutching his staff.

The light in Traissell's eye flared and then dimmed abruptly. He could not press his advantage. He sank to his knees, clutching at his heart, his face contorted.

Karash-Kabey tried to raise himself but could not. He fell gasping and groaning, drooling bloody froth, and then he tried again. This time he managed to prop himself on an elbow, and there he paused with his head lowered. He was recovering, and Traissell showed no sign of awareness.

Brondin saw, and knew in an instant what his role was to be. He pulled himself to the dais and worked his way to where the Iron Angel jutted from the cairn. When he gripped the sword hilt, he felt its power sing within him; with a single tug, he drew it free.

The Iron Angel was a massive blade, yet it rode lightly in his hands. He turned to where Karash-Kabey lay, and, raising the sword, he started forward.

The fallen sorcerer turned at the first sidelong glimpse of motion. At the sight of the blade, his eyes widened in terror. Quickly, desperately, he swept his staff around in a gesture, not at the Iron Angel, against which he was helpless, but at Brondin.

A lash of fire coiled around Brondin's ankles, jerking him backward. He fell to the dais, landing hard, and his momentum sent him rolling off the edge, where he lay stunned for a moment. The Iron Angel flew free and rang on the stones at Traissell's side.

When Brondin recovered, both wizards had regained their feet. Blood-spattered, sweat-soaked, panting for breath, they faced each other poised for a duel that sent a shudder through Brondin. Before each, hovering in the air head-high as if wielded by an invisible giant, was a sword: the Iron Angel for Traissell, the blade of Korang for his opponent. Slowly, cautiously, the blades glided toward each other. Then, moving too fast for Brondin's eye to follow, they clashed.

The chamber filled with the harsh arrhythmic clangor and the auroral flash of swordplay, but this was a match no mortal swordsman could have sustained. The speed and ferocity of stroke and counterstroke dazzled Brondin. Faint and dizzy, he averted his eyes and shrank into the shadow of the dais, scarcely daring to draw breath.

Back and forth beat the swords, weaving a web of flashing light between the motionless wizards. Then, in a stroke, the battle ended. The blade of Korang laid open Traissell's stomach, and as he collapsed and the Iron Angel fell to the floor, Korang's blade struck a second blow at the base of his neck. He dropped forward and lay motionless in the spreading pool of his own blood.

Brondin limped to the old wizard's side and knelt in the dark pool, but he could do nothing for his friend. Traissell was dead, and already his magic was fading and the years so long held at bay were claiming their due. His hands were scrawny yellow claws; his face was sunken and skull-like, and his hair lay in clumps in the congealing blood.

Instinctively, Brondin took up the Iron Angel. Holding it before him, he moved slowly to where Cabanard lay and motioned for Ciantha to join him. Standing astride his unconscious comrade, Ciantha close at his side, her dagger drawn, he awaited Karash-Kabey's attack.

The victorious wizard still leaned on his staff, looking down on his fallen enemy like one entranced. The sword of Korang hung in the air before him, unwavering, the red of Traissell's blood darkening as it congealed.

Then Karash-Kabey began to laugh, a low, deep laugh that was chilling to hear. "I've won," he said softly. Then louder, "I've won. The only man I ever feared is dead. There's no one to stop me." And then he cried, "I've won!"

He turned to the cairn and laid the crystal stone against it. "Come forth, lord of the cairn!" he said. "I give you freedom and the children of your enemy to punish. Come forth and pour your power into me and in my flesh walk the world again. I set you free!"

He stepped back, and a low laugh burst from him. Then, as he stood expectant by the cairn, the sword of Korang swung slowly in the air until its point was at the wizard's breast. He started and attempted to strike it aside with his staff, but the blow had no effect. The sword eased forward smoothly and inexorably. As Karash-Kabey screamed in astonishment and pain, it pierced him just beneath the breast-bone and sank steadily into his chest.

Flinging the Doomstaff aside, Karash-Kabey seized the crosspiece of the sword to hold it off. Brondin and Ciantha heard the snap of dislocated bones as the blade drove forward. Ciantha buried her face in her hands, but Brondin, for all the horror he felt, could not look away. He saw Karash-Kabey topple from the dais, arms limp at his sides as bits of rope, and land on his back. The blade of Korang sank deeper, ever deeper, until the muffled squeal of metal on stone set Brondin's teeth to chattering. When the crosspiece touched the wizard's robe, the sword rested.

Brondin lowered the Iron Angel and drew Ciantha to him. Neither could speak for a time. They clung together, trembling with relief at their deliverance.

"Is he dead?" Ciantha asked.

"Dead and rotting, like Traissell."

"Awful . . . just to disintegrate. . . ."

"They were alive in the time of the Stone Hand. That's ten generations ago," Brondin said, his voice hushed.

Ciantha felt the sudden tension that drew Brondin taut as a bowstring. She looked up and cried out sharply. Darkness was pouring from the cairn, dropping like a viscous fluid from the dais, oozing across the stones. Already it had enclosed the scanty remains of the fallen wizards, and it crawled ever nearer to where they stood, and Cabanard lay helpless.

The Cairnlord was coming forth.

CHAPTER TWENTY-FOUR

INFINITY IN A LITTLE ROOM

It was the last and greatest peril. Brondin could not know what the touch of the spreading darkness might do, but he feared it, and his fear fed on itself until he could feel panic gnawing within him.

The blackness flowed around them, dividing, and then closed upon itself to encircle them. They stood like castaways on a rock in the midst of a flood. Brondin fought his growing terror; he knew that if he succumbed now, they were lost. But his mouth was dry, and his hands trembled on the Iron Angel.

The black tide was rising, and the chamber was filling with a thick gloom, like frigid sullen smoke; yet the stone floor was clear around the three who waited at bay, and the air above them was a dome of light. It came to Brondin that the power of the Iron Angel was protecting them from the ancient enemy, and he saw a way to escape.

"Ciantha, I'm going to try to carry Cabanard out of here. I want you to take the Iron Angel," he said.

"I could never lift it!"

"You need only hold it. Rest it on your shoulder. You see how the blackness stands off. I think we're safe as long as one of us holds the sword."

"But if the darkness follows?"

"When we're outside, we'll lay the blade across the doorsill. The blackness won't be able to pass. We'll find a way to seal this chamber off so it can't escape."

Sudden fear broke over them like a wave. He knew that it came from the encompassing blackness, but reason was no defense against the onslaught of terror. He trembled, and the sword wavered. Ciantha reached out frantically, herself

231

in the grip of the same overwhelming fear, and her hands closed on Brondin's.

The terror vanished on the instant, and reassurance flowed through them like water through a parched land, bringing strength and new will. A light appeared in the gloom. It grew in size and brightness, and the darkness drew back and gathered into itself, clotting into impenetrable black, dense as stone yet churning with inhuman life.

The chamber shuddered and was gone. They stood on nothingness in an infinite void where light and darkness poised for a timeless interval before the clash and then came together like the bursting of all the storms since creation met in one. Colossal powers whirled around them, and sound unheard before by mortal ears vibrated in their bones. They felt the cold of the void between the worlds, and all that was reasonable and human in them feared for life and sanity; but something else within them glimpsed the truth and understood what was required of them in order that things sundered might be made whole.

They faced a new dilemma. To do what they must do, they had to enter the darkness together; but they could not leave Cabanard helpless to the dark tide that would surely engulf him once their protecting presence was removed. All the ponderous weight of duty urged them onward; friendship held them rooted fast.

They looked at each other and saw their anguish reflected in each other's eyes. Brondin shook his head helplessly. Ciantha clutched his arm and pointed to a golden gleam an arm's length from Cabanard's side.

"The cloak pin!" she cried.

It had lain forgotten since Cabanard's fall; it was now to be his protection. They reached out and caught it on the sword point, and Ciantha quickly affixed it to Cabanard's tunic.

Now they were ready. Hands linked on the Iron Angel, arms firm around each other's waists, they stepped into the abyss that was at once the arena of a cosmic battle and the chamber beneath the High City. The nothingness beneath their feet was prosaic flagstone; the howling whirlwind that shrieked and tore was the still air of the low vault; the great gulf that divided them from all things was a matter of a few confident steps. Calm and chaos were one.

They reached the cairn. It stood as before, on the dais in the center of the chamber, yet it and they hung suspended in the emptiness of infinity, and they did not question how this could be. It was impossible, yet it was so. A gap in the close-packed stones was before them. Gripping the hilt of the Iron Angel with both hands, they held it poised for an instant, set it carefully into the opening, and then, with all the force in them, plunged it deep into the cairn. It flowed into the stone as smoothly and soundlessly as a blade entering its proper scabbard. Around them a great cry arose and faded to a mournful wail, ever fainter and more distant, until it died in a peaceful sigh.

The walls of the chamber encircled them. Overhead hung the single cresset, swaying gently, and by its light they saw two scatterings of rotted rag on the dusty flagstones. No other trace of the wizards remained, and no trace at all of the blackness. The sword of Korang was gone. Cabanard sat dazed on the floor beneath the lamp, looking in bewilderment at his blistered hands.

A tall figure stood behind Cabanard, unseen by him. He was broad of shoulder, and his long hair was white. His simple robe, too, was white. At his side hung an empty scabbard.

He reached out and made a slight gesture over Cabanard's head. The warrior slumped forward, and the man in white laid him out carefully. He knelt over Cabanard and took the injured hands in his, one by one; then he crossed them on Cabanard's chest and rose to face Brondin and Ciantha.

"He will heal, and live to serve you long and faithfully," he said. He came to their side, smiled fondly, and held his hands out to them. "The worst is over. You've done well."

They knew him at once. Although they did not understand, they felt the link between them and reached out to him.

"Staver Ironbrand," Ciantha said, clasping his hand in hers.

"I am he. And you're the last of my kin. I can see my brothers in you both. You're of the line of Ordred, no mistaking that," said the mage to Ciantha. To Brondin he added, "And you look enough like Colberane to be his son. It's long since I saw them, but I remember."

"It's ten generations since the sons of Vannen came from the Headland to do battle with the Stone Hand," Brondin said.

"A long time by your reckoning. I sense time differently now."

"But you came back to save us."

"You summoned me."

They glanced at each other in surprise and then looked up into his strong, broad-featured face, which was still smiling on them. "But we knew nothing. We came here to . . . to . . ." Ciantha began, and then faltered in confusion.

Brondin finished for her. "To face the wizard. And something more. . . ."

"The memory will return," Staver assured them. "You've been through an ordeal few could survive, but you've done what was required of you. All have played their part, and for a time the dark power is checked."

"But what part . . . what use were we to someone with your power?" Ciantha asked.

"You brought me here. No one else could have done that," Staver replied, releasing their hands. When they looked at him, uncomprehending, he explained. "Your hands joined on the Iron Angel and opened the way for me to pursue the Cainlord, and only you, together, could replace the sword in the stone to imprison it again. Your part was great indeed."

"You speak as if all were foreordained," said Brondin.

"The way is plotted, but the end is unknown. Each of us has a duty, Brondin, and we cannot escape it. The creature we call the Cairnlord will spend eternity struggling to break free, and I will stand watch as long as it and I exist. There is much I cannot make clear, but believe this—the life you know is not the only life. Powers beyond our imagining are aware of all we do and have done and will do. I have been chosen by those powers to be their instrument. So have Ambescand, and my brothers, and my parents, and many others whose names are unknown to us. So have you."

"And the others: Cabanard and Traissell?"

"They, too, had their role. Cabanard gave his strength, Traissell his magic. Even the thief and the storyteller had their parts to play."

"The thief," Brondin repeated, struggling to remember. "Yes, there was a theft from Balthid's Keep. That's how it all began. I came north, searching."

"And because of the theft, you met the others. Traissell had a glimpse of what was to be. He knew that you and Ciantha had to be here when he confronted his enemy, but he never saw the pattern whole. He brought you together and led you here. That was sufficient."

"Poor Traissell," Ciantha murmured.

"Do not mourn him. He did the thing he was born to do, and then he died. Few men are so fortunate."

"So now it's over at last," said Ciantha.

"For a time. A battle is won, and the dark power has been driven back, but the war is unending. The Cairnlord is powerful and dangerous. Even when it was bound in stone, it was able to reach out to the mind of that unfortunate man, draw him here to uncover the sunken, scattered stones and rebuild the cairn. It will try again."

"Then all we've done might be in vain."

"Never think that," Staver said in a stern voice. "Evil is real, Brondin, real and powerful. It will not fade away of its own accord, because it's proud and hungry and believes it will overcome. It must be fought and beaten, again and again, as long as good and evil exist." He laid his big hands on their shoulders, gently but firmly, and said, "Terrible as the Cairnlord is, it is not the ultimate evil. It serves a master that is evil incarnate, just as you and I and all the others in our cause serve the good. And no blow against evil is struck in vain. If we ever think that our efforts are futile, the struggle is lost." He dropped his hands and held Ciantha and Brondin for a moment with the fierce light in his green eyes. Then he turned away, saying, "I can tell you no more. We have work yet to do."

"Halssa . . . the assault on the High City," said Brondin as memories came clear and began to fit into place.

"The alliance is gathering, and we came to prevent a siege if we could," Ciantha added. "I remember now."

"But we had no plan. We knew that we must come here, but we knew nothing more."

"There is a way," Staver said. He knelt at Cabanard's side

and took the unconscious warrior up in his arms as if he had been a child. "Come," he said, and started for the doorway.

They retraced their path, the way illuminated by a light that lay around them, moving with them, as if the air itself were aglow. As they walked, Staver spoke with Ciantha. His voice was subdued. Brondin overheard nothing; he assumed that Staver was instructing her in what she was to say and do once they were outside. Staver said not a word to him. Brondin wondered at this, but he remained silent.

When they came to the end of the storm drain, the sky was bright with the early light of a misty spring day. Staver put Cabanard down gently, cushioning his head on his traveling cloak.

"Cabanard will wake soon," he said to Ciantha. "When he does, you and he are to go to the leaders of the alliance and tell them what I told you."

"Will Cabanard be well enough? His hands were terribly burned," she said.

Staver smiled and nodded. He lifted one of Cabanard's big stubby-fingered hands so that the light from the entrance shone full upon it. The flesh of the palm was a healthy unscarred pink.

"What magic causes, magic can cure," he said. As Cabanard stirred and groaned, Staver rose. "Tell him nothing of me or of what happened after he was stricken. Trust him to guide you."

"Will they listen?"

"When they see the cloak pin, they will listen," Staver assured her.

On the moist morning air came a deep throbbing sound. It stopped, began again, and then settled to a steady rhythm, like the beating of a giant's heart.

"The siege drums," Brondin said.

"Go as quickly as you can. Remember, there must be no attack for nine days," Staver said. "I will wait out of sight. Join me, Brondin."

As Staver vanished into the darkness, Cabanard blinked and rubbed his eyes. He sat up and then stood and stretched like a man rising from a long sleep. He looked at his hands and turned confusedly to his friends.

"They were hurt. Burned. But there's nothing. . . ."

"It was enchantment, all of it, Cabanard. All illusion," Ciantha said.

"There was a wizard . . . a pile of stone. He . . . knocked you down."

"He's gone. We've done what we came for. Now you and Ciantha must go to the leaders of the alliance. She has a message for them," said Brondin.

"How long have the drums been beating?"

"They just began. There's still time, Cabanard, but none to spare. The armies are assembled."

"What about you?"

"I must go back inside. There's no wizard to fear now. I'll be all right. You'll have to go with Ciantha, to guide her. Seek out Henorik and tell him I'm safe. He'll see that you meet the chiefs. Go now, quickly."

As the slight, quick figure of Ciantha and the broad bulk of Cabanard vanished into the early mist, Brondin turned and made his way into the darkness without torch or lantern. Before long, he saw Staver ahead, and all around him was a pale haze of light.

"They're on their way. What task do you have for me?" he asked.

"We must go to a farther chamber. There's work for us both."

They walked on. At the entry to the upper passage, Staver helped Brondin up and then jumped and drew himself up without assistance. He smiled boyishly and explained, "It feels good to be in my body again. I've never managed to forget this world."

This time they followed a different route; and they soon descended long flights of stone steps that took them far beneath the level of the storm drains. Brondin, who had never set foot in the High City, marveled at the immensity and complexity of the passages beneath the palace. It seemed impossible to him that any ruler could ever have known them, and he voiced his doubts to Staver.

"They knew these ways in the time of the Old Kingdom, but since the days of Aluca, the rulers of the city have had too many other things on their minds. Very few of the rulers since Ambescand ever set foot on the lower levels. The last few have posted guards at the entrances and persuaded themselves that the lower levels are full of ghosts and demons," Staver said, and laughed softly.

"But isn't that true?"

"I don't think of myself as a ghost. And I'm certainly not a demon."

"I meant Karash-Kabey's servants and the Cairnlord. There might be other things like them down here."

"There are not. As a matter of fact, just below the chamber where we fought the Cairnlord is a treasure room full of precious stones and bars of gold. It was put there by Marduran, the third king, and forgotten when he died. And not far from Marduran's vault is an even greater treasure for those who can penetrate its secret."

"Magic?"

"Something at once simpler than magic and far more potent. A scholar named Serne, who lived in the days when the Old Kingdom was at its height, discovered ways to release and control immense power from ordinary objects. He could make air, water, and fire work for him."

"But that's magic!" Brondin insisted.

"Perhaps it is," Staver said carelessly. "But it's a different kind of magic than any before or since. Serne's workshop lies forgotten and sealed. All his devices are there, just as he left them, waiting to be discovered."

Brondin went on for a short distance in thoughtful silence and then bluntly asked, "Why do you tell me these things, Ironbrand?"

"When you and Ciantha rule in the High City, you must know what you rule over. You must know what you can pass on to your descendants. The lords of the city have too long been ignorant."

"We don't rule yet. If Halssa rejects the challenge and the city is besieged, there may be little left to rule," Brondin said gloomily.

"Halssa will accept. A single combat of champions is the sort of solution men like Halssa prefer."

"I only hope we have a champion to match his."

"We will, Brondin. Have no fear of that," Staver said.

The passage ended in a deep well, with a flight of narrow
steps coiling downward around its inner surface. Staver led
the way with a confident unhurried step, and Brondin kept
pace with him, though not without pain to his leg. Their
steps echoed and reechoed off the enclosing walls, and
neither of them spoke as they descended.

The steps ended far below in another smooth-walled passage fashioned by the hands of men in a forgotten age. The
air was cool and fresh, with only a trace of moisture. Recalling the stale air of the tunnels beneath the Fastness,
Brondin wondered how this could be. Staver spoke as if responding to his thoughts.

"Do you notice how pure the air is? That's the work of
Serne. He has a device that harnesses the power of the tides
to bring good air into the passages underground."

"After all those years when no one walked here, it's still
working. Serne was a man of great power," Brondin said
earnestly.

"I hope you'll seek out his workshop."

"I'd be willing to seek it right now if you like. Perhaps
he knew some way to create a champion for the alliance."

"What would happen, Brondin, if the alliance offered to
pit leader against leader in single combat, and you fought
Halssa yourself?" Staver asked.

"Halssa would kill me," Brondin said without hesitation.

"For a man with blood of Ambescand in his veins, you
have little faith in yourself, Brondin."

"I have no illusions. I grew up a cripple in a world of
warriors, and among the first things I learned were the things
I could never hope to do. If ever I forgot, I had only to look
at those around me."

"And this is your way of saying that you fear Halssa, is
it?"

"No, Ironbrand. If we could meet on even terms. . . . I'm
as strong as Halssa, I'm sure of it. A lifetime of using
crutches and a cane and dragging myself up after I've fallen
for the hundredth time has given me strength in my arms.
My swordsmanship is good. Balthid saw to that. But I'm a
cripple, and Halssa has two good legs. He'd win," Brondin
said. He spoke evenly, with no trace of self-pity, but there
was bitterness in his voice that he could not conceal.

"You've kept up with me all this way. It may have hurt, but you've done it," Staver pointed out. When Brondin offered no reply, he went on. "You walked hundreds of greatmarks over ice and snow. You climbed cliffs and descended into caverns and walked ledges no wider than your finger. You matched a man like Cabanard step for step. Impressive feats for a cripple."

"I'm not helpless. Ironbrand. But all the walking in the world is not the same as single combat. That requires agility."

"You've gone into single combat with three assassin demons and slain them all. No man has ever done such a thing before."

After a time Brondin said, "All you say is true. And I think you say it to goad me into facing Halssa in single combat."

"You must. You've known that all along."

Brondin's pent-up feelings exploded. This man who had come out of legend to deliver him and his friend and the woman he loved from monstrous death, this godlike figure who seemed father and brother, teacher and friend all in one, was showing himself to be no different from the scheming men whom Brondin had dealt with all his life. He had his own plans and purposes, and Brondin had a place in them. He treated Brondin like a creature without intelligence or will, to be manipulated like a dog sent chasing after sticks.

Brondin had had enough of such treatment. He turned on Staver angrily. "Do you think I haven't wished every day of my life for the chance to confront Halssa on equal terms and win back for myself what's rightfully mine?" he cried. "What kind of man do you think I am, Ironbrand? Do you see me as someone who can live comfortably knowing that his throne and his power and the wife at his side were won for him by another man's sword?"

"I know you're not such a man, Brondin."

"Then why do you taunt me with impossibilities? I know that I'll never rule in peace if other men fight my battles and win my victories for me. Ciantha and our children will never be secure, but I can do nothing to change that! I'll tell you this and swear it on any oath you name: If I had two good legs, I'd fight Halssa or any champion he sent against me. If you want that so much, use your magic and heal my leg. Do it, Ironbrand!"

Staver laid his hands on Brondin's shoulders and looked into Brondin's flushed, angry face for a moment before he replied in a gentle voice, "Magic can only heal the injuries magic has inflicted."

"But you're a healer, too. Is there no way you could make my leg straight with your healing skill?"

"I could, Brondin, but it would take far more time than we can spare now."

Brondin pulled free and stepped back, looking coldly into Staver's eyes. "I thought you came to help me."

"You must fight Halssa on your own two feet."

"I understand that now. All I ask of you is that you lead me out so I can join the others and prepare myself."

The look of concern passed from Staver's face, and he smiled and gave a sigh of relief. "Don't be in such a hurry," he said. "Now that you've freely chosen, I can help you."

"You can't heal me in time for the combat."

"No, but I can do other things. Come, we're almost there."

"Where are we going now?" Brondin asked, falling into step at Staver's side.

"To a very ancient place."

Staver said no more. They walked on a short way and turned a curve, and Brondin saw a faint red glow in the distance. As they came nearer, he could distinguish the outline of a massive iron door, with deep red light shining through a grating at the top and a narrow crack along the sill. When they reached the door, it swung wide at the motion of Staver's hand.

Against one wall of a small chamber a forge glowed deep red. An anvil stood in the center of the floor. At the realization of what place it was, Brondin felt a chill of awe. That forge had glowed for Ambescand, and the anvil had felt the power of his blows when he forged the blades of liberation. What other magic had been worked here in ancient days he did not dare imagine. He looked apprehensively at Staver, who gestured for him to enter.

Within, as his eyes grew accustomed to the dim light, he was able to make out the tools of the swordsmith hanging on the walls or leaning against them. He saw no spot of rust. Everything was in readiness.

"Come, Brondin. There's much to be done here and little time," Staver said, unbelting his robe.

Brondin tugged at his tunic. "Are we going to forge a blade for me?"

"A blade and something more. Let's get to work."

CHAPTER TWENTY-FIVE

A TIME TO STAND ALONE

Halssa stood on the topmost platform above the western gate of the High City and looked out at the camp of his enemies. The morning sun was warm on his back. The mist was fading from the plain, and he could see the clusters of tents, in a variety of sizes and colors, extending westward to vanish in the last far traces of white.

"More than I expected," he said. "They must have a man for every one of ours."

"The reinforcements will come," said the commander of the city guard, who stood at his side.

"There's no word of them, and we can't wait forever. This is the best way. Once I've defeated their champion, the alliance will fall apart."

"That may be so, but if you could delay...."

"I never did like the idea of bringing a lot of strangers into the city to do my fighting. That was all Karash-Kabey's idea, and now he's chosen to vanish. If he's lost faith in his easterners, I see no reason to wait for their help. No," Halssa said as the commander turned to respond, "I've won all this by myself, and I'll defend it myself. A man who can't do that, or won't do it, isn't fit to rule."

"Who will their champion be?"

"Their leader, whoever he is. I believed all along that Balthid's limping brat was their leader, but it appears I was wrong. They would not send a cripple to face me," Halssa said. He paused for a moment and then laughed grimly. "Though it would give me great satisfaction to lop off Brondin's withered leg and maybe an arm or two. He's caused me much trouble. Every time he seemed to be dead, he showed up again. As for the rest, there isn't one of them who's a match for me. They lost their best when Balthid died."

"Could it be a trick, this offer of single combat?" the commander asked.

"How?" Halssa asked, and there came no reply. Both men looked out at the cleared level space where the champions were to meet.

It lay three hundred marks from the city walls, outside the range of the best bowshot, at the edge of the rise on which the city stood. Beyond it, the ground sloped gently to the plain, and there was no place where a man could move unseen from the city walls.

The field was oval, outlined by posts driven in the ground at intervals of about a mark. Along its northern and southern sides stood a row of tents for the champions, their guards and healers, and the chosen judges. From the tents to the south, Halssa's red and black colors hung. The others were unadorned.

A gentle land breeze stirred the pennants. It brought to the men on the platform the sharp tang of campfires and the low pounding of the hooloom, the great hooped siege drum brought to this land by the men of the west.

"I don't see how they could trick us," the commander admitted, "but with the odds in their favor, I don't understand why they offer single combat. They stand a greater risk than we do, and it's unnecessary."

Halssa shrugged. "Maybe they just want to make sure there's something left worth the winning. I don't care. It's better for us this way."

"True. But all the same—"

"Stop worrying. It will all be over by midday," Halssa said.

He took one last look at the encampment and the field of combat and then turned to the rear of the platform, where he paused to look down on the High City, glowing under the morning sun. Halssa was not a man sensitive to beauty, but he was moved by the sight nonetheless, touched by pride and possessiveness. The city lay like a bowl of golden light, the honey-colored stone of its walls and the copper of its domes flashing in the low-hanging sun. It was the loveliest city in the world and the richest, and it was his, he thought fiercely. He had won it and held it by his strength and his cunning, wresting it from the grip of squabbling usurpers. The people might grumble about his severity, but under his rule they and their goods were safe from attack, and they ate regularly. That was more than the last half dozen legitimate rulers had done for them.

And now they wanted to place a crippled youth with a few drops of Vannenson blood on the throne in his place. Let them try, Halssa thought. He would cut down their champion, and then, when they were demoralized and divided, dispose of the pretender. And he would do it all without the aid of that skulking wizard who had fled with his bag of conjurer's tricks just when his help might have been of some use. So much for wizards, he muttered to himself, and spat contemptuously. In the final reckoning, it comes to sword against sword.

"See that there's a close watch on those tents," he said to the commander. "I'm going to rest a while." He turned and strode to the stairs.

When the sun was midway to the zenith, Halssa marched from the western gate at the head of two score men. He wore a loose robe, and his sword was at his side. Two men carried his fighting gear. Two healers walked behind them, and three observers. His trainer walked beside him. Of the rest, fifteen were picked guardsmen, ready to fight at the first sign of treachery, and the rest were Halssa's chiefs, unarmed.

Drawing near the field, he saw pennants flying from the tents of the enemy. They bore three green stripes, the colors of Brondin of Balthid's Keep. He wondered at that but said nothing. He saw the alliance leaders and scorned to greet them. But when a familiar figure emerged from one of the tents, he squinted, shaded his eyes, and gave a shout of recognition.

"Cabanard! Is it you?"

The big thickset man waved a burly arm in response. "It's I, Halssa. Are you ready?"

"I thought you'd wandered off long ago, you old pirate. Don't tell me. . . . You're not the champion of these bumpkins, are you?"

"No, not I. I've had my share of fighting."

"But you're with my enemies," Halssa said. When Cabanard merely nodded, he went on. "Too bad for you. You'd do better to be with me than against me. From your colors, you serve Brondin now."

"I've been helping him train."

"Train?" Halssa laughed loudly. "Helping him crawl, you mean. What other training does a crooklegged boy need?"

"He's Balthid's son, Halssa."

"I know that. And he's not the man his father was. Balthid wouldn't have spent year after year hiding behind his walls, plotting and scheming to have other men do his fighting. He'd have come out and grabbed for what he wanted. We'd have settled all this long ago."

"Brondin needed time to grow up. You'll settle it today."

Halssa gaped at him and shook his head slowly in disbelief. "Does he really dare to face me man to man? Much as I'd like to gut him in front of his followers, I have little taste for fighting cripples."

At that moment, from one of the tents on Brondin's side, the three observers chosen by the alliance emerged. Raising their hands in the gesture of peace, they joined their colleagues from the High City, and all six drew apart to confer. To be chosen observer was the highest tribute to a man's integrity. On their word hung victory and defeat, and their word was beyond question.

Their appearance silenced Halssa. He stood uncertainly for a moment and then ordered his armorers and healers to their tents to prepare. As he turned to bid farewell to Cabanard, Brondin stepped from his tent and came forth to join them.

Halssa had never seen Brondin before, but he had known his father well, and he recognized the son. He was surprised at the first sight of his enemy. This was no crippled boy, hobbling about with the aid of a crutch. He was as tall as Halssa and even broader in the chest and shoulders. His arms were corded with muscle. He walked with a perceptible limp, but not ungracefully and not on crutches. One leg was encased in a construction of iron strips and bands, hinged at the knee and fastened with padded leather straps to his upper and lower leg. In his face and voice there was no trace of fear. He might have been welcoming a guest.

"We meet at last, Halssa. I'm Brondin of Balthid's Keep," he said.

"You look like Balthid. I doubt you'll fight like him."

"We'll soon find out."

"Believe it, boy, I've long looked forward to this day," said Halssa.

The two champions, unattended, walked to where the six observers waited. The observers wore identical robes of dark blue, with the hoods drawn forward. They had fixed dark cloths over the lower part of their faces to conceal their features more completely. To be an observer was to abandon all allegiance except fidelity to truth, to be no longer an individual man but a pair of watchful eyes and an impersonal judgment.

"Are you steadfast in your wish to meet in battle?" asked one observer. When they replied in the affirmative, another asked, "Do you agree to abide by our judgment in all matters concerning this combat?" Again they agreed, and a third hooded figure commanded, "Go then, and arm yourselves. We will summon you to the combat."

As he returned to his tent, Halssa asked his trainer, Delbas, "What do you think of Brondin?"

"He looks strong. He may try to outlast you."

"He won't. I'll take him fast."

"Don't underestimate him. He must have learned a lot from Balthid. Cabanard could have taught him plenty, too."

"I'm not underestimating him, Delbas. He's twenty years younger than I am, and that will help him. But I've got twenty years experience on him. And I've got two good legs. A cage on his leg doesn't make him a match for me."

Delbas grunted and nodded his shaven head. He knew that Halssa was unmatched in battle, but there was something about the son of Balthid that made him hesitate to speak of an easy victory. Even with that contraption on his leg, the youth moved easily. With two healthy legs, he would have been an even more formidable warrior than his father. Delbas was certain of only one thing: Whoever won, the combat fought this day would be long remembered and spoken of.

When they were fully armed, the two champions were summoned once again to the presence of the observers. Both were lightly armored, and each carried a sword and dagger and no other weapon. Halssa's shield was slightly larger than Brondin's; Brondin wore a shoulder piece to protect his sword arm. In all other respects they were equally fitted out.

"We ask again: are you steadfast in your wish to meet in battle?" asked an observer.

"I am," each champion replied.

"Then you place yourselves and your separate causes under our judgment," said a second observer. He signaled, and the guards of both sides began to string a black rope from post to post, enclosing the field of battle.

"Hear, now, and follow these precepts," said a third. "Until we have pronounced judgment, neither of you is to leave the field. Cross the black rope and you will be slain."

Another observer said, "You will fight to the death or until one yields. There will be no pause and no rest and no help from those beyond the rope."

"If both are mortally wounded, the last to die will be proclaimed victor," said a fifth.

"Now, before us, swear to accept these terms and abide by our judgment," said the sixth observer, stepping forward and placing his fingertips on each man's forehead. "Swear by all the gods and powers you know and by all that move unknown in the air and on the earth and over the waters; by the powers that move beneath the waters and in the secret places of the earth; by those named, and the unnamed, and the unnameable; by those which move in the light and those which work in darkness. Swear by your blood and your name and your honor, and by the honor of your family, and the love of friends. Swear by your strength and your battle prowess and your hope of victory and fame."

"I swear," said the two with one voice. Brondin added, "And may Wrothag guide my hand."

"Retire and await my signal," said the oath giver, pointing to opposite sides of the field.

Halssa and Brondin walked to the black rope, turned, and gazed across the open space at each other. The observers stepped outside the black rope and spread out around the circle, where guards already stood by each post, swords drawn. Now that the oath had been taken, the guards were under the direct command of the observers. If anyone outside the black rope tried to interfere or offer assistance, he would be slain. If either champion attempted to flee, his own men were equally bound with his enemy to cut him down.

At the signal, both men moved forward cautiously, dropping into a fighting crouch as they closed. When they were a mark apart, they began to circle slowly, and then Halssa opened the attack with a series of overhand blows that drove Brondin back by their sheer ferocity and force.

Brondin blocked four hard blows and then slipped aside and slashed at Halssa's legs; Halssa brought his shield around in time and cut backhanded at Brondin's head. The blow glanced off Brondin's helmet, staggering him momentarily; but he recovered before Halssa could press his advantage, and he landed a solid stroke that sent Halssa reeling backward.

They had taken each other's measure, and they moved more warily. Having each felt the other's strength, they dodged strokes rather than attempting to parry them. Though the sun was not yet overhead, both men shone with sweat; their breathing was loud.

Twice more Halssa attacked, but Brondin held him off both times. Then he took the offensive, forcing Halssa back step by step, until Brondin stumbled and nearly fell. By the time he had recovered his footing, Halssa was a safe distance away; but blood ran from the shoulder of his shield arm.

They clashed again, and each struck at the other's weak points: Brondin at the shield arm, Halssa at the head and leg. Halssa's stroke was turned by the metal of the leg brace, but his blow to the helmet left Brondin dizzy. When they drew apart, Brondin wiped his brow with his forearm, and the forearm came away covered with bloody sweat.

Another furious passage of arms left both men bleeding from fresh wounds. Their harsh, strained breathing could be heard all around the arena as they gathered strength for the next exchange.

Halssa, guarding his injured shoulder, struck again and again at Brondin's leg, but the metal brace kept his hardest strokes from doing more than barely breaking the skin. Then, with a furious blow, Halssa shattered his sword on the iron framework. He flung the useless hilt aside and drew his dagger.

The blow had not fallen without effect. It had struck the outer hinge of the knee joint, bending the metal, driving it into Brondin's leg and jamming its movement so that he could not move his leg freely. What movement was possible could be achieved only with great pain, as the metal ground into the flesh behind his kneecap. As soon as he saw the shattered sword on the ground and the dagger in Halssa's hand, Brondin threw his own shield aside and pulled off his helmet to leave himself unencumbered.

Halssa stayed just out of reach, and Brondin did not rush after him. Both men waited. Brondin knew that the situation was not favorable to him; Halssa, with his experience of battle, was every bit as dangerous with dagger and shield as an immobilized man with a sword. Everything depended on one solid blow.

Brondin lurched forward, crying out fiercely to mask the groan of pain wrung from him by the metal that ground into his raw flesh. Halssa caught the powerful two-handed blow on his shield and turned it aside, and his slashing dagger barely missed Brondin's neck. Brondin hammered blow after blow on Halssa's shield and helmet, stumbling after him as Halssa fell back step by step.

Then Halssa sprang aside, and as Brondin's blow fell on empty air, pulling him off balance, Halssa brought his shield around edge-on to smash into the bloody knee with all his might. Brondin's agonized cry cut the air like an omen of death. He fell to his good knee, his braced leg jutting out awkwardly. But he broke his fall with one hand. With the other, he brought his sword around to catch Halssa just under the buttock, in the back of the leg. The blade drove in bone-deep and tore down the leg, past the knee.

Halssa's leg gave way, and he pitched over on his back. Struggling to his feet, Brondin stood over him, sword point at the fallen champion's breastbone.

"Yield," he said in a dry, croaking voice.

"And rot in a cage? For you . . . to gloat? Kill me, cripple."

"No prison. Exile. I'll swear to it."

Halssa glared at him and then laughed. "You'll have to kill me, and you have no stomach for it."

"I can kill you if I must."

"Then do it, boy. Stop talking."

"You were once a friend to my father. Before the sorcerer warped your will. For that I'd spare you."

"I had Balthid killed."

"I think your will was not your own."

Brondin held the sword point steady, reluctant to kill this lifelong enemy and begin his reign with an act of blood. Halssa's hand swept around from behind his back, and as the sand and pebbles flew into Brondin's face and Halssa tried to roll aside, Brondin thrust. The blade slid into Halssa's chest with his full weight behind it. Halssa gaped at him, wide-eyed.

"I wanted to spare you," Brondin said.

Two observers came on silent feet and stood over Halssa until he fell back dead. The other observers were now once more inside the black barrier. They converged on Halssa's body, made certain of his death, and left, three to each side, to proclaim the outcome.

Brondin threw down his sword and hobbled painfully to where Cabanard waited. As he stumbled forward, clutching at the post to keep from falling, Cabanard let out a cheer. The others took it up. Peace had returned to the north at last.

Toward evening, as he lay in his tent alone, lulled by wine, his wounds washed and oiled and bound, Brondin listened to the excited talk that buzzed all around him, made half audible by distance and his drowsiness. All afternoon he had heard praise and acclaim for his victory. Stallicho and Witigense had frankly admitted their astonishment at his achievement. Henorik was ecstatic; he could speak of nothing but how proud Balthid would have been to see this day's work. Young Zantorne had thrown himself at Brondin's feet and sworn lifelong fidelity to his warrior-king. Moorook, a dark and gloomy-looking man, had offered his loyalty in terse, restrained words. Even Parhender was liberal with his praise; but Brondin was certain that once outside the tent, Parhender would dismiss the victory as a cripple's luck.

He fell into a light sleep. Awakening with a start, he looked up into Ciantha's face. She was frowning with concern, and her eyes gleamed.

"Brondin, are you all right?" she asked earnestly.

"I won, Ciantha. It's all over."

"But are you hurt?"

"I'll heal," he said. He started to sit up and grunted at a stab of pain. At once she knelt by his pallet, arranging cushions to support him and then helping him up with smooth, cool hands.

"Cabanard told me all about the combat. He said you were magnificent!"

"Halssa was pretty good, too. There were moments when I thought he was going to be too good."

"Cabanard said you were better than Balthid ever was. And you offered to spare Halssa's life."

"No point in killing him. I wasn't fighting for revenge. He was a brave man, Ciantha. If he hadn't been influenced by that wizard, we might have settled long ago and been friends."

She took his face in her hands and kissed him gently. "You're safe. And the High City is safe. There'll be no more bloodshed, thanks to you."

He pulled her close. They lay in silence for a time, full of the quiet contentment of one another's nearness. He thought of all they had endured together, and it seemed like part of a tale told long ago in another world. Even the blood and rage and pain of the day's combat were fading from his memory, dimmed by the vivid image of their hands joined on the Iron Angel while darkness howled and clutched at them and all things fell to nothingness but themselves, the sword, and the struggle.

"People will always think that today was the climax of the struggle," he said dreamily. "And it was only a clash of men for the prizes that can be won by the sword."

Ciantha raised her head and looked at him, puzzled. "But it was a great victory, Brondin. You brought peace. You saved hundreds of lives."

"The true victory was won in that dark chamber. It was our victory, ours together. You and I and Staver Ironbrand touched eternity. We saved more lives than we can imagine, won freedom for generations to come, and no one but the three of us will ever know. Today was simply the last step. It had to be done. But it was not the great feat people will call it."

"It was a great feat," Ciantha said flatly. "And when Orannan comes to make a tale of it, don't try to stop him. You've earned the honor."

"You deserve as much honor as I do."

"I didn't fight Halssa. Stop arguing with me."

"I only did what I had to do." Brondin kissed her again and ran his hand through her bright hair. He sighed and said, "Ever since Balthid's death, I've had one obligation after another imposed on me. It's been much the same with you, I think—never free to say, 'I will do this, or that, because I please,' always fulfilling duties, doing what others say you must. Now there's only one obligation left to both of us, and I look forward to it with joy. It makes all the rest worthwhile."

Ciantha drew herself from his arms and gazed at him coolly. "And yet you call it an obligation. Is it nothing more?"

"Ciantha, Ciantha," Brondin said softly, reaching out to take her hands. "It needs no obligation, no oath, no claim of duty to the future to make me want you for my wife. I love you, and I want to be with you from now on. If Ambescand himself stood before us and said we must not marry, I'd defy him. I'd meet him on the field as I met Halssa, and I'd defeat him."

Her expression softened. She looked into his eyes for a moment and said, "I believe you, Brondin."

"Then let's choose a day and summon the chiefs and tell them to make ready for a wedding in the High City," Brondin said, taking her in his arms and holding her close.

The transition from Halssa's rule to the reign of Ciantha and Brondin was relatively smooth and peaceful. Here and there a pocket of diehards refused to accept the outcome of the combat, but they were few and were soon quieted. The city folk, even the guardsmen, accepted the change with something like relief. The names of Ambescand and the brothers Vannenson were much loved and respected in the north, and the return of their descendants to the throne was welcomed.

Cabanard was a changed man in those peaceful times. He had wielded the sword of a wizard and had faced another wizard in battle—deeds done by the likes of Ambescand. There could be no greater adventure, and he saw no purpose in seeking what no man could find. Cabanard did not have the words to explain his feelings, and so he became ever more silent and private as the years passed. He took to spending much time, in all weathers, on the city wall, looking sometimes out to sea and sometimes to the far mountains, rubbing his shoulder as if to ease an old wound, alone but never seeming lonely. He had a vague memory of a great moment in his life, something he could not fully recall but could not abandon to oblivion. He was like a man who has visited, in a dream, the great good place where all wish to go and finds the waking world a pallid place ever afterward.

Orannan, once back in the city, became quite respectable. Upon the death of the venerable Espar, he was appointed chronicler of the High City. He studied much, and his songs and tales were now of high deeds and noble motives, of sacrifice and duty and honor. Now and then, with his old friend Cabanard or the companions of his youthful days, he sang a bawdy song or told a tale to freeze the blood of the bravest; but for the most part, his behavior was exemplary.

In the deep of a winter night some years after their wedding, when they had a young son named Colberane just beginning to walk and an infant daughter, Meragrand, still in the cradle, Ciantha and Brondin donned heavy cloaks, took lanterns, and descended to the lower levels of the palace to revisit the chamber of the cairn. The way was tangled and confusing, and their memories were dulled by time and the concerns of state, but at last they came to the room where they had once faced Karash-Kabey and his master. It looked small and bare in the lantern light. The cresset hung overhead, dark and still, and the dais stood where they remembered it. Nothing else remained. Of their struggle, of the cairn and the Iron Angel, there was no trace.

After a time, Ciantha spoke, and her hushed voice echoed eerily off the stone walls of the barren chamber. "So this is how it ends. Emptiness."

"It is not ended," Brondin said.

Ciantha turned to him, alarmed. "Will the Cairnlord return? Will our children have to face him, and their children?"

Brondin limped to the dais, where he rested. "While we worked at the forge, Staver told me that in some remote day, when we and our world and all we've done are long forgotten, a man will be tempted by a sword in a stone. He will be a good man, and his purpose will be a high one. But if he draws the sword from the stone, disaster will follow. He and those he loves will suffer greatly. All the good he has accomplished will be undone, and a long age of misery will come upon the world."

"Worse than the time of the Cairnlord?"

"Worse than anything we can imagine," Brondin said.

She raised her lantern and looked into his face, into his care-narrowed eyes. "And must this be?" she asked.

"It may be, or it may not. The man is free to choose. But if the evil should return, the good will resist. The struggle will never end."

She reached out to take his hand. They stood for a time in the gloom, silent, remembering. Then they left the chamber to return to the cold, clear light of the world, to take up their duties once more.